WITH LOVE, LOUISA

WITH *LOVE,* *LOUISA*

ASHTYN NEWBOLD

THREE LEAF
PUBLISHING

Copyright © 2021 by Ashtyn Newbold

All rights reserved.

No part of this book may be reproduced in any form or by any electronic or mechanical means, including information storage and retrieval systems, without written permission from the author, except for the use of brief quotations in a book review. Any references to historical events, real people, or real places are used fictitiously. Names, characters, and places are products of the author's imagination.

ISBN: 9798536288474

Cover design by Ashtyn Newbold

Three Leaf Publishing, LLC

www.ashtynnewbold.com

CHAPTER 1

A lady had only two respectable choices when faced with poverty. She could enter into a hasty marriage without any hope of future happiness, or she could call upon her relatives, no matter how distant, for their hospitality. Being the romantic of all romantics, the first was not an option for Louisa Rosemeyer.

Tapping her chin, she thought arduously over how to address her letter. She had already thrown out one sheet of foolscap, cringing at the way *My dear aunt* had appeared on the paper. Millicent Irwin was indeed her aunt, but she was not *dear*. Louisa had never even met the woman. Her aunt didn't care to associate with her relatives, which did little to bolster Louisa's hopes of the woman taking her in. Perhaps it would be best to keep her request professional, distant, and straightforward, with as few endearments as possible.

Mrs. Irwin, she began in a neat hand.

I have not yet had the privilege of making your acquaintance, but I am your great niece, Louisa Rosemeyer.

She chewed her lower lip as she forced herself to be as concise as possible. The likelihood of a response was slim already, and she didn't want to get her hopes up.

I have fallen upon difficult times, and have no place to belong or call home, at least not without causing disrepute to the friends that are currently offering me their hospitality at Larkhall, an estate in Surrey. I am writing my humble request to live with you in Folkswich. I would do all I could to make you comfortable and happy while I am living under your roof. I am often described as quiet and reserved, so you should not expect me to be bothersome in your company. My presence in your home would only last for as long as you allow.

Louisa felt the color drain from her face as she wrote. But then where would she go?

She shook her head fast. She couldn't think so far into the future. She had been offered hospitality from her sister Alice and her husband, but Louisa couldn't help but feel burdensome living among a newly married couple with a child on the way. She wanted to have a purpose. If her elderly aunt had been alone for so long, perhaps she desired the company. Louisa would feel helpful.

After all, she had never been to Folkswich. She had heard the small village in Yorkshire was lovely in the summer.

Please inform me of your decision at your leisure.

Her quill paused, and she rubbed the feather against her lower lip as she thought of how to sign the letter. How cold and distant did she really wish to be? For all she knew, her aunt might like to know Louisa cared about her and claimed her as a relative.

Dipping her quill in fresh ink, she pressed the tip to the paper.

With love,
Louisa

"What the devil is this?" Jack Warwick muttered under his breath. His blurry eyes skimmed over the letter in his hand. He sat at the dining room table beneath the small chandelier, a soft glow filling the room. Had the butler brought this letter to him? Yes. He could vaguely recall the starched old man walking in with a salver.

The writing was neat…almost *too neat.* Had he ever seen such a neat hand in his life? Words jumped from the page, tangling together in his lopsided vision. Jack blinked hard, trying to clear his sight before attempting to read again. He clamped his lips around the rim of the bottle in his other hand, throwing his head back for yet another gulp of brandy.

When his eyes managed to focus, he read the first line.

Mrs. Irwin,

A deep chuckle rumbled through his chest. Why exactly he was laughing, he could not entirely say. All he knew was that he most certainly was not *Mrs. Irwin*. He had let her manor, Benham Abbey, but from what he had gathered about the woman, she was not one to receive letters—or visitors for that matter.

Ever.

And if she did, she likely would have driven them out with her cane. Or even with a sword and pistol.

His laughter continued to rumble through his chest without his consent. He continued reading down the page, his eyes focusing on the name of the poor girl requesting to live with Mrs. Irwin. *Louisa Rosemeyer.* What a hopeless young thing. She sounded entirely too desperate. Was she a young woman? Or a spinster? How could he know? At any rate, she must have been very desperate indeed to be soliciting a request to live with Mrs. Irwin, even if she did happen to be the woman's great-niece.

Jack rubbed his jaw, pausing to swallow what remained in his bottle. The room spun, adding to his delirium. It wasn't kind to laugh at the misfortunes of others, but it was serving well to distract him from his own.

He bunched the letter up in his hand, pushing away from the table and taking unsteady steps toward the door.

"May I assist you to your room, Master Warwick?" Jack ignored the offer, not even looking to see where the voice had come from. He could make it to his blasted room on his own. He was not a child any longer.

He stumbled over the first step of the staircase, landing on his outstretched hands. He recovered, picking up the letter that had fallen with him, taking hold of the bannister with his other hand. When he finally made it to his bedchamber, he sat down heavily in the chair at his writing desk.

Parchment.

Quill.

Where the devil was the ink?

He gathered together his supplies, the strange urge to laugh still hovering in his throat. His head pounded as he thought over what to say, struggling to create sentences in his muddled mind. Miss Louisa was fortunate that her letter had fallen into his hands instead. If Mrs. Irwin had received it, she wouldn't have hesitated to turn the girl away. Jack would make certain she was invited, and once she arrived, Mrs. Irwin would be forced to contend with the situation.

He would pay a great deal of money to see that.

His chuckling resumed as he scrawled on the parchment.

Dear Miss Louisa,

Do come to Benham Abbey as soon as you wish. I will be most eagerly anticipating your arrival.

Sincerely,

Mrs. Irwin

He looked over the incredibly short correspondence, his head aching too much to write more. It would be quite exciting to rattle Mrs. Irwin. The entire town would thank him for doing so. That unpleasant woman would finally have to consider caring for someone other than herself. If Miss Louisa traveled so far, Jack doubted Mrs. Irwin would send her back to where she came from.

Where had she come from?

He glanced at the address and copied it down, sealing the letter and preparing it to be posted in the morning. If he left it on the edge of his desk it would be carried off before he even awoke—and by the pounding in his head, he would likely sleep most of the next day.

Without bothering to change, he staggered to his bed, falling on top of the blankets rather than under them. An odd, unwelcome smile still tugged on his lips. Perhaps it was because he had forgotten his own troubles. What *had* he been so upset about earlier? He could no longer recall. His brow furrowed as his eyes closed. Just before everything went black, a familiar voice chanted through his mind, one that he heard every time he closed his eyes. At least this time he wouldn't remember it when he awoke.

The chant grew louder even as his consciousness faded.

You killed him.
You killed him.
You killed him.

CHAPTER 2

A pair of navy blue eyes met Louisa's over the rim of her teacup. "You wish to leave Larkhall?"

She swallowed the scalding liquid, nearly choking as she did. *Compose yourself.* Now was not a time for appearing inept. If she could not swallow her tea properly, then she most certainly could not travel across England on her own. "Yes. That is indeed my plan. I have already written to my aunt in Yorkshire and she has sent her reply. It was brief, but she did confirm that I was welcome at Benham Abbey." Her voice was softer than she intended. No matter how hard she tried, she could not sound anything but timid, especially when being questioned by Matthew. She was still surprised that her aunt had written back at all.

She unfolded the letter from her lap, showing the one sentence to Matthew. Once again, she was reminded of the horrendous penmanship. Her aunt was quite advanced in years, so that could excuse part of it.

"What ghastly writing," Matthew muttered, echoing her thoughts. "But I suppose it is indeed an invitation." Was it relief she saw in his eyes? Or perhaps a mixture of relief and worry? Matthew sat up straighter, interlocking his fingers in his lap from where he sat across the tea table from her. The long case clock in the corner of Larkhall's Peacock drawing room ticked five times before he spoke. "Are you certain you wish to leave?"

"Yes."

"I will not have you travel there alone if that's what you mean." Matthew's gruff voice was inarguable. Ever since his younger sister Bridget had married a few months before, he had seemed to replace her presence in the house with Louisa, treating her as he had always treated his younger sister—as if she were fragile and in constant need of protection.

He was not wrong; to travel to Folkswich alone would be extremely daft and improper, but what other choice did she have? Louisa didn't belong at Larkhall any longer. She had been Bridget's companion, but now Bridget was living across the country as the new mistress of Thorncarrow. Louisa's parents had died years before, her stepfather was in debtor's prison, and her sister Alice was married as well. Louisa couldn't bear the thought of being an inconvenience any longer. Not at her sister's home, not at Larkhall.

Matthew knew as well as Louisa that rumors had already begun circling town about what a young lady like

Louisa was doing at Larkhall. Soon Matthew's younger brother, his wife, and their two children would be moving to a house of their own. With only Matthew's elderly aunt in the house, it would appear to all the gossiping mouths of society as though Louisa was some sort of mistress of Matthew's. She couldn't bring that sort of suspicion and disrepute upon a friend who had been so generous toward her.

"Do you mean to suggest you would accompany me there? You're not actually my brother, Matthew." Louisa's eyes fluttered down to her lap. Surely he understood what she meant by that. The two of them traveling together alone would be equally frowned upon as if she went alone.

"I am the closest thing to your guardian." Matthew leaned back on the sofa, his long legs stretching out in front of him. "And the closest thing to your brother. During your time here at Larkhall you have become something of a sister to me regardless of whether or not you view me with the same sentiment." He gave a half smile. "My conscience would not be clear if I sent you across England on your own. No matter what you think, you are welcome here. Do not feel as though you have to leave."

"I do." She cleared her throat, trying to excuse the quick way her words spilled out. "I do have to leave." She had burdened his reputation long enough already. "I thank you for your hospitality these months since Bridget was married, but I do not belong here any longer. You know that. I must find my own way before you begin inviting suitors to dine with us in an attempt to marry me off." She cast him a knowing smile. He had done the same to his sister before she was married, but fortunately Bridget had possessed the cleverness to fend off all his suitors of choice. Louisa didn't know if she would have the same ability to fend off a man like Bridget had so effortlessly. It would require a boldness of speaking and confidence that Louisa lacked.

Matthew gave a low chuckle. "I suppose I do have a propensity to do that." He paused for a long moment, his smile fading. "I must see that you are well cared for one way or another. Marriage *would* be the best way to secure a comfortable future for you."

There was a time that Louisa had wanted to marry Matthew. When she and her sister had first visited Larkhall, it had been their goal—to secure husbands and comfortable futures for themselves. Louisa's heart, however, had quickly abandoned the effort. Love was all she would marry for, especially now that she had seen both her sister and Bridget married so happily and so madly in love with fine gentlemen. There was nothing Louisa wanted more and nothing she wouldn't sacrifice for it. She and Matthew were like siblings, and at times she even considered him a fatherly figure, one who would protect her as no one ever had before.

She *did* feel at home at Larkhall. That was why it was so difficult to leave behind.

"I would be willing to fund your Season," Matthew suggested. "You could then find a suitable husband rather than live with an aunt you have never even met."

"That is too generous, Matthew." Louisa shook her head fast. "You have shown me enough kindness already."

"Is there such a thing as *enough* kindness?" He cocked one eyebrow.

She sighed. "At times too much kindness can make me feel rather helpless. I should like to feel capable of creating my own plans and executing them properly."

Matthew seemed to relent, fixing his dark blue eyes on hers with a sigh. "Well, if you would like to execute them *properly*, you must not travel to Folkswich *alone*."

In the hallway beyond the open drawing room door, the children of Matthew's brother Oliver chased one another, their giggles echoing. Their governess, Margaret, hurried behind them, her pale cheeks flushed from chasing the children, straight blonde hair sticking out both sides of her cap. She was only a few years older than Louisa, and the two had become dear friends, especially since Bridget had left Larkhall.

Margaret paused in the doorway, her eyes flooding with curiosity. She gave a quick curtsy before interrupting the conversation. "Pardon me, but did I hear you speaking of Folkswich?"

Matthew turned, giving a nod. "Louisa intends to travel there alone. Am I so ridiculous to persuade her against it?"

Margaret gave a visible swallow, shaking her head. "Oh, no, dear Louisa. That is a long journey." She paused. "I made the journey alone when I first came here, and I would not recommend that."

Alone? Louisa shifted, studying Margaret's downcast gaze. Margaret was rarely caught without a smile, but something appeared to be troubling her now. Her fingers twitched around her skirts. Her blue eyes lifted, and her lips parted. Before she could speak, a soft crash sounded in the hallway. It was followed by a shriek of laughter.

Margaret's expression transformed to one of concern, and she excused herself with a quick curtsy, darting down the hallway toward the children.

Louisa laughed under her breath. "Poor Margaret has her hands quite full. I ought to go help her." She made to stand, but Matthew stopped her.

"I worry for Margaret as well," he said in a heavy voice. "Oliver has found a house to rent in Bath. He and Julia and the children will be moving soon. My brother seems to have the same desires as you—being unwilling to stay here and accept my kindness." Matthew looked down, lowering his voice. "They haven't yet told Margaret that they will be unable to afford keeping her on as governess once they move away from Larkhall."

Louisa's gaze traveled out to the hallway, her heart sinking. From what she had learned of Margaret's past, she was in straits just as dire as Louisa's. She had nowhere else to go. Perhaps it would be off to a workhouse for both of them. It would be better to go with a friend. Louisa bit her lower lip, resisting the idea. No. She was wise enough to find a different solution. So was Margaret.

"Perhaps Mrs. Crauford would like a companion? It would allow Margaret a place to stay."

Matthew laughed under his breath. "I did think of that, but for you. Unfortunately, my great-aunt feels that to have a companion would deem her unable to keep herself entertained, which was an insult to her pride. In truth, I think she will miss you once you leave Larkhall."

Louisa's heart stung. How could she be missed in a place as grand as Larkhall? She was like a fleck of dust, floating around the house without reason. All that fleck of dust could do was cause inconvenience. "Fortunately, *my* great-aunt seemed to appreciate the idea of me coming to stay with her." Louisa thought back to her aunt's letter. *Had* she seemed appreciative? She had been direct and brief, and that was all. Though Louisa would not admit it to Matthew, the thought of traveling to Yorkshire set her stomach twisting in knots.

Overwhelmed by her thoughts, she decided she would be better off fretting over the problems of someone else rather than her own.

"I will go assist Margaret with the children." Louisa excused herself from Matthew's presence with a bow, walking into the hallway.

Margaret stooped over a broken vase on the floor, one hand pressed against her forehead. Strands of her straight blonde hair clung to her reddened face. She exhaled slowly in exasperation before she noticed Louisa's approach. She quickly put a smile on her face. "I suppose I will be sent packing after this." She gestured at the vase that was now a pile of shards on the floor.

Louisa swallowed. Little did Margaret know that she *was* to be sent packing, but for other reasons.

Louisa stooped down to help Margaret gather up the blue shards, carefully pinching them and piling them on the nearby corridor table so as not to cut her hands. "I don't think the Northcotts would dismiss you for a vase." Louisa scowled at the floor.

Margaret was silent for a long moment before speaking. "I wish I could accompany you to Folkswich. My parents live there, you see. My parents and my three little brothers." Longing stole over her features. "I haven't seen them in a very long time."

"I had forgotten you were from Yorkshire." Louisa sat back on her heels, pausing her work for a moment. Her mind raced. "Perhaps—perhaps you can accompany me there. I am certain Matthew would take the journey with us, but it would not be so improper if you traveled with us. Then you could visit your family."

A spark of hope entered Margaret's eyes before she blinked it away. "Oh, no. The children need me here." Her gaze flickered to the children who still played riotously in the corner. "I must earn my wages. I'm afraid my family cannot persist without them."

A heavy stone of dread dropped through Louisa's stomach. When would Oliver and Julia tell Margaret that she would be excused? It did more harm than good to keep it from her. Difficult conversations were necessary at times. As much as Louisa wished she could tell her, it was not her place.

"Have you considered seeking employment closer to your family?" Louisa asked. "Now that you have experience and a very reputable reference, perhaps you could find a position in Yorkshire."

"How could I leave Susanna and Cecil?" She laughed. "I adore them, despite their mischief." Coming to her feet, she dusted off her skirts.

It took all of Louisa's strength to hold her tongue. Matthew, who must have been eavesdropping from the other room, made a sudden appearance behind her, his tailcoat catching in the corner of her eye. It was not entirely Matthew's place to tell Margaret either, but he didn't seem to care for such matters. In fact, he wasn't often one to abide by rules at all.

"You ought to come to Folkswich," Matthew said.

Margaret looked down. "I—I do not see how that would be possible."

"Oliver and Julia are moving to their own home soon. Julia's inheritance will only provide them with enough to live on, not enough to afford the expense of a governess. I know Oliver intended to inform you of that matter soon."

Margaret's face lost its color. Louisa inched closer to her, touching her forearm in an attempt to comfort her.

Matthew's voice softened, as if he were recognizing his tendency to speak too bluntly. "I will accompany you both to Folkswich and ensure you are well recommended for a position near your family before I return to Larkhall. I promise."

It seemed as though Margaret had lost the ability to

speak—or breathe for that matter. She stared down at her feet, her shoulders slumping before she appeared to compose her thoughts. "I could not ask so much of you."

"You did not ask, did you?" Matthew gave a soft smile. "It is an offer, one that you would do well to accept."

Margaret's shoulders straightened, and she gave a firm nod. "I would be most grateful for your assistance. And to come to Folkswich."

"Home." Louisa gave her arm a soft squeeze. "It shall be my home soon too. You will have to tell me all that I have to look forward to about the place."

Worry still etched itself in Margaret's forehead. Perhaps she didn't yet understand the significance of a promise from Matthew. He would look after them both as he would his own sisters. They had nothing to fear.

Louisa took a calming breath, repeating those words in her head. Yes. She had nothing to fret about. So long as her aunt was even just the smallest part kind and hospitable, she would be quite content.

CHAPTER 3

"They are coming to work for *me*." Mrs. Millicent Irwin lifted her chin, jowls wobbling. Her grey eyes flashed dangerously, staring down her long pointed nose straight into Jack's soul. "It was agreed upon while you were too drunk to comprehend it."

Jack scoffed, watching with complacence from the doorway as Mrs. Irwin stood on the steps of Benham Abbey, explaining why he was still left with only a few servants to run the household. He would have to hire his own after all, it seemed. It had already been a fortnight of the housekeeper pestering him about the matter of her working twice as hard to make up for the lack of servants. It was not his fault she had to actually work to earn her wages.

At any rate, how did Mrs. Irwin even know Jack had been drunk? He was never without his wits about him, not even after he had been drinking. He could recall their conversation fully. He squinted against the sun. Couldn't he? Perhaps there were a few events in the past his drinking had caused him to forget.

"Very well, take the servants," Jack said. "It matters little to me." He waved his hand through the air. "Maids are not so difficult to find."

"They won't simply drop themselves on the doorstep." Mrs. Irwin nearly snarled. "They must come with experience and references."

"I am letting this house." Jack raised his eyebrows. "I shall do with it and manage it how I wish. Good day." With one swift step backward, he threw the front door closed, clearing that vexing woman from his view.

A long, exasperated sigh came from behind him. "Oh, Jack. Could you not be a little kinder to Mrs. Irwin?"

His expression flattened as he turned to face his sister, Cassandra. Her long, ginger hair was arranged in a disorderly pile atop her head, the pile adorned with wild flowers that she had likely found on her walk to his house. Tendrils hung around her face. He had nearly forgotten she had taken the long walk from their family home to see him. Her eyes, a pale brown, bore into him with disapproval. That was the only way people seemed to look at him of late. His heart had once ached in resistance when he was looked at in that manner, but now he was accustomed to it.

"She is a vile, ridiculous, inhospitable woman, and she has taken nearly all of the household staff," he muttered. "It is women like her, with far too much money than they know how to spend, who vex me greatly." Mrs. Irwin owned multiple properties, two in Yorkshire alone, one of which she had just purchased within a few miles of Benham Abbey.

Cassandra planted her hands on her hips. "It is quite telling that nearly all the staff would rather work for her than for you, wouldn't you agree? Perhaps they fear that you will soon gamble away your means to pay their wages."

Jack ignored the prickle of realization that climbed his skin. He *did* have a game or two planned for that evening. But he would never stake *everything* he had; he was not that foolish, no matter how much the pompous men at the parties pressured him.

"This home is temporary," Jack said in a flat voice. "If Father's health declines soon, as would be expected at his age, then I shall soon not need this place." He gestured all around the entry hall.

Cassandra gasped. "And are you counting down the days until his death?"

"No, I am counting down the minutes, dear sister." Jack sauntered toward the cabinet against the wall, surprised to find it empty. He whirled to face his sister, hot anger in his chest. "Where is the port?"

Cassandra lifted her chin. "I disposed of it. You have a severe problem, and since you will not take any action toward fixing it yourself, I have given you a place to start."

Disposed? He took a step toward her, his jaw tightening. "You—"

"I accept your gratitude most humbly." She swished her skirts as she turned toward the front door, humming as she passed him.

"I will be purchasing more and locking the cabinet," he snarled as she reached for the front door.

She gave a thoughtful look, glancing heavenward. "That may be difficult since I have also hidden the key."

His jaw hung open, fury rising in his throat. It was not Cassandra's place to mother him, to steal his property as though it belonged to her. She was his elder sister, but only by two years.

Two years that seemed to have given her all the permission she needed to treat him like a child.

His anger continued to rise, and the bottle in his throat that held all his horrible words came unstopped. "It is no wonder you have failed to find a husband. No man in the world would choose to marry a tyrant."

Cassandra turned on him, a twinge in her brow. His words had struck hard. Perhaps too hard. Guilt stabbed at his heart, but he ignored it. Cassandra was nothing short of a spinster at twenty-six, but she claimed she had no desire to marry. Jack had suspected her declarations of happy spinsterhood were simply a way to cover the pain she felt at the rejections she had faced, but only now did he realize how true his suspicions were.

He exhaled. "Cassandra…"

She marched down the first step, her skirts flowing upward with the breeze for a moment, revealing her bare feet. It wasn't even quirks like that which had caused her to be a spinster. She never wore shoes when walking outside if she could help it, having her skirts hemmed a little longer to hide her feet. But Jack knew the true reason Cassandra had not yet found a match.

It was Jack's fault.

Reaching back, his sister tugged the door shut, blocking him from her own view just as he had blocked Mrs. Irwin from his.

He raked a hand over his hair, closing his eyes. Cassandra was the only person who could make him feel ashamed. There was a moment—a fleeting one—where his heart pinched with remorse. And then Mrs. Chamberlain's croaky voice interrupted his brief fit of contrition.

"Where have my scullery maids gone?"

Jack's eyes shot open. Not only did Mrs. Chamberlain sound like a toad, but she resembled one too, with her wide-set round eyes and small nose and mouth. She was short and broad, frowning up at him in dismay.

"Mrs. Irwin has taken them," he said with finality.

"Taken?" The housekeeper shuffled closer. "Where are the replacements?"

"I have none."

She sputtered, glancing about in shock. "I cannot do all the work alone. Please…" she inserted a curtsy, as if to excuse her frank way of speaking, "Please employ a few more hands."

"You will have assistance eventually." Jack rubbed his forehead. He did not wish to fret about the matter that day.

He had planned on an entertaining evening visiting his favorite gambling party with his friends.

"Eventually?" Her skin paled. "I'm afraid it is a matter of urgency. I—"

Jack raised a hand to silence her. "You will have your maids soon enough. But if you pester me about the matter again, you shall never have maids in this house, nor a position of your own." Out of habit, he strode toward the cabinet again before remembering Cassandra's untimely antics. He would have to fill his cups elsewhere. A trip to the market would provide what he needed.

Before Mrs. Chamberlain could say another word, Jack took his beaver from the wall and placed it on his head, keeping his gaze downward as he started out the door.

Clouds rolled across the Yorkshire sky, pale grey, like smoke. The late afternoon sunlight, tinged orange with the sunset, filtered through them like fire.

Louisa had scarcely seen such a colorful landscape as the sky and rolling green hills of Yorkshire. Their coach had been rumbling down the same rugged path for an hour, the scenery finally changing to reveal houses tucked among the hills and what Margaret had pointed out as the River Derwent. Grey stones piled up to create walls on both sides of the path, the sunlight glowing on the rocks, reflecting off of the moisture from the earlier rain.

Even from inside the carriage—if Louisa breathed

deeply enough—she could smell the earth, crisp and raw and inviting.

Matthew's head lolled to one side, resting against the side cushions. His eyes were closed, but Louisa doubted he was asleep. The slightest jolt of the coach would have him alert, sitting straight up.

Margaret shared the same side of the carriage as Louisa, her eyes fixed on the landscape just as Louisa's had been. What a joy it would have been to grow up in such a lovely area as this. Margaret must have missed it terribly. Even by the way her posture had straightened, Louisa could see that Margaret was in her own territory. Her family was nearby. The thought sent a string of shivers over Louisa's arms, a smile pulling on her lips. Uncertainty still twisted her own stomach into a knot, but Margaret's joy was enough to untie it.

Seeing the joy of others could either be a balm for an aching heart, or the root of envy. Though Louisa wished she had a loving family to come home to, she would not wallow in self-pity.

"They will be overjoyed to see you," Louisa said. She didn't need to specifically mention Margaret's family. Surely she was already thinking of them.

Margaret turned, a half-smile on her lips. "I'm afraid they will be more distraught than anything else. Until I find work again." Her eyes traveled to Matthew, her voice lowering to a whisper. "Do you suppose he will keep his promise? I hope he does not. It is too much kindness for him to stay here until I am employed."

Before Louisa could reply, Matthew's eyes opened.

"I am staying until you are both happy and comfortable." He raised his eyebrows in a way that invited no argument. Seemingly satisfied, he closed his eyes again.

Louisa laughed, covering her mouth to muffle the sound. Margaret did the same, shaking her head as she looked out the window. Her eyes rounded and she pointed. "Look! That's the market I shopped at often with my family. May we stop for a moment?"

The idea of escaping the stuffy carriage made Louisa sit up eagerly. Her legs were stiffer than the wooden sign to the right of the coach, dangling above the gin shop.

Matthew rapped his knuckles against the roof of the coach, and it began to slow.

Once her feet were on solid ground, Louisa scanned her surroundings, pressing her hands against her lower back and stretching as she did. The market square was lined with rows of shops, as well as booths at the center with food and costermongers.

"Shall we take a quick turn about the square?" Margaret asked, looping her arm through Louisa's.

Louisa nodded, grateful for the opportunity to exercise for a minute or two. Matthew remained by the coach as they walked, apparently unaffected by the cramped carriage seating, despite the fact that his legs were the longest by far.

"Perhaps my favorite shopkeeper will still be here," Margaret said. "She used to slip me a sweet each time I came to the market with my mother."

Louisa laughed, surveying the many faces that passed them. "Is that why you wished to take a walk? Perchance she has another sweet for you?"

Margaret's smile grew, a giggle escaping her. Had Louisa ever heard her laugh before? If Margaret felt so free here, perhaps Louisa would too. The sense of lightheartedness was contagious, and Louisa's own smile grew, unreserved and wide as they walked across the cobblestones. The stiffness in her legs had already faded, and a new sense of hope expanded in her chest. She adjusted her straw bonnet as a light breeze made it tilt to one side. The peach ribbons under her chin billowed as another gust passed over them. Just as Louisa grasped for the ribbons, she realized she had untied them in the carriage. In her haste to step outside, she had forgotten to tie them again. The wind pushed under the brim of her bonnet, sending it spiraling off her head.

"Oh, drat," she muttered through a laugh, stopping abruptly. "My bonnet!"

Margaret pressed a hand against her own head, preventing her bonnet from flying away as Louisa's had. "It didn't seem so breezy only moments ago."

Louisa turned, searching the ground for her bonnet. Despite it being worn and old, it was one of the only ones she had. How had it disappeared so quickly? Had someone snatched it? She couldn't imagine why anyone would wish to steal such a worthless old thing. Her brow furrowed as she walked, scanning every inch of the cobblestones. Was she missing something? Perhaps Margaret had seen it.

Turning fast, she opened her mouth to speak. "Margaret, did you see—" She stopped, glancing up at the person in front of her.

It was most certainly not Margaret.

Margaret was not a broad-shouldered, finely dressed, dark-haired, shockingly handsome man. Louisa stared up at the man in front of her, her mouth buttoning itself closed.

Where had he come from?

She studied his dark brows, deep set blue eyes—crowded with lines as though he had spent many hours of his life smiling—a perfectly straight nose and full, rather serious lips. The lower half of his face showed the result of what must have been at least a week without shaving, but for a strange reason, it suited him.

Heaven. That was where he had come from.

She blinked, tearing her gaze away from his face for long enough to notice what he held in his hand. Her bonnet.

"I presume this belongs to you?" His voice was deep and slightly gruff, like he had made a habit of swallowing jagged stones or glass.

Or fire.

Drat it all, Louisa, she scolded herself. The sight of a handsome man would not set *every* lady into a fit of shyness and wonder—only a true romantic like herself. She let out a breath and straightened her arms at her sides before pulling them back in, crossing them in front of her. The motion helped gather her wits about her like a hen gathering her chicks.

And she would need her wits conversing with a man with a face like his.

"Yes," she said in a quiet voice. She willed her voice to sound more confident. "I lost it to the wind."

Margaret stood a few paces behind the man, wringing her hands together as she watched the exchange. What did she have to be nervous about? Louisa was the one whose bonnet had been retrieved by a gallant young gentleman, one who was now staring down at her with his deep blue eyes. She shrugged away the unease that crept over her shoulders at Margaret's expression.

Hmm. Despite what the creases at the corners of the man's eyes suggested, he seemed to have lost his habit of smiling. He stared down at her with that same serious look as before, saying nothing, making no move to return her bonnet to her.

Louisa rocked on her feet. "I thank you for fetching it for me." She reached for the headpiece. A jolt of surprise struck her stomach as he lifted the bonnet upward, away from her extended hand.

Was he? —no. He was not intentionally keeping it from her. Her gaze flitted up to his face.

He was grinning.

It was not any ordinary grin, but one almost undetectable. Louisa only recognized it because of how it contrasted with his previously brooding expression.

Her confusion must have played out clearly on her own features. Words lodged in her throat as she frowned up at him.

"If your gratitude is genuine, you must allow me another moment or two," he said in a low voice. "It is not common to see a face as bewitching as your own. I would prefer it uncovered by the wide brim of a hat."

Heat climbed Louisa's neck, but she refused to let any color reach her cheeks. Who was this gentleman and how could he be so…shamelessly flirtatious? She thought back to all the times she had observed her friend Bridget at parties and gatherings as gentlemen had attempted to flirt with her. With all her practice, Bridget had become quite skilled at deterring unwelcome suitors.

But was this man's attention…unwelcome? It was unexpected, certainly. And Louisa hadn't the slightest idea of how to react.

Rather than increase her confidence, his words only made her wish to hide her face from his view even more. She was accustomed to being ignored by gentlemen, hiding behind her elder sister or Bridget. Impulsively, Louisa lowered her chin. "I am rather in a hurry, sir."

"Jack Warwick," he said, shifting her bonnet from one of his hands to the other. She glanced up as he tipped his head to one side. "And who might you be?"

"A pleasure to meet you, Mr. Warwick." She kept her voice polite. She would not forget her manners nor propriety, even if this man did. "I am Louisa Rosemeyer."

"Ah. Only a lady so lovely could be called *Rose*meyer."

A man so confident in his compliments could only be well-practiced. The romantic in her swooned, but the wit that remained in her brain protested his attention. It was likely that he had already exhausted his flirting on every other lady in town, and Louisa was new to Folkswich. That was the only explanation for why a man like Jack Warwick, as he had called himself, would be so attentive to her at first glance.

She remained silent, still too shocked to speak.

"What brings you to Folkswich, Miss Rosemeyer?"

"I am visiting my aunt."

"Well, I hope your visit will not be too brief." That gruff, deep voice could make even the reading of a recipe for roasted pigeon sound flirtatious. His words were not excessively flirtatious, but his manner of speaking made them so. "Who is your aunt?"

Louisa grew impatient, watching him pass her bonnet from one hand to the other, all while drowning in the discomfort of knowing he was enjoying his view of her face. Or so he had said. "Mrs. Irwin. Perhaps you know her."

The bonnet stopped, halfway toward his other hand. "Mrs. Irwin has invited you to stay with her?" A smile of disbelief passed over his lips. "I would never have imagined her to be hospitable toward anyone."

Louisa's face fell, dread landing heavily in the pit of her stomach. "Why not?"

He shrugged. "She is perhaps the most disagreeable woman of my acquaintance. She disapproves of everything and everyone, and I am fairly certain she has never loved anything but her own achievements." He chuckled.

Oh, no. This was not a laughing matter. Louisa had

only just begun to feel calm about her situation, but now worry had begun spiraling through her once again. Her mind rattled with the reassurance that her aunt *had* accepted her request. She had written back inviting Louisa there, hadn't she? So Mrs. Irwin could not be entirely disagreeable. And who was this man to share his opinions of Louisa's relative so freely and without remorse?

"I am sorry to hear you have formed such opinions of my aunt," Louisa said.

"They are not opinions." He laughed under his breath. "They are facts."

She studied his face. He was not quite so handsome as he was before, not even as he smiled down at her, still chuckling at the thought of her aunt taking her in. He had misjudged Mrs. Irwin, and Louisa had misjudged him. He was not a hero from one of the novels she read, gallant and romantic, retrieving her bonnet for her.

He was quite possibly the villain.

She looked him squarely in the eye, providing him a clear view of her face. Perhaps she could *bewitch* him into giving her bonnet back to her.

"I must be going." She extended her hand, taking hold of the brim of her bonnet. With one swift motion, she snatched it from his grip.

He stepped back in surprise, his chuckling persisting. Whether he was still chuckling about Mrs. Irwin, or about Louisa's abrupt bonnet-snatching, she didn't care. Anger bubbled beneath her skin, and she was rarely angry. Although he didn't know it, he was crushing her hopes for a happy life here in Yorkshire. She shunned her unpleasant thoughts. Why should she trust this *Jack Warwick* and his opinions of Mrs. Irwin?

"Good day." Her face burned as she turned around, and an overwhelming sense of pride enveloped her. She was never so bold as that. A smile tugged on her lips as she approached Margaret, returning the bonnet to her head. Glancing back at the disagreeable man—for what else could possibly be his new name in her mind? —she tied the ribbons under her chin with one quick tug. He cast her an amused smile before sauntering toward the doors of the nearby gin shop. When he was out of sight, Louisa turned to Margaret, letting out a huffed breath.

"At first I thought he was quite handsome," Louisa whispered. "But I do not like him. Not one bit."

Margaret shook her head ruefully. "I should have helped you escape him sooner."

"You know him?"

"Everyone in town knows Mr. Jack Warwick." Margaret cast her gaze upward, sunlight glinting off the blonde strands on her forehead. "Especially the young ladies and every owner of every gin establishment within fifty miles. I have heard a rumor that he recently moved away from his family…that they forced him out. My mother writes to me all the gossip she hears of their neighbors," Margaret explained, laughing. "If his father could disinherit him, he surely would. He gambles. Steals hearts he has no intention of keeping. And then he drinks it all away."

Louisa grimaced. What was the purpose of such a

dreadful man being born so handsome? Was it a disguise to mask the monster within? "Is his family wealthy?"

"Oh, yes. He has wanted for nothing his entire life. That is the problem. He is quite the eligible bachelor by all opinions of society, but will he ever marry?" Margaret wagged her finger. "Not unless his bride is a bottle of brandy."

Louisa let out a loud laugh, slapping her hand over her mouth. "Oh, Margaret."

She threw her hand in the air. "It is true."

Louisa's nerves began to dwindle with her laughter. She didn't even feel guilty laughing at Mr. Warwick's expense. He had been amused at the fact that Louisa was about to go live with a woman he called 'the most disagreeable woman of his acquaintance.' So she had a right to be amused at the thought of him marrying a bottle of brandy.

"I wonder if the modiste would make a wedding gown so small," Margaret mused.

"Oh, I am certain she would, for Mr. Warwick would be willing to pay a large sum so his beloved bride could be presentable on their special day."

The image of Mr. Warwick gazing lovingly at a bottle dressed in a white gown made another laugh bubble from Louisa's chest. Perhaps he had been drunk during their exchange today and that was why he had spoken so freely. Did people remember what they said and did when they were drunk? It was an experience she never wished to have. With any luck, Mr. Warwick would forget their conversation that day. He would forget her 'bewitching face.' She would do all she could to forget his.

With any luck, she would never see him again. If he despised Mrs. Irwin so much, he wasn't likely to come near Benham Abbey.

Margaret made another jest at Mr. Warwick's expense as they approached Matthew and the waiting coach, whispering so Matthew wouldn't overhear. Louisa threw her head back in laughter. Her heart felt lighter now, floating on her laughter like a ship atop a calm sea.

"What joke have I missed?" Matthew asked, raising one eyebrow.

"We were discussing the likelihood of a man choosing to wed a bottle of brandy over a woman. Would you make such a choice?"

The crease between Matthew's eyebrows deepened. It was a ridiculous question, and the half-smile on his lips betrayed his amusement. "I would choose not to wed at all."

Of course that was Matthew's answer. From what his sister Bridget had told Louisa, he was quite determined never to marry, despite how eligible of a bachelor he was. He pretended his lack of motivation to marry was his own choice, but Louisa suspected it was the result of his fear of being hurt. Love had scarred him once before, though he never spoke of it.

"What prompted such an odd topic of discussion?" Matthew asked as he opened the coach door. He extended his hand to help Louisa up, then Margaret, before stepping inside and closing the door.

"I met a most vexing man just now." Louisa gazed out the window. "Margaret knows him and can attest to his disagreeable character."

Matthew's eyes narrowed.

Oh, drat. She should have known not to tell him.

"Was he pestering you? I would have come to your aid had I known."

"He told me my face was bewitching."

Margaret gasped. "You did not tell me that part."

Louisa shook her head, feeling a blush climb her cheeks. "It was ridiculous."

"You must take care around such men," Matthew grumbled, shaking his head. "Will being under your aunt's protection be enough? It would be a greater comfort to me if you were married to a good man before I leave Yorkshire."

"No, no, no." Louisa laughed. "Please do not begin searching for a suitor for me as you did for Bridget."

He shrugged. "She found a good man to marry and I now have little to worry about on her behalf."

"And she found him without your assistance." Louisa was again surprised at how bold her words were. Was there some sort of magic in the grey Yorkshire sky? Or was she simply tired?

"Very well." Matthew sighed, leaning his head back and closing his eyes. "So long as you do not marry that disagreeable man you met today, I shall be content."

Louisa laughed. "You may rest assured on that matter."

One of Matthew's eyes opened as he smiled. "Good."

Her thoughts traveled back to Mr. Warwick's pompous smile and glinting blue eyes. He and his bottle of brandy would live happily ever after indeed.

CHAPTER 4

Perhaps she had been a bit too optimistic. Louisa's stomach tied itself in knots as she looked out at the night sky from the tiny window inside the Lovell family's cottage. She would have to go to her aunt's house soon. Her back ached from sitting on the low, lumpy sofa, but her cheeks also ached from smiling. She did not wish to leave. Margaret's family was delightful.

Seeing how little they had, Louisa and Matthew had refused the family's attempt to offer them any of their meager dinner of boiled potatoes and stew. While Margaret played with her little brothers and Louisa distracted Mr. and Mrs. Lovell with conversation, Matthew had sneaked a generous amount of money under the towel that covered their bread basket. It was obvious why Margaret needed to find work in a household that would provide shelter and food for her, as well as wages to help her family. Louisa wanted to ask what had brought such poverty upon them, but she couldn't do so in any manner that wouldn't be deemed impertinent.

"It has been a pleasure to meet you all." Matthew stood from his place on a wooden stool. He glanced at Mr. and Mrs. Lovell, then at their sons who sat on each side of Margaret. Two of the boys had straight blond hair like their sister, and the other had ginger curls and freckles. All three boys wore clothing slightly too small for them, the knees of their trousers torn. They gazed up at Margaret with wide smiles, and there was no questioning whether or not they had missed her.

Louisa would have gladly lived in a home as cramped and old as this one if it meant she could be as happy as Margaret appeared now. To be among family, to be loved, to know there was a place she belonged. Her heart ached as she reflected back on the life she had once lived as a child. She and Alice had known their mother loved them, though their father had never been as attentive and kind as Mr. Lovell was with his children. Louisa couldn't recall being nearly so distraught over her father's death as she had been over her mother's years later. Being left with her stepfather as her guardian had been the day she realized those happy days of her childhood were gone.

That was when she and her sister Alice had first escaped to Larkhall. A temporary home. Louisa was still in search of where she belonged, but she feared she would never find it. She would always be trespassing on the hospitality of *someone*. Even marriage now seemed like an unlikely possibility. As a girl, she had dreamed of falling in love with a noble and kind gentleman, but what man would want to marry a woman with no connections, one who was passed from guardian to guardian with not a penny to offer?

As she watched Margaret, she considered the idea of seeking work as a governess. At least then she would not feel like a burden to anyone. Least of all her aunt—a woman she had never even met.

Her worry heightened as she stood from the sofa. What if her aunt did not like her? What if she regretted inviting her to live at Benham Abbey? What if she had only done so out of a feeling of obligation? Louisa recalled the description that flirtatious man in town—*Jack Warwick*—had given of Mrs. Irwin. What if she was as disagreeable as he had said she was?

Louisa nearly returned to the sofa, wishing she could sink into its lumpy cushions and disappear. No. She had to face the challenge before her. Oh, how Louisa envied tortoises. They could retreat into their shells and avoid the world anytime they wished to.

"It is late," Louisa said in a quiet voice as Matthew approached her. "Will Mrs. Irwin be upset that I am arriving at this hour? What if she is asleep?" She fiddled with a loose string on her dress. She had worn such an old gown—it was nearly falling to shreds like the trousers Margaret's brothers wore. Why had she not thought to make a better impression on her aunt by wearing a better dress? Hopefully Mrs. Irwin was already asleep.

Louisa touched a hand to her head, cringing. She had played blind man's bluff with Margaret and her brothers outside that evening, as well as nine pins with a stack of wood and a rock. As a result, her hair arrangement had fallen excessively loose, strands spilling out all over her shoulders and forehead. She groaned inwardly, begging the heavens to let her aunt be asleep. That way the staff could let her in, and she could meet her aunt when she was presentable in the morning.

"Not to worry," Matthew said in a reassuring voice. "I will walk to the door with you to ensure you are well-received."

"Oh, no." Louisa shook her head. "I must go alone. It is a short walk from here." She did not have to explain why. Matthew often forgot his place. As much as he acted the part, he was not her real brother. Louisa could only imagine what her aunt might conclude from their relationship.

Matthew scowled. "You cannot walk there alone in the dark if that is what you mean."

Louisa nearly huffed a frustrated breath, but she remained as stoic as she could. It was no wonder Bridget was often fit to be tied over her brother's protectiveness.

"I couldn't help but overhear your plight," Mrs. Lovell craned her neck to see over Matthew's shoulder. Her blue eyes sparkled. "My husband and I will accompany you if you wish. You must be quite tired from your travels, Mr. Northcott. And my boys have surely worn you out." She laughed. "You should make your way straight to the inn so you can sleep. I believe the inn is a short distance from Miss Rosemeyer's destination. We will walk with her from there. I cannot resist an evening walk in the summer rain."

Was it raining? Louisa looked outside, relieved to see that it was just a light drizzle that pattered on the window.

"If you're certain it's not too great of an inconvenience," Louisa said.

"We are certain." Mr. Lovell smiled, rising to stand beside his wife, his movements slow and labored. He farmed for a nearby estate, his leathery, tan skin a testament to his hard work in the sun. He must have been even more tired than his movements showed.

After bidding farewell to Margaret and promising to come visit again soon, Louisa, Matthew, and Mr. and Mrs. Lovell started out the door. Once Matthew had stopped at the inn, the other three exited the carriage, each taking one of Louisa's small trunks. She didn't have many possessions to boast of, so it would be easy to carry them the rest of the way to Benham Abbey. If they could find it. The sky was awfully dark that evening.

Louisa hid her worry as best as she could, though Matthew likely sensed it.

"Don't wait for us, Mr. Northcott," Mrs. Lovell said. "We will walk home after accompanying Louisa to Benham Abbey."

He hesitated before seeming to relent. Mrs. Lovell was capable, and she seemed intent to prove that through her actions. Louisa admired her already.

"If anything is amiss, inform me immediately,"

Matthew said as Louisa began walking away with the Lovells.

She nodded, swallowing the nervousness that rose in her throat.

She took a deep breath. Nothing would be amiss. Yet she could not seem to shake Jack Warwick's opinion from her mind. *Do not listen to that cad*, she said to herself.

"Cad?" Mrs. Lovell raised her eyebrows, pulling Louisa out of her thoughts. "Mr. Northcott did not strike me as a cad."

Louisa shook her head fast, putting a hand to her forehead. Had she really said that aloud? She was more tired than she showed as well. "Oh, no, not Mr. Northcott. I was speaking my thoughts aloud concerning another man I met today."

"I do not tolerate cads." Mrs. Lovell raised her chin. "Who was this man?"

Perhaps calling him a cad had been a bit harsh. She bit her lip. All he had done was pay her a compliment or two. His gaze had not strayed anywhere it should not have, and his words hadn't been anything scandalous. "Mr. Jack Warwick."

Mr. Lovell let out a scoff, and Mrs. Lovell had a gasp to match it. "It is no wonder you found him so disagreeable," she said. "He is always drunk as a wheelbarrow, going about causing mischief."

"Mischief?" Louisa gulped.

"Gambling and the like," Mr. Lovell said. "I've heard

that he recently let a house in this area, moving away from his family's estate for unknown reasons."

That was what Margaret had told her. But she didn't know it was *this* area he had moved to. Hopefully he didn't live close enough to Benham Abbey to have another encounter with her.

Mrs. Irwin would be agreeable and kind. *Agreeable and kind,* she repeated in her mind as they walked along the path. The rain droplets grew in size, falling a little faster. Louisa's already ruined hair became plastered to her forehead. She was afraid to ask the Lovells their opinion of her aunt, considering that they had such a strong opinion of Mr. Warwick. She would rather meet Mrs. Irwin and develop her own opinion for herself. Perhaps she would find much to like about the woman that others overlooked. The cheerful monologue in her head was interrupted by Mrs. Lovell's voice.

"Oh, yes, you would do well to avoid Mr. Warwick." She spread out her free arm, the one not holding Louisa's trunk, catching raindrops on her sleeves.

"Indeed." Mr. Lovell said. "I have given Margaret the same advice."

"Oh, not to worry. That is my intention." Louisa gave a polite smile, watching the ground as she walked to avoid slipping. The last thing she needed was a muddy dress to add to her disheveled appearance, but the hem of her gown was beyond help already.

As they walked over the crest of a hill, the house came into view. Symmetrical and square, the manor stood among two rows of trees, with a handsome garden on the front lawn. The windows were almost all dark. Surely her aunt was already asleep. *Please let her be asleep.*

"I must confess I was surprised to hear Mrs. Irwin offered to take you in," Mrs. Lovell said. "I was also quite surprised to hear of your relation to her. I daresay the two of you could not be more different."

She must have noticed the fear creeping into Louisa's expression. Mrs. Lovell quickly added, "Perhaps it has simply been too long since I have seen her. She rarely ventures out."

Louisa's stomach pinched with dread.

Mrs. Lovell continued to try to dig herself out of her first statement. "But how could she not adore you? I am certain you will become dear friends in no time at all."

They stopped walking when they reached the front steps of the house. "You are very kind. Thank you." Louisa offered a smile before turning toward the door. She paused to listen, hoping to hear some sound from behind it. How improper was it to come knocking at this hour? In Mrs. Irwin's letter, she had told Louisa to come as soon as she wished, and that her arrival would be *eagerly anticipated*. So what was she so worried about?

With a deep breath, she raised the knocker and struck it softly against the door three times.

Within seconds, the door was tugged open at the hands of a short, slouching woman, her wide-set eyes taking Louisa in with scrutiny. If not for her tell-tale cap and apron, Louisa might have thought she was Mrs. Irwin.

"Good evening. I am Miss Rosemeyer. I'm sincerely sorry to be arriving so lat—"

The woman's croaky voice stopped her. "You have actually arrived much earlier than I expected." Her eyes took in Louisa's dirty, worn dress and disheveled hair. "The house has been so empty, you see, with Mrs. Irwin's staff being so disloyal to this house." The woman let out a huffed breath, shaking her head.

Disloyal staff?

"You must promise you will stay for a long while," the woman said. "It has been difficult to find anyone to stay."

Louisa gulped, gripping the handle of her valise a little tighter. "Yes. I plan to stay as long as I am welcome."

The woman—Louisa assumed was the housekeeper—let out a quiet laugh. "Well, you will stay as long as you fulfill your responsibilities soundly."

Responsibilities? Louisa frowned, but didn't inquire, feeling suddenly intimidated by the woman and her intense gaze.

"Are these your parents?" The housekeeper asked, nodding toward Mr. and Mrs. Lovell. Louisa had nearly forgotten they were there. She was somewhat shocked at the housekeeper's casual way of speaking to her, considering Louisa was her mistress's guest.

"No, they are my friends."

The housekeeper gave a jovial grin. "Well, I thank you for bringing her here. She is most desperately needed."

Louisa's composure was wearing thin. She took a deep breath to calm the turmoil in her stomach. What was she desperately needed for? Perhaps her aunt was so lonely that her housekeeper had grown concerned for her health?

Mr. and Mrs. Lovell appeared to be just as confused as Louisa, but they returned the housekeeper's smile, setting Louisa's trunks inside the door. "We will see you soon, Miss Rosemeyer." Mrs. Lovell waved as they walked down the steps.

Louisa thanked them, walking inside the house with the housekeeper, whose name she had yet to catch. Since the woman hadn't fetched Mrs. Irwin yet, Louisa could only assume her wishes had been granted. She had already gone to bed.

"I am very surprised you arrived so soon, though it is a pleasant surprise." The woman seemed flustered, turning to a nearby footman and instructing him to pick up Louisa's trunks and follow them. "I had a few rooms prepared in the hopes that they would soon be filled."

"Multiple rooms?" Louisa's brow furrowed.

"Of course. You can't expect to be the only one coming. This is a large house, you know."

Louisa's head pounded. She had never been spoken to so frankly by a servant of any house. It was all so strange. She followed behind the housekeeper as they walked down a set of stairs in the dark. Louisa could barely see, but she walked faster, afraid the footman behind her would stumble in the darkness and crash into her. Where were they going? Had Mrs. Irwin really had a room prepared for her below stairs? Did she think so little of her?

"Here we have your room, Miss Rosemeyer." The

housekeeper gestured at the cramped space. A low-sitting bed was nestled into the far corner. As tired as Louisa was, even that bed looked comfortable. Her eyes already drooped as she looked at the thin quilt and flat pillow. She sniffed. Was that rodents she smelled?

The footman set Louisa's trunks inside the room before leaving. The housekeeper held the only source of light in the room, a small candle. "Go to sleep promptly, and plan to arise at dawn." She touched the tip of her candle to the one at Louisa's bedside, bringing a small flicker of light to the room.

Louisa's confusion doubled, and she turned to examined the space again. Realization sprung atop her shoulders, and her eyes widened. The housekeeper thought she was a maid. It was obvious now. With Louisa's dreary clothing and hair, she hardly looked like a lady that day. She was timid like a maid too, submissive, allowing the housekeeper to give her orders. Louisa nearly explained the misunderstanding, but she paused.

What if that had been Mrs. Irwin's plan? What if she had only invited Louisa there on the condition that she earn her place?

She swallowed, her breath catching. Well, if that was what she had to do, then she would do it. And if it really was just a misunderstanding, then she could sort it out when she met her aunt in the morning. Cold fear settled between her shoulder blades, but she didn't let it show.

By the time Louisa sorted through her thoughts, the housekeeper was gone, the door closed firmly behind her.

CHAPTER 5

Finding a decent gambling hall outside of London had been a difficult task, but Jack had found one a few months before. It wasn't a traditional establishment, not like the ones in London, but in the parlor of Lord Bridport's estate. Men were only welcome by invitation, and Jack had earned his place at the table by offering stakes that kept all the games interesting. His life had not been filled with luck in any other sense, but when it came to gambling, he was notoriously lucky.

He had a place among the chandeliers, red velvet curtains, and dark walls with ancient paintings. Lord Bridport provided food and drink, and plenty of it. Cassandra was mad for suggesting he stop coming there. It was all he had. It was all he truly found joy in from his life. That, and beautiful women.

He grinned at the thought of the young lady in town

that day. Miss Rosemeyer. He wouldn't forget that name, nor her large brown eyes, nor the way she had snatched her bonnet from his hand. The poor girl was out of her mind to be living with Mrs. Irwin. The fact that Mrs. Irwin had invited her there at all was incredibly puzzling, and the unlikelihood of it hadn't ceased to leave his thoughts alone all evening. And why did the entire matter concern him at all? He had let Mrs. Irwin's house, but that was the only connection he had to her. Still, the entire situation rattled through his brain with familiarity. Had Mrs. Irwin *told* him she had a great niece coming to live with her? He couldn't recall such a conversation. Then why did it all feel so blasted familiar?

He shrugged his strange thoughts away, focusing instead on the game at hand.

As he sat back in his chair at the round table in Lord Bridport's parlor, he blinked to see past the smoke that hung in the air from a newcomer to the table, Mr. Evan Whitby's, pipe. According to Lord Bridport, he had invited Mr. Whitby in an attempt to befriend him. Mr. Whitby was guardian over the woman Lord Bridport hoped to marry, so it was in Lord Bridport's best interest to please him with an invitation to his exclusive party. And how could a man's approval not be won by free port?

"An extraordinary roll, Whitby." Lord Bridport groveled to Mr. Whitby like a mouse to a slice of cheese. "Perhaps if I wish to keep any of my money I should never invite you here again." He slapped the table, laughing.

Mr. Whitby turned up his nose, half his mouth rising

in a smug smile. "I *am* known for my luck, especially in hazards." The man's voice reminded Jack of an opera singer, each word drawn out and oddly musical.

"It appears we will all have a challenge tonight," Lord Bridport said, chuckling. He gestured at Jack with his cup. "Especially you, Warwick."

Jack crossed his arms over his chest, scoffing under his breath. Now he had to make absolutely certain Mr. Whitby lost all that he had wagered. Every last shilling. And he would be proud to erase the smug smile from the man's face as well.

Jack inhaled deeply, grimacing. He had never liked the scent of smoke. It reminded him of gunpowder.

"Ah, Warwick, is it?" Whitby paused, his eyes narrowing as he studied Jack from across the table. His mouth hung open as he squinted, as if he couldn't see him clearly through the puff of smoke he had caused to float in the air between them. "*Jack Warwick?*"

Jack stiffened. He didn't recall ever meeting this man before that evening. Was Jack really so famous in town? "Yes, that is what I am called." Jack raised his eyebrows. "Have we met?"

At Jack's confirmation, Whitby wagged his pipe in front of him, an eager glint entering his eyes. "This—this is the man who killed Simon Warwick." His eyes darted around the table.

Jack's stomach turned over, flipping like a fish on dry land. His skin went cold, and pain burrowed itself into the familiar hovel in his heart. He took a deep breath, gripping his cup to keep his hand from shaking.

"I do not understand," Lord Bridport said, his voice uneasy as he glanced at Jack. "I am not aware of a man named Simon Warwick."

"Because *this* man," Whitby pointed a harsh finger at Jack, "killed him before you'd have had the chance to make his acquaintance. Haven't you heard the story?"

Jack's eyes closed, the walls crowding in on him. His chair felt like it was sinking slowly into the ground. The *story*. By the way Whitby described it, one would think it was an exciting tale, one to be told over drinks in a room such as the one they were in now. Jack wished it were only a story, but it was a piece of his life, one he relived every time he closed his eyes—one he would undo even for the price of his soul.

"The law should have been more involved in the ordeal if you ask me. I'm surprised he'd even show his face in public after what he did." Whitby's musical, almost cheerful tone scraped at Jack's composure like a dull knife.

Jack's eyes shot open. "Do you think I revel in it as you do? My uncle died that day, and I was to blame. It was accidental." His voice cracked on the last word, and he took a swig from his cup, wiping his mouth with the back of his hand before slumping back in his chair. His head pounded. Each time he defended himself, his guilt gained weight, falling heavier on his shoulders. Accidental or not, he was to blame. It was his fault. There was nothing to defend.

"Accidental. Hmm. The papers had a different theory," Whitby mused. "Would you all like to hear it?"

Jack's jaw tightened, his teeth nearly cracking with the pressure.

The other men at the table remained silent, staring with wide eyes at Jack. They knew him well. Or so they thought. They didn't wish to betray him by asking for the story, but their curiosity stopped them from denying Whitby's offer. They hardly knew the deuced Evan Whitby who sat so condescendingly with his pipe and lofty dark hair. Could the man have possibly piled it higher atop his head? His broad shoulders and short neck gave him a squat appearance as he surveyed the others at the table.

"Well, I will tell you anyway." Whitby cast a knowing glance at Jack, one that dripped with disgust. He turned to Lord Bridport. "It was five years ago…likely before you moved to this estate, which must be why you have not been made aware of this before now."

Jack's jaw loosened long enough for him to interject. "If you plan to tell the entire table against my will, then I will tell it," he grumbled. "I was the only one who was there and therefore the only one who has the truth." Jack's voice shook. His breath came in short gusts, his lungs never filling all the way. He could hear his heart pounding, each beat pulsing hard against his ribs. Could he tell it? He hadn't spoken of the incident aloud in years. He hadn't been able to. Each time he let the memory back in, it made his entire body ache, and he could hardly bear to even breathe. He didn't deserve to.

Whitby smirked. "Is it the truth you will tell? Or are you attempting to pass your own sins off as an accident? I was surprised the inquest found you innocent. I never believed it."

Jack bit the inside of his cheek, glancing at Lord Bridport. Would his friend really remain silent while Jack was being attacked like this? Accused so blatantly of something as serious as murder? It was unpardonable, yet Lord Bridport couldn't dare speak a word that might convince Mr. Whitby that he was not worthy to marry his ward. Whitby must have known he had Jack trapped. No one would risk upsetting Whitby at the risk of upsetting Lord Bridport and being unwelcome at his gambling parties. So the table was quiet, waiting, stiff as the pomade in Whitby's hair.

"I was nineteen years old," Jack said. His legs shook beneath the table, his heart still beating faster than an Arabian racehorse. He drew a deep breath. "My father and my uncle took me on their traditional fox hunt. There was an accident." Jack rubbed a hand over his face, fighting the horrific images that entered his mind. Every image from that day was painted in vivid color, hanging in the gallery of his memories. These were paintings meant to be covered by a sheet. A black, heavy sheet. But as he spoke them aloud, the sheets fell, and a wave of dread pressed against his chest until he could hardly open his mouth. "I was startled. My gun fired. My uncle was shot. He did not survive the wound." Jack's jaw clamped shut again, and his breath rushed through his nostrils audibly. He tried to calm the turmoil within his chest, but his heart and lungs continued to work hard, as though he were physically running from the past.

All the eyes that watched him from around the table were filled with shock, caution, and no small measure of dismay.

"How unlikely is an accident like that?" Whitby said, breaking the heavy silence. "I daresay it is nearly impossible."

Anger rose in Jack's throat, and he leaned forward like a bull pawing the ground. "Are you accusing me of murder?"

Whitby lifted both hands in surrender. "Oh, no. It is not my accusations. I am simply repeating what the gossip papers theorized about that day." He turned his attention back to Lord Bridport and the others. "You see, Simon Warwick was the elder brother of Jack's father. He was set to inherit the family estate, an enviable property indeed. With his own business struggling, Jack's father stood to gain much if his brother were no longer alive. He would inherit everything since his brother hadn't yet produced an heir, and then his own son, Jack, would be the next heir. Together, they devised this plan to stage the death as a hunting accident."

Jack fisted his hands on the table, nearly rising from his chair. "That is not true." Society loved a gruesome story, especially one that was fabricated. Jack remembered the day that story had been published in the gossip papers. It was the day his father had stopped speaking to him altogether. It was the day Cassandra had given up hope that she would marry. It was the day Mama had paced the house at least a dozen times, hiding her sobs between her quiet exclamations that they were forever ruined.

"I think it is far past time you owned up to it," Whitby said. "You are among friends. Let us hear your confessions. We will not judge you harshly."

Jack swallowed, his chest rising and falling fast. "You will hear no confession from me."

"This money you gamble with tonight...how does it feel to know it belonged to the uncle whose death stains your hands? How much morality can one man lack?" He turned to Lord Bridford. "My lord, I should hope you reconsider inviting him here again. I choose not to associate myself with criminal men."

Confound it. Jack leapt from his chair, lunging to where Whitby sat atop his throne of condescension. No man had ever needed a firm facer more than he did. Even the gasp that came from Whitby's mouth sounded like a musical note, but the only music to Jack's ears was the thud of his fist against Whitby's jaw.

The man had more strength than Jack had given him credit. Only a moment after recoiling in pain, Whitby sprung out of his chair, tackling Jack to the floor. His broad shoulders and short, wide neck should have been an indicator of some measure of strength. It wasn't long before Whitby's fist collided with Jack's nose, then his jaw, then his eye. Jack's vision blurred, and he tasted blood. Pain pulsed through his entire face, but he managed to throw a blind punch upward, striking something solid and wet.

Whitby grunted in pain, rolling to the side,

clutching his hand over his mouth as he screamed. Jack shook out his hand, cringing at the teeth marks on the tops of his fingers. He wiped under his nose, pulling back a streak of blood. His head spun, his pulse ringing in his ears.

"Out!"

Jack blinked as he was tugged upward by the arm. Lord Bridport's face came into view, fury raging in his features. "Get out of my house."

Jack had never seen him so angry before. The image startled him into silence, ebbing the anger that flowed through his own veins.

"Now!" Lord Bridport thrust him away.

Jack wiped at the blood on his face again, walking several paces away from Lord Bridport. Whitby stood hunched over, glaring up at him. His own face was swollen, his lip split and bleeding. Jack stepped toward him before Lord Bridport caught him by the back of his jacket. Jack met Whitby's eyes. "If you really think me capable of murder, you ought to tread a little more carefully, don't you think?"

Lord Bridport tugged Jack backward, handing him off to two footmen, one taking each of his arms. Jack jerked his elbows free. "I'll see myself out."

His face felt numb to the pain, his nose throbbing softly without aching as he walked out into the warm evening air. The sky was blacker than his horse's hair, the smallest crescent moon hanging among the sparse stars. Jack normally would have smelled the rain that trickled down around him, but at the moment he could not breathe through his nostrils.

He found his horse and mounted, staunching the flow of blood from his nose as he dug his heels into the horse's flanks. As he rode away, he stole a lingering glance at Newton Hall, regret enrobing his heart like iron. Those parties had been all he had to look forward to. A place among Lord Bridport's table had been the only place he was welcome. And now, because of Evan Whitby—that *deuced nodcock*—Jack was banished from the property. He couldn't show his face in London. Those who remembered the stories in the papers would never let him near their establishments. He would be driven out of town and treated like a sewer rat.

He wiped angrily at his nose, unsure now what was rain and what was blood. The pain was settling in now, extending through every nerve in his face. He had no doubt his nose was broken. He tightened his grip on the reins, slowing his horse's pace enough that he could reach up and gingerly touch the bridge of his nose. Devil take it. That bump hadn't been there before.

He could barely see through the rain and darkness. It must have been past midnight by now, and he still had a thirty minute ride ahead of him. The pain in his face was rather blinding too, and he couldn't rid his mouth of the taste of blood. At least he had the comfort of knowing he had caused similar pain to Whitby. He could only hope it was worse. Only then would it be worth losing the only place Jack was welcome to visit—the only friends he had.

Were they his friends? Bridport's pursuit of Whitby's sister had been more important to him than Jack's dignity.

The sense of betrayal dug into his heart like a dagger, bringing his thoughts back to the present. He blinked the rain from his eyes, squinting. The jarring realization hit him—he was not on the path back to his new house. Without thinking, he had taken the path toward his childhood home, where all the windows were darkened. Jack's family always had retired early each evening. Haslington estate was hunched beyond the path ahead, tucked among the hills. In the darkness, Jack could barely see the water of the nearby river, blackened by night, and the stone bridge that arched over it.

He stopped his horse, pausing to stare at the front doors beyond the iron gate. How many times had he walked through them? Mama had greeted him with a hug each time, and Papa had slapped him on the shoulder with a smile because he was not the sort to hug. Cassandra had been the one to tease Jack, not to scold him as she did now.

Back then, there had been little to scold him about.

If Jack were to walk through those doors now, he would be greeted like an intruder, at least by his father. His entrance would likely be met by the same words Bridport had used that night. *Out. Get out of my house.*

He urged his horse forward, his heart pounding. Had his father turned Mama against him too? If she saw him now, would she even pity him? He recalled a day when he was a child, when he had broken his arm falling from a tree he had climbed on the property. He had gone running inside, and Mama had held him while he cried. Papa had stayed beside him and held his hand when the physician came and set the bone into place.

Atop his horse in the dark rain with a broken, bleeding nose, Jack was that child again. His heart thudded in his ears as he stared at the facade of the dark house. How could Mama look at him the same way now? He had failed her. He had failed everyone.

She would not hold him in her arms.

Papa would not stay beside him for anything.

Hot tears burned in Jack's eyes, rolling down his face. He wiped them away in one swift motion, appalled that he had let them spill at all. The quiet loneliness of the night had caused his hold on his emotions to weaken. How the stars must have laughed seeing him in such a state.

It had been a long day.

Picking up the reins once again, he turned his horse back, guiding it toward the path that led to Benham Abbey. Although he would inherit Haslington one day, the house he had let from Mrs. Irwin was the place he would have to learn to call home for the time being. It was the only place he could ensure he was not banished from. At Benham Abbey, there was no one there to tell him whether he was welcome or not, no matter how much the housekeeper tried to make clear that she did not like him.

At the thought of his housekeeper, he made a mental note to begin working toward hiring new staff the next day. As much as he liked to spite her, they really did need more help in the house as soon as possible. At least the cook had stayed.

His stomach growled. His first order of business when he arrived home would be to visit the kitchen. He needed food.

And a few drinks.

CHAPTER 6

"Drat it all," Louisa muttered under her breath. She let out a sigh as she grasped angrily at the back of her dress. Her candle had already burned out, and changing in the dark was proving a difficult task. Why had she worn this old, out-of-fashion dress? The many buttons down the back were much more difficult to manage than the dresses of current fashions. She tugged at the fabric, no longer caring to preserve the gown. If it tore, then she wouldn't feel guilty throwing it out.

But the buttons held firm, surprisingly well-sewn. She stopped struggling, blowing out a puff of air. It seemed she would have to try to fall asleep with her dress half-unbuttoned down the back. She couldn't see enough to accurately unbutton it, and even if she could, she doubted she could reach. With the new strength of a good night's sleep, she would attempt the task again in the morning. Her eyes had begun drooping again.

Working quickly, she felt all around her head, pulling out the pins she could manage to find. Her hair fell heavily over her shoulders, and she massaged her scalp as she sat on the edge of her bed. It was quite a…firm mattress. She shifted, kicking aside the thin blanket to crawl inside. Shivers ran over her arms. She would not even be able to see if there were any insects or spiders in bed with her. A scuttling sound across the room made her freeze. Was that a rodent?

She shunned the horrific thought, wrapping the blanket around herself. So long as she didn't feel any tickle on her skin, she would be safe. But that thought caused her skin to tickle all over, and she slapped at her arms and legs each time she felt it.

Stop, Louisa. You are imagining things. She drew a calming breath. She would most likely not have to sleep in that bed again. There had simply been a miscommunication between Mrs. Irwin and her staff. Yes. Louisa refused to believe any different.

She stared at the dark ceiling for a long moment before closing her eyes. How could she sleep with the way her thoughts were racing? By now it was far past midnight, perhaps even later, and the housekeeper had told her to be awake at dawn.

She tossed and turned, attempting to relax her mind. After at least an hour without success, she gave up, sitting up at the edge of her bed. She pushed her hair back from her forehead. What a mess she was. Her dress was half-buttoned down the back, her hair hung loose and tangled, and her stomach grumbled viciously. Had she eaten anything at all the day before? The Lovells had offered to feed her but she had felt too guilty to take any of their food. Her throat was also dry…she needed water. If she could find something small to eat and drink, perhaps then she could finally sleep.

The idea set her stomach grumbling again. Of course. All she needed was a full stomach and she would be able to finally relax.

She stood up too fast, a faintness coming to her head. She stumbled through the dark, but hesitated at the door. Was it wise to wander through the house in the middle of the night? What if she awoke Mrs. Irwin? Or worse…the housekeeper? How embarrassing would it be if her aunt found her sneaking through the kitchen like a stray cat? She couldn't even begin to think of how she might explain herself.

As if in protest of her hesitation, her stomach gave a furious grumble, much like a child throwing a tantrum. "Oh, hush," Louisa whispered. Oh, dear. She was speaking to her stomach. Was her hunger causing madness now? Her fingers slid over the door handle, and much to her surprise, the door didn't even creak when she opened it. Thankfully, her eyes had adjusted to the darkness already, so she didn't need a candle as she walked on the tips of her toes toward the stairs.

One benefit to being so small was the ability to sneak around when necessary. The floorboards made only the rare creak as she walked.

The house was quiet and still. She would have believed she was completely alone inside it if she didn't know better. The trees outside the windows cast faint shadows over the floor by the staircase, causing an army of chill bumps to cascade over Louisa's arms. It still rained outside, heavier now, and the wind carried a slight whistle, combing through the branches that hovered by the window. Her heart picked up speed and she walked a little faster. With so little light, her mind had begun creating all kinds of scenarios involving ghosts and monsters.

At Larkhall, the kitchen was on the second floor. Louisa decided to try the same here, despite the manor being much smaller. She hurried up the stairs, careful to keep her steps light.

Kitchen. Kitchen. Kitchen. She scoured all the doors that she passed, walking with quick steps.

A sound made her pause, her heart leaping to her throat.

A man's voice. Deep and mumbling—so quiet that she wasn't certain if she had really heard it or if it had only been a product of her imagination. She strained her ears, pressing a hand to her chest in an attempt to quiet her heart.

There it was again. The mumbling. Then the sound of two staggering footsteps. A thud.

"Devil take it," the voice muttered.

Louisa jumped back like a spooked horse, moving backward. A door down the hall had a small flicker of light beneath it. To her dismay, the door began to open. Was that the kitchen? She certainly couldn't go toward it now. Her pulse hammered as she slipped down the adjacent hallway and pressed her back against the wall. She hadn't been seen. Had she?

Cold fear wrapped around her chest, making her breath come faster. Mrs. Irwin was not married, so there should not have been a man in that house, aside from the servants. Could it have been the butler? Or a footman?

Louisa froze. A ghost?

She nearly laughed at the ridiculous thought, but her laughter stopped in her throat when she heard the staggering footsteps resume…

…down the hall toward where she was hiding.

Her hiding place was not much of a hiding place at all if the man were to come around the corner. She was standing against the wall in the open hallway. All she relied on was the darkness to conceal her, but it wouldn't be enough. Her gaze darted to the staircase that led to the next floor. If the man was indeed a servant, he would be going down, not up.

With quick steps, she sneaked up the stairs, too afraid to look back. She cringed at the way her skirts rustled. Turning the corner, she stopped by a closed door, one that likely led to a bedchamber. Was it her aunt's room? Louisa held her breath, careful not to make too much noise.

A groan and a cough echoed in the empty house. Louisa's skin went cold. It had come from the bottom of the stairs.

Thud.

Thud.

Thud.

The shadow of the top of a man's head came into view, moving up the stairs with that same staggering gait.

Had he seen her? Was he following her? Something was amiss. If this man was a servant in the house, he would not have been making so much noise. Only a madman would be so loud and be muttering to himself for so long. Could it be an intruder? The idea sent a spiral of terror through Louisa's head, bringing back the faintness she had felt from her hunger. Without thinking, she eased open the nearest bedchamber door. She had no choice if she hoped to remain unseen.

The moment she was behind the door, she scanned the room. To her relief, the bed was empty. At least she hadn't trespassed on her aunt's bedchamber. The large room was neat and empty, aside from a large bed, fireplace, writing desk, and tall wardrobe. The drapes were drawn open, letting in the smallest hint of moonlight.

Her heart still hammered as she listened for more sounds from the hallway. The thick door drowned out any noise. How would she know if the man was close? She backed away from the door, pausing by the fireplace to grab the steel poker. The wardrobe caught her eye, the wide doors beckoning her like a warm blanket. She would feel much safer if she were hidden in a smaller place, one that completely concealed her.

It would merely be a precaution.

Her mind raced as she darted toward the wardrobe,

pulling open the doors and slipping inside. With a tug, she brought both doors in toward her until they settled into place.

She let out the breath she had been holding, inhaling deeply to calm her nerves. Her hands and legs shook. Why had she left her room? Could she not have waited until morning to eat? Now she had no food, and she was hiding from an unknown man in an empty wardrobe. She scolded herself in a whispered voice as she tried to calm her heartbeat.

She gripped the fabric behind her with one hand, tightening her hold on the poker with the other.

Fabric?

Her brow furrowed as she touched the clothing inside the wardrobe, rubbing the starched material between her fingers. Was that a collar? She reached to the other side, tracing her fingers over the long row of buttons on a silk piece of fabric. The inside of the wardrobe brought a new level of darkness, so she couldn't even see her hand in front of her face. There was no telling exactly what her fingers touched, but in her blindness, it reminded her of a waistcoat. Her hands moved more frantically now. Thick, soft, leather. Breeches? A long line of wool buttons. A tailcoat, perhaps? She was sure of it now.

This was a man's wardrobe.

Her skin went cold as the realization washed over her. Could it be...*the* man's wardrobe? The man who—

Her heart jumped to her throat. A low creak indicated that the bedchamber door was opening once again. Then came the staggering footfalls, thudding heavily across the room. Had he seen her? Was he following her? She turned the poker over in her palm, letting the cool metal keep her alert and anchored. Had she missed something? Had her aunt married and she hadn't known? Why else would this man have a room in the house? Dread crept up her throat, and she felt very near to vomiting.

Louisa closed her eyes, even though she could already scarcely see a thing. Her breath shook, but she kept it as quiet as possible. If she remained silent enough, he might not find her. She would wait until he fell asleep and then slip out of the room. That was all she *could* do. She was not, under any circumstances, leaving her hiding place until she heard the man let out a loud, monstrous snore. A man with such a heavy gait and deep, muttering voice could only be of the snoring sort. He was probably short with a round belly, with his facial hair far too overgrown. At least that was how she imagined him as she listened to him muttering curses under his breath.

She opened her eyes. A candle had been lit in the room; she could see a faint glow in the crack between the two doors of the wardrobe. If she leaned her eye close enough to the crack, she would probably be able to see into the room. *No.* She didn't dare move a single inch and risk being heard. She had already acted with enough stupidity for one day.

The candlelight flickered brighter, then dimmer, as the man moved, his footfalls still ridiculously loud. Louisa held her breath as the sounds moved closer.

The man inhaled deeply, then groaned, as though it had caused him pain. Fabric rustled, then fell with a soft thud to the floor. As she listened, her horror intensified. Was he—was he...undressing?

An even more unsettling thought followed. If he was indeed undressing, then he would soon be opening the wardrobe for his nightclothes.

She stifled the squeaking noise that had begun escaping her throat with each shaky exhale.

Compose yourself, she ordered, standing up straighter. Before she could gather more than a small portion of her wits, the wardrobe doors jolted open.

A chest. A man's bare chest and shoulders were the first things she saw. Lean and muscled, the torso was far from what she had imagined from hearing the man's staggering gait. Then she saw his breeches, thankfully still in their proper place. She witnessed all of it in a flash, leaving only one instant between her shock at seeing his bare torso and the shock at seeing his face.

Although the round belly was absent, the beard was not. The man held a candle in one hand, lifting it to illuminate the inside of the wardrobe, and consequently, his own face. Louisa gulped, her breath catching in her throat with horror.

It was not a beard.

It was blood, covering the entire bottom half of his face.

His *familiar* face.

Her skin went cold, and her heart all but stopped. It was the man from town.

Jack Warwick.

Her heart flipped when she saw what he held in his other hand. A white bundle of fabric, stained with even more blood.

Oh, no, no, *no*. Dread puddled in Louisa's stomach. Her throat dried up like an autumn leaf. *Dash* it all.

All the signs could only point to one thing.

Jack Warwick—the deranged, wicked, *mischievous* man—had broken into Benham Abbey and murdered Mrs. Irwin.

CHAPTER 7

Louisa's thoughts swirled too fast to make sense of a single one. Panic tore across her mind. She clutched the poker with both hands. Within seconds, she saw the light of Mr. Warwick's candle pass over her own face, and she let out a shriek, crashing against the back of the wardrobe.

Mr. Warwick's eyes fell on her, darkened by the shadow of his candle. They rounded, and he jumped back. And then he let out a deep, thunderous scream, the likes of which Louisa had never heard in her entire life, at least not from a man.

He tripped over the jacket, waistcoat, and boots he must have discarded on the floor, landing on his back with a thud. A deep groan escaped him, and then he became still, his head lolling to one side. The candle he had been holding clattered to the ground.

Louisa's heart pounded. She clutched her poker as she

stepped out of the wardrobe, lunging forward to pick up the candle before it could set the house on fire. She held the light out in front of her, keeping Mr. Warwick fully illuminated from where he lay on the floor. If she dashed away quickly enough, he wouldn't be able to catch her.

She paused on his closed eyes, his mouth hanging agape. Was he...dead?

She crept forward, afraid to blink as she observed him. He stirred, his brow furrowing.

She gasped, biting her lip against the sound. He was alive, but unconscious, it seemed. She recalled Mrs. Lovell's words from earlier that evening. *He is always drunk as a wheelbarrow, going about causing mischief.*

Was *this* the sort of mischief he caused? Breaking into houses that were not his own? His chest rose and fell, each movement shallow. His skin was covered in a sheen of sweat, and the beard of blood seemed to be originating from his nose.

Louisa inched forward again, studying the bundle of blood-stained white fabric he had been holding. It now lay on the floor near where the candle had fallen. She picked it up, pinching one clean corner of the fabric between her thumb and forefinger. It was a shirt. His shirt, no doubt. Another square of starched fabric sat beside it on the floor, this one even more reddened. His cravat.

Relief cascaded through her chest. The blood, it seemed, was all his own. Perhaps he had not murdered Mrs. Irwin after all. But that still did not explain what he was doing in Benham Abbey. He was drunk—that much was obvious now by the way she had heard him walking and muttering to himself. Had he simply become confused and entered the wrong house?

With careful steps, she circled around to have a better view of his face. Oh. *Oh*. Her stomach lurched. His nose was certainly not as straight as it had been earlier that day. One of his eyes was swollen as well, but there was no question his nose was the source of the blood, and it was undoubtedly broken. A surge of pity enveloped her heart, but she pushed it away. This was a madman. A raging, dangerous, deranged man. She studied him again. How had he acquired such a...figure? Did it simply come as a natural companion to his unjustly handsome face? She tore her gaze away from his torso, appalled that she had even let it linger there for a moment. She eyed the door. How could she leave him like this? Should she fetch the housekeeper? If he committed crimes such as intruding into homes that were not his own, he ought to be held responsible.

A deep, rattling sound came from his nose, making her jump. In perfect rhythm, the sound repeated itself.

Of course. She had guessed that the man she had heard outside the wardrobe would be the snoring sort. Well, she had made that assumption before she had seen him. She wouldn't have guessed that Jack Warwick was the snoring sort, not from their first interaction. But one man could not be physically perfect; no indeed. Mr. Warwick's once perfectly straight nose, now crooked, was further proof of that.

Louisa grimaced as she realized his nose hadn't stopped

bleeding. She needed to elevate his head. Unconscious as he was, he could choke. That was all she would do to help him before hurrying to find the housekeeper. It was against her nature to leave anyone alone who was in need of help, even someone who had just caused her a great deal of terror. But Jack Warwick was obviously not right in the head.

Not right at all.

His snoring continued as Louisa hurried over to the bed, snatching a pillow from it. She paused when she saw the bowl of water and rag on his desk. Had he brought that in with the intention of washing his face? He must not have been terribly drunk to have thought to do that. Louisa had never been so far into her cups to lose her mind, so she couldn't pretend to understand what his level of comprehension was at the moment. All she knew was that he seemed far from capable of harming her. She was no longer afraid of that ridiculous man. She only pitied him. Once he was discovered, he would be in severe trouble. It was all she could do to make his last moments of freedom a little more comfortable.

With a deep breath, she crouched behind his head, setting down the poker before forcing the pillow under his dark hair. He moaned, but didn't move. Louisa stood, brushing her hands over her skirts. There. His breathing had become steadier, but the amount of blood on his face was still ghastly. It was fortunate for him that she did not become faint around such things. Her stomach turned, sending a rush of lightness to her head. Or did she?

No. Louisa had secretly prided herself on her ability to

not faint at the sight of things she was expected to faint at. And ladies were expected to faint at nearly everything unsightly. As a child, she had witnessed a boy in town fall from his horse and break his arm. At the sight of the injury, Louisa's friend Emma had collapsed to the ground faster than a lady could collapse a fan in her hand. Louisa had helped walk the boy to safety, and everyone had been amazed at the levelness of her head. Louisa was nothing if not levelheaded and optimistic. And despite every reason not to, she couldn't leave Jack Warwick here bleeding. She would help him quickly without waking him, then hurry back to bed. It would be better to do that than to wake the housekeeper or find her aunt and wake her. How could Louisa explain what she was doing in this room in the middle of the night?

She almost laughed. Almost.

To think that she had been afraid of making a poor impression on her aunt before was highly amusing considering her situation now.

With soft steps, she walked to the bowl of water on his desk. She fetched a blanket from his bed as well. When she returned to her place beside Mr. Warwick, she draped the blanket over his bare torso, grateful for the barrier to make the situation seem a little more proper. The impropriety of it all still burned on her cheeks, but she ignored the sensation. Despite his madness, this man *had* helped retrieve her bonnet in town earlier that day. This could be her way to repay the favor—by not allowing him to die on the floor.

She wrung the excess water from the rag, shifting on

the floor until she sat to the right of his head. His breathing continued, slow and shallow, but he did not seem keen to wake any time soon. The water was warm enough that she doubted it would wake him, but she still hesitated as she held the rag over his nose. If he started to wake, she would simply dash out of the room.

Rolling the rag into the shape of a sausage, she tucked it under his nose, wrapping the ends around and applying a slight amount of pressure. His brow flinched, and she nearly jumped back. Her heart hammered. Why did she feel as though she were treating a tiger's broken nose? Would he attack her if his eyes opened now? She would not put it past him. She gulped. Every noise made her jump, even if she was the one who made the sound. She could hardly believe his scream hadn't awoken the entire household.

She removed the rag from his nose, checking beneath it. The blood no longer flowed from his nostrils, so she set to wiping clean the rest of his face. With gentle strokes, she cleaned the bridge of his nose, now twisted slightly to the left. Oh, dear. A physician would need to set it back in place, no doubt. That would not be a pleasant experience.

With each stroke of the rag, she watched his brow, careful that he didn't stir too much. His facial hair was indeed overgrown, but not by more than a fraction of an inch, though it did make his face more difficult to clean. She blushed as she washed his lips, feeling excruciatingly awkward. Once his face was clean, she set the rag back in the bowl of water, sitting back on her heels. She ought to be rewarded from the heavens for her good deed. It was undeserved on Mr. Warwick's part.

She scowled down at him, watching the way his long, straight eyelashes shadowed his cheeks. A crease still marked the space between his two dark eyebrows. In that moment, she couldn't quite recall what color his eyes had been.

She surveyed the room, confusion rising to her mind once again. This was certainly a man's room. With the candlelight now burning, she couldn't see any sign of a feminine touch to the decorations. It was Louisa's downfall, being too timid. She should have asked for answers from the housekeeper, no matter how intimidated she was. Something was certainly amiss. There had been a misunderstanding, or several. Mrs. Irwin would have much to explain in the morning. Could Mr. Warwick be a guest in this house? The idea was preposterous. He despised Mrs. Irwin.

The Lovells' words came back to Louisa's mind from earlier that day. *I've heard that he recently let a house in this area.* Her heart thudded. Had he—had he let *this* house? She glanced at the wardrobe again, seeing clearly now the array of fine, masculine clothing inside. But how could he be letting Benham Abbey if her aunt had replied to the letter Louisa had sent here?

It simply did not make any sense.

Panic took root inside her again as she glanced at the bowl of reddened water and was reminded of where she was. Her stomach gave a lurch. If Mr. Warwick did indeed live here, as difficult as it was to believe, then it was not *he* who was the intruder. It was Louisa.

She needed to leave the room. Now. Urgency flooded her limbs, but she managed to move only an inch before her gaze settled on Mr. Warwick's face, checking to ensure he was still unconscious.

Louisa was fairly certain unconscious people did not open their eyes, and two blue ones were staring straight up at her.

It was Louisa's turn to scream.

CHAPTER 8

Had he died? Jack blinked, his vision becoming blurred. Was he in heaven? Who else could be hovering over him but an angel? A deep chuckle started bubbling in his chest, but never left his throat. Gads, his face hurt. The back of his head hurt just as much, throbbing against the hard floor. Had he hit his head? His vision cleared enough for him to examine the angel above him. Her dark hair hung long around her shoulders, her large brown eyes flitting around the room. His room.

What the devil was she doing in his room?

Dread filled his stomach as the possibilities roamed through his mind. No, he was not so much of a rake. He hadn't even been drinking as much as usual that evening; if he had, he would have been a little number to the pain in his nose. As his mind cleared, so did his memory. He had been at Newton Hall at the gambling party. That atrocious man, Evan Whitby, had begun spreading rumors, and they had both shared a few facers. Then he had come home to eat, but had taken a few drinks instead. What had happened after that was hazy. He examined the angel above him again, finding her more familiar by the second. As if she sensed his gaze, she looked down, catching his eyes.

The sound that escaped her mouth was a mixture of a gasp and a scream, ringing in his sensitive ears.

Angel? *Demon*, rather.

Jack cringed, rolling to one side. Perhaps he was not in heaven, but somewhere else entirely.

"Do I truly look so hideous?" Jack muttered, propping himself up on one elbow. He touched the bridge of his nose gingerly, appalled at how much larger it felt under his fingertips.

The woman had scrambled back a few feet, still kneeling on the floor. She was not well-dressed—wearing what appeared to be an old gown, the fabric covering her shoulders loosely and nearly falling down. The light of one candle was all that illuminated the room, so he couldn't quite recognize her face in the dimness. He had certainly seen her before, that much he knew. He studied her further, sitting up slowly.

"What are you doing in this house?" she asked in a squeak.

"Pardon me?" Jack cleared his throat. "I believe I should be begging that question of you." He rubbed his forehead. One of his eyes was swollen, so he couldn't see as clearly as he would have liked as he examined the woman in front of him. She was turned slightly away from him, terror gleaming in her eyes. The buttons on the back of her dress were undone.

Had that been *his* doing?

As he sat up, a blanket slid off his chest and onto his lap. Where had his deuced shirt gone? He swallowed. What sort of a man had he become? He had never been a rake, but what excuse could he have now?

The woman before him looked frightened out of her wits. His memories continued to flood back to him from that evening. After he had gone to the kitchen, he had walked straight back to his room. Alone. Then he had opened his wardrobe for a change of clothes and…

Oh, yes. That had been frightening, indeed. There had been someone inside. He recalled the round brown eyes and dark hair, and the steel poker that had been pointed straight at his heart. He recalled her high-pitched shriek. Or had that been his own shriek? Then he had hit the floor.

"What on earth were you doing in my wardrobe?" His voice came back to him, and he inched toward her on the floor, eager for a closer look. He had seen her somewhere before—somewhere other than the wardrobe.

"I—I am very…very confused." She put a hand to her forehead, all the while keeping one eye fixed on him.

"Ah, I remember now." He raised one finger. "You lost your bonnet in town." How could he have forgotten such a pretty face? In truth, there was little he hadn't forgotten from that day. But it was slowly coming back to him now. He raised one eyebrow, unable to prevent a sly smile from pulling on his lips. "Miss Rosemeyer, was it? Did you follow me here?"

"No!" Her voice was quick, the horror on her face strangely endearing. Jack was just as confused as she seemed, yet that couldn't stop his amusement with the situation. If she truly had followed him here, then she was a madwoman. Shouldn't he be at least a little afraid?

Her tiny fingers fiddled with the fabric of her skirt, a dimple denting her round cheek as she stared at him with her lips pressed together.

No. He could have been more afraid if a puppy were sitting across from him. At least now that she wasn't pointing the steel poker at his chest, that was.

"My—my aunt lives here," she said in a quiet voice. "Mrs. Irwin. I arrived too late to see her. The housekeeper…it is embarrassing to confess, but I'm afraid she mistook me for a maid." Her voice continued rambling, picking up speed. "I was hungry and couldn't sleep, so I was in search of the kitchen when I heard you. I ran here to hide." She kept her round gaze fixed on him. "You startled me."

"*I* startled you?" Jack scoffed, rubbing the back of his head. "It is not every day I find a pretty lady hiding in my bedchamber."

She frowned.

"Only every other day."

Her eyes grew impossibly wider.

Jack chuckled, unable to help himself. "It was a

pleasant surprise to see you again, I must confess, even under the circumstances."

Her look of surprise turned to a scowl, and for a moment, he worried she would reach for the poker again. "Why did you fail to mention you lived with Mrs. Irwin? Are you her relative?"

He groaned. "Please refrain from speaking such profanity again. I have no relation to Mrs. Irwin whatsoever. I do not live with her. I'm letting this house. She lives across town now."

Miss Rosemeyer's face went whiter than a clean serviette. "M-my aunt is not here?"

"No, indeed." Jack grinned, the movement causing his nose to throb again. He sniffed, wiping beneath his nose, surprised that the blood was gone. He glanced at the bowl of reddened water beside him and the rag floating in it. "Did you wash my face?"

The question brought a little color back to her cheeks. "Yes, though I was tempted to leave you there on the floor."

"Is there anything else you were tempted to do while I was at your disposal?" He gave a half smile, to which she responded with a glare he never would have imagined possible on that sweet face of hers.

"I was tempted to give your right eye a bruise to match the left if that is what you mean." Her sudden confidence seemed to be a facade. She still fiddled nervously with the fabric of her skirts. Even so, her gaze could have cut stone.

"Well..." Jack swallowed. "I thank you for not succumbing to such temptations."

She said nothing, tucking strands of hair behind her ears as she took a shaky breath. She really did seem terrified. He should not have been tormenting her so.

"If my aunt is not here, then how did she receive my letter? She wrote her reply and sent it from this address." Miss Rosemeyer shook her head, taking her face in her hands as she stared into space. "Would she have invited me here as a cruel trick?"

Jack shrugged. He would not have put it past Mrs. Irwin to do such a despicable thing. "Perhaps you misunderstood her letter."

"It was very concise." Miss Rosemeyer let out a long puff of air. "I did not misunderstand."

"Well, then. On the morrow, we will walk to Mrs. Irwin's new residence and sort out this—er—misunderstanding." A surge of pity bloomed in Jack's chest. What would Miss Rosemeyer's life be like living with Mrs. Irwin? He could hardly believe the woman would be hospitable. What had brought Miss Rosemeyer to such a desperate situation?

Miss Rosemeyer wrung her hands. "If you tell me where to go, I will go without your assistance, thank you."

"Just as well." Jack sighed, stretching his legs out in front of him. "So long as you end up where you belong."

The corners of her mouth tipped downward, her hands stopping their movement on the fabric of her skirts. "I don't belong anywhere." She glanced up, her eyes meeting his, solemn in the dimness. She looked away fast, her gaze flitting over his chest and shoulders. Her cheeks reddened.

Jack grinned.

"Least of all here. I—I will go back to my room. Well, I suppose it is not my room, only the place your housekeeper had prepared for a new maid." She put a hand to her head. "Perhaps I should sleep outside."

"You may stay in that room tonight," Jack said around a chuckle. Each laugh made the bruises on his face ache more. "I will not *banish* you yet. My housekeeper has been desperate for new maids, so I imagine that is why she mistook you for one. I don't see what in your appearance or manner of speaking could have caused her to make that mistake." His gaze swept over her smooth skin and bright, intelligent eyes. She was a lady, that much was certain. A young, frightened, and confused one. Also a very attractive one. He looked away, noting again how her dress was coming undone down the back. Did she know? He almost chuckled again. After seeing her in town that day, seemingly quite distressed over losing her bonnet, he never imagined he would see her in this state, with her hair completely loose and her dress nearly the same. She likely hadn't planned on being seen like that either.

He certainly hadn't planned on being seen in his current state. He caught Miss Rosemeyer's gaze flicker below his neck once again.

"I put that blanket there for a reason," Miss Rosemeyer blurted. "You might use it to cover yourself." She gave a quiet huff, as though disgusted, nodding at the blanket in his lap.

Jack made no move to retrieve it, thoroughly enjoying the discomfort on her face. *Be a gentleman*, a voice in his head—his mother's voice—demanded. How many times had she told him that? He tugged the blanket up over his shoulders, tucking it under his chin.

He eyed her. "Are you able to breathe now? Has your heart slowed just a little?"

Miss Rosemeyer's brows shot up. "P-pardon me?"

He resumed his chuckling. He was doing it again—frightening the poor girl with his flirting. Why was it so dashed entertaining?

She finally seemed to catch his meaning, and her brows leveled over her eyes. Her lips pressed together, hiding what seemed to be gritted teeth. He could almost read her mind from that one look. She was wishing for *his* heart to slow… until it stopped entirely.

"I will find my way back to my room now." She stood in one swift motion, her skirts sending a breeze toward the nearby candle on the floor. The only light in the room extinguished in an instant.

"Drat," she whispered in the dark.

Jack staggered to his feet.

"Stay back!" Miss Rosemeyer's panicked voice echoed.

"I'm not a rabid beast. I will not attack you. Might I remind you that *you* were the one pointing the poker at my chest when you pounced out of my wardrobe."

"I did not *pounce* out of the wardrobe. I fell backward when you startled me."

"I assure you, it was not intentional." Jack glanced heavenward with a sigh. Fortunately, she couldn't see his exasperation. When would she realize that it was he who had been more startled? All he had expected to see inside was a row of unmoving, clean clothing, not a madwoman with a weapon. No, Miss Rosemeyer was not a madwoman, she was simply very lost and confused.

"How can I know you are being honest? I cannot take your word. You could have followed me here from town yesterday afternoon." Her voice was frantic as her feet paced quietly in the darkness. "I don't know where I am, and I have never been so hungry," she finished in what Jack could only call a snarl.

He stepped back in surprise, his eyes adjusting enough to see her outline and the whites of her eyes. She fell silent.

"Ah. So it is your hunger which has led you to this state."

"This state?" she asked, her voice fatigued.

"Madness."

A quiet giggle filled the air, and he took another step back.

"I am not mad." Her laughter continued, growing higher with disbelief. "I am perfectly sane. *You* are mad. And you are drunk. Drinking to excess is a disagreeable habit to have, you know."

"Let us find you some food, shall we?" Jack said in a cautious tone. He glanced at the window. It wasn't his eyes adjusting, but the first hints of dawn sending a faint glow into the sky. It would still be quite some time before the sun rose fully, but the night was slipping away. Once Miss Rosemeyer was fed and asleep, he could plan how he was going to get her out of his house and where she belonged without further damage to her reputation. Except she had said she didn't belong anywhere. Empathy unfolded in his chest. He knew the feeling well.

"Come with me," he said, marching to the door. His head spun from the sudden movement. He opened the door swiftly, turning toward Miss Rosemeyer.

She stared at him, eyes wide.

He looked down, realizing he had left his covering behind again. Quite frankly, he was too exhausted to care. "Yes, I am aware that I am still not wearing my shirt, but we will make quick work of this and then I plan to go to sleep."

Miss Rosemeyer's expression didn't change. How could he see her so clearly? A shadow flickered on her face. There was light behind him, the glow from a candle bouncing through the room. Oh. She wasn't looking at him at all. She was looking at something behind his shoulder.

He turned, locking eyes with none other than his housekeeper, Mrs. Chamberlain.

A rattling gasp escaped her, and her hand flew to her chest. She only looked at Jack for a brief moment before turning her attention to Miss Rosemeyer, who still stood, just a few paces away, her hair loose and gown unbuttoned down the back.

Confound it, this did not look good.

Jack cleared his throat, but it was too dry to formulate words.

Mrs. Chamberlain curtsied, averting her gaze. "Master Warwick. My apologies." The shock of her expression bled into her voice. "I heard a great deal of commotion and thought it prudent to investigate." She looked up at Miss Rosemeyer again, her eyes fuming.

"There has been a misunderstanding," Jack said in a slow voice. "This—" he gave a hard laugh. "This is not as it appears. I—she—" He gestured at Miss Rosemeyer. Why could he not speak? His mind raced. The gossip of servants was impossible to stop; Miss Rosemeyer was ruined already if he did not find the right words to say.

"Mrs. Irwin would have never stood for such promiscuity in her home," Mrs. Chamberlain blurted, as though she could not help herself. "How dishonorable. How scandalous!" she spat. "It is no wonder you hired her. I did think she was too pretty to be a maid."

Jack's eyes widened. He had never heard such frank words from a servant before. He wouldn't even have expected it from Mrs. Chamberlain, even if she was the least well-mannered of his staff.

"If you care to keep your position in this house, you will hold your tongue." Jack glared down at her. "You are mistaken. Miss Rosemeyer was lost and confused. She's not a maid at all. She's a relative of Mrs. Irwin's."

A gasp even more thunderous than the first came from

Mrs. Chamberlain. Her brows shot up over her frog-like eyes.

Jack's stomach sank. What had he done? He could not have possibly said anything more condemning. It would have been better for Miss Rosemeyer if she were believed to be a maid.

"You have ruined the girl! In Mrs. Irwin's home, no less." Mrs. Chamberlain appeared near to fainting.

"This is my home at the moment," Jack reminded her in a stern voice. "And I assure you, you misunderstand the circumstances. Miss Rosemeyer was invited to Folkswich by Mrs. Irwin, and there was a bit of—er—confusion concerning the location of her residence. You mistook Miss Rosemeyer for a maid when she arrived this evening. She was wandering the house, quite confused, and—"

"And she found her way to your bedchamber accidentally?" Mrs. Chamberlain continued to speak far out of her bounds. "It appears you welcomed her arrival." The dismay in the housekeeper's voice grated on him as her eyes flickered between Miss Rosemeyer and Jack, heavy with disapproval.

Jack chuckled, unable to stop himself. "What has occurred here is far from romantic, I assure you."

Miss Rosemeyer's quiet voice piped in from behind him. "I hid in his wardrobe because I thought he was an intruder. H-he fainted when he saw me and I stayed to ensure he was not dead and cleaned the blood from his face."

"I have never heard a more ridiculous tale in my life,"

Mrs. Chamberlain said, turning up her nose. "Mrs. Irwin will be ashamed to hear you are masquerading as her relative."

"I promise, I am who I say," Miss Rosemeyer pleaded.

"Upon my word," Mrs. Chamberlain shook her head. "If that is true, she will never wish to soil her hands with you."

Miss Rosemeyer shrank back.

Anger rose in Jack's throat as he returned his gaze to Mrs. Chamberlain. "Let us hope Mrs. Irwin wishes to 'soil her hands' with you, because you are not permitted to work in my house another day."

"I didn't plan to." The housekeeper lifted her chin. "Mrs. Irwin has already been asking me to return to work for her, where I'm appreciated. My loyalty's now to her, not to this house and the sorts of scandals existing here."

Jack had a few more facers up his sleeve. If Mrs. Chamberlain were a man, he might have planted them. "It is no wonder you and Mrs. Irwin are so compatible. Go, please. Once Miss Rosemeyer is ready, bring her along. Mrs. Irwin will be glad to see her niece has arrived in Folkswich."

Mrs. Chamberlain scoffed. "This girl won't be receiving such a warm welcome from Mrs. Irwin after what I've witnessed tonight. I daresay this girl has her cap set on you and this was her plan to ensnare you."

Miss Rosemeyer gasped. "I was lost. That is all. I will explain it all to my aunt today. Surely she will understand." Her voice wavered.

Jack closed his eyes. No. Mrs. Irwin would not understand. She despised Jack, and would have every reason to believe he was the rake Mrs. Chamberlain claimed him to be. Mrs. Irwin prided herself on her solitude. There was a reason she did not associate with others, and it was to keep her own reputation spotless. To think she would take in Miss Rosemeyer now was almost humorous.

But Jack couldn't laugh. Not when he saw the desperation in Miss Rosemeyer's wide brown eyes.

"All will be well," Miss Rosemeyer said as she walked past him with quick steps, straight into the hall. "I have no doubt Mrs. Irwin will be true to her word in allowing me to live with her." She seemed to be speaking more to herself than to him or Mrs. Chamberlain. "Matthew will help me. He will ensure nothing goes awry."

Jack watched her with concern. "Who is Matthew?"

"My—well, my friend. I was under his protection at his estate in Surrey before coming here."

"A mistress, no doubt," Mrs. Chamberlain muttered, her voice barely audible.

Miss Rosemeyer's cheeks flamed. "No. How dare you make such an assumption." Her nostrils flared, and she marched farther into the hall.

Jack studied her carefully. It wouldn't have surprised him if Miss Rosemeyer had the temptation to plant a facer or two on the housekeeper as well. He cleared his throat. "Miss Rosemeyer—wait. I will assist you in any way I can."

She glanced back at him, wariness still hovering on her features. "Matthew will help me."

Jack gave a swift nod. Matthew. Who was this *Matthew*? Did Jack trust him to sort out this situation with Miss Rosemeyer and Mrs. Irwin? Would Miss Rosemeyer be well cared for? He set his worries aside, appalled that they had even come. Miss Rosemeyer's well-being was not his concern. She was practically a stranger to him. And she had turned his night into a living nightmare, at that. He should be happy to be rid of her.

Mrs. Chamberlain ushered Miss Rosemeyer forward and farther away from Jack. With a huff, the housekeeper shut the door, blocking Miss Rosemeyer from his view.

Jack stared at the grain of the wood, his mind reeling.

Poor Miss Rosemeyer.

If she thought she still had a place with Mrs. Irwin… she was far too optimistic for her own good. The nervous crease in her brow, her tiny fiddling fingers, and wide eyes were seared in his memory, and he found himself reflecting on them far too much as he tried to fall asleep.

CHAPTER 9

A folded square of parchment sat outside Louisa's door. The sun had fully risen now, and she had managed to change into a different dress without assistance, styling her hair as presentably as she could. Despite how tired she had been from her frightful night, she had still struggled to sleep at all. Rubbing her eyes, she picked up the parchment from the floor, turning it over.

Miss Rosemeyer,

I have had a coach prepared to convey you to Mrs. Irwin's new residence. Under the circumstances, I do not think it prudent that I accompany you there. With all sincerity, I hope your aunt will see sense and believe your story of the events of yesterday evening. I am afraid people are often inclined to believe the worst possible scenario instead. If you have any need of my assistance, do not hesitate to call upon me again, although I would beg that you come at a more reasonable hour next time, and without a weapon in hand. If I am to never see you again, please take one piece of advice from me in parting. Do refrain from hiding in men's wardrobes in the future; it is a disagreeable habit to have, you know.

J. W.

Louisa cast her eyes upward, folding the letter briskly in her palm. *Ridiculous.* Why had Jack Warwick assumed she would want him to accompany her to Mrs. Irwin's house? There was nothing she wanted less. His uninvited *advice* grated on her as she took her valise in hand, shoving the letter inside. She could hear the hint of amusement in his voice almost as clearly as if he had spoken aloud.

Of all the emotions—terror, worry, anxiousness—that had been tearing through her, nothing reigned like embarrassment. She cringed each time she remembered the moment Mr. Warwick had opened the wardrobe and when he had told her that it was indeed his residence, not her aunt's. And then the fact that her dress had been unbuttoned down the back the entire time? Her cheeks warmed just at the thought.

There had been so much occurring; she had forgotten all about that. It was no wonder with Mr. Warwick's state of undress even exceeding hers that the housekeeper had suspected a scandal.

Louisa blew a puff of air past her lips, shaking her head. It was over now. There was nothing she could do to change the past. All she could do was vow to avoid Mr. Warwick at all costs, if for no other reason than to ease the sting of her humiliation.

Fortunately, she managed to gather all her things into the coach and set out toward Mrs. Irwin's residence before Mr. Warwick could find her. She almost instructed the coach to stop by the inn where Matthew was staying, but she stopped herself. She could do this alone. She couldn't pull Matthew into this mess she had made.

The drive to her aunt's house was surprisingly short, just through a grove of trees and straight to the other side of the river. When the coach stopped, Louisa hurried toward the door, hardly stopping to notice the immaculate grounds surrounding the quaint structure. The red brick was charming, the size of the house much more suitable for a woman who lived alone like Mrs. Irwin did. With the rows of pretty flowers beneath each window and the vines growing up the sides of the house, Louisa felt welcome already.

She drew a deep breath and rapped her knuckles on the door.

While waiting for an answer, she adjusted her curls and gloves, hoping her eyes were not too puffy from lack of sleep.

The door swung open. The butler stood tall, his eyes

lowering to her without his head moving an inch. Before Louisa could say a single word, her eyes caught on the white frilled cap and wide-set eyes of Mr. Warwick's housekeeper, standing just a few paces behind him.

Dash it all.

She had beat Louisa there. Louisa had even hurried that morning, but she hadn't been quick enough.

The housekeeper stepped forward with a curtsy and rankling smile, one that was meant to appear polite, but was far from it.

"I am here to see Mrs. Irwin," Louisa said, keeping her voice confident. "Where is she?" Rather than addressing the housekeeper, she fixed her attention on the butler.

Each servant standing at attention watched Louisa with wary eyes. The housekeeper must have already relayed the events of the previous night to them all. Louisa swallowed. "Take me to her please."

The butler nodded, dispatching a footman to lead the way down the right hall, stopping at the door of the morning room. The footman announced Louisa's entrance before retreating away, leaving her to walk past the threshold alone.

A solitary ray of light filtered through a gap in the sheer drapes, beaming down on the grey curls of Mrs. Irwin.

She sat like a queen at the center of the blue sofa, two heavy circles of rouge on her high cheekbones. Her weathered hands sat in her lap, fingers linked like sausages, with just the tips of her fingers touching as she examined Louisa from head to toe.

"Ah, Miss Rosemeyer. I was told you would be coming today." Her face didn't show a single hint of expression.

Louisa calmed her shaking legs by taking a deep breath. She had only been in the woman's presence for seconds and already she was intimidated. "I—I am here in response to your invitation, ma'am. D-do you recall receiving my letter?"

Mrs. Irwin made a sound, a small grunt. "I have no recollection of receiving a letter from you, nor of extending an invitation to you. Unfortunately, you are not permitted on this property. I do acknowledge your relation to me, given your name, but I have no wish to claim you as my ward given your unscrupulous behavior witnessed by my housekeeper last night."

Louisa took a small step backward, struck by the harshness of Mrs. Irwin's reply. "Well—I'm afraid what the housekeeper witnessed only *appeared* to be scandalous. You see, I was lost. When you wrote your reply inviting me to come stay, you did not inform me of your change of address, and—"

"I did *not,* in fact, invite you." Mrs. Irwin's eyes flashed. "I am ashamed that you would fabricate such a story in order to trick me into providing a home for you. Frankly, I must confess, I would not have wanted you here even if you were a woman of spotless repute. I have lived a long life, Miss Rosemeyer, and I have already extended my share of generosity and kindness. I daresay I have earned my existence of solitude." She picked a hair from her dress, flicking it away just as easily as she was flicking Louisa away. "You might have convinced me to take you in if you had not spent the night in Mr. Warwick's bedchamber." Her lips curled with disgust.

"You misunderstand—"

Mrs. Irwin's eyes lifted from her dress and back to Louisa with scrutiny. "Why are you still standing there? Go." She waved a hand, and the footman opened the door again. "Your reputation has already stained me." Mrs. Irwin lifted her nose. One rouge-darkened cheek rotated away from Louisa, ending the conversation.

Louisa's jaw hung loose. As stunned as she was, she could hardly make sense of her thoughts. This was what she had traveled all the way to Yorkshire for? A rejection? Her stomach lurched. Matthew had come, and so had Margaret. Mrs. Irwin was just as cruel and disagreeable as Mr. Warwick had said. Perhaps even more so. How could she not remember writing that letter to Louisa?

The letter.

Louisa dug through her valise, pushing aside Mr. Warwick's letter from that morning. At the very bottom, tucked inside a book, she found Mrs. Irwin's reply. Looking at the woman now, Louisa wouldn't have guessed that her writing could appear so disorderly. The words were difficult to read, but Louisa presented the paper to her aunt. "This is the letter you wrote to me. See? You invited me to come. You said you were eager for my arrival."

Louisa drew a deep breath, stepping back as Mrs. Irwin snatched the letter from her hand. The woman's eyes narrowed as she examined the page. "I did not write this."

"It is signed from you."

"Forgery, that is all it could be." She sniffed, handing the letter back to Louisa. "I am appalled that you would think my penmanship to be so unsightly. I am well-bred, you know."

Louisa's frustration bubbled over. She had lost her ability to keep it at bay of late. "I must politely disagree. A well-bred woman would be true to her word. She would show generosity, or, at the very least, compassion for those in need. She would carry her manners with her, no matter her age. And she would agree that acting with kindness is a privilege, not a burden." Louisa's voice was quiet, but it somehow managed to keep Mrs. Irwin's rapt attention. "And," Louisa took a deep breath, "she would know it is no longer fashionable to wear so much rouge."

Mrs. Irwin's face darkened another shade, her thin lips sputtering. Flecks of saliva spewed into the air. Louisa had read about volcanoes, and she did not want to be near this one when it erupted. Crumpling the letter and throwing it back inside her valise, Louisa gave a quick curtsy, stumbling awkwardly out of the room.

Her heart pounded. She had never, *ever* spoken so freely before. Something had come over her since the night before when she had spoken with Mr. Warwick. It was impossible not to develop a bit of cheek while dealing with him, but she hadn't thought it would carry over into other dealings she had.

Out the door, across the lawn, Louisa stopped a few paces ahead of the waiting coach. What was she doing?

How could she tell Matthew what had happened? He would insist that she come back to Larkhall, even when it came at his expense. Would he offer to marry her out of pity? She laughed under her breath. That was the one thing Matthew would never offer anyone.

Alice. Her sister. She could write to her again. Louisa hadn't wanted to ask for Alice and her husband's hospitality, even though she knew they would give it. Their child would be born soon, and they were not wealthy. Louisa had assumed any woman living in solitude like her aunt would be lonely and in want of companionship. But it seemed that solitude did not always equal loneliness.

Louisa was the only lonely one.

Her heart pinched as she took one more step toward the coach. How could she get to Matthew's inn? She bit her lip, waving a hand to capture the coachman's attention. She scoured her mind for the name of the inn.

"Please take me to the White Swan."

The coachman doffed his hat in greeting, revealing his head—bald as a coot—and two concerned eyebrows. "I'm 'fraid the master's orders say otherwise."

Louisa frowned.

"He said when Mrs. Irwin turned ye away, ta bring ye back ta 'is house."

"His house?" Louisa could hardly understand the man's words, and certainly not what they meant. "*When* Mrs. Irwin turned me away?" She glowered at the ground. Had Mr. Warwick really been so sure of her failure that he had already given his coachman orders to bring her back? Well, there was no possible way she was complying with his orders, that much was certain.

"That's what 'e told me, miss." The coachman sniffed, squinting against the sun. He waited several seconds. Louisa didn't move.

"The inn is a short drive from here," she said, willing her voice to sound confident. "It will not be far out of your way."

"I'm sorry, miss. I can't go 'gainst the master's orders." He gave a discreet nod toward the door of the coach.

Louisa shook her head. "I have no wish to return to Benham Abbey."

"I was told ta convince ye to come by any means necess'ry. It's yer only transportation, miss. I was told not to take ye anywhere else."

Louisa's patience was at its end. She still hadn't eaten. She could hardly keep her eyes open. She had just been harshly turned away by the woman she thought would be her new guardian. Her defiance reared its head. How dare Mr. Warwick assume the role of her guardian? Did he think he could transport her wherever he chose? Oh, certainly not.

She eyed her two small trunks that were still strapped to the coach. Could she carry them both as well as her valise? It was unlikely, but she would try. Moving with quick steps, she untied the trunks from the coach, letting them fall to the ground with a thud. Fortunately she hadn't packed anything valuable. Even if she hid the trunks somewhere nearby, she could walk to the inn and fetch

Matthew, then return for the trunks once she had his assistance. The Lovells' house was even closer than the inn, so perhaps she would start there instead. She had a very sharp memory. She could find her way there with what she recalled of the surrounding hills and river.

"What're ye doing?" The coachman's voice was quick. "Master Warwick said—"

"I do not care what that man said." Louisa let out a puff of air as she dragged her largest trunk closer to her feet. "Perhaps you can relay a message to Mr. Warwick from me. Tell him I do not need his assistance, for I have two perfectly capable legs beneath me. They can walk, they can run, and they can give him a swift kick where he does not wish to be kicked if he dares try to stop me."

The coachman's eyes grew larger than saucers. He swallowed.

"His broken nose," Louisa clarified. She cleared her throat, brushing the hair from her eyes.

"I—I see. I'll be sure to tell 'im." The coachman doffed his hat once again, keeping one eye on Louisa as he drove away, as if he feared she would kick him where he did not wish to be kicked as well.

She sat down on the edge of her trunk, lowering her head to her hands. She was stranded. Utterly stranded. With a deep breath, she stood, ignoring the gnawing in her stomach. Sitting and wallowing would not solve her problem. She picked up the first trunk, walking across the path to a large hedge on the property. If her aunt would not allow her to stay at her house, then at least she could provide a hiding place for her belongings until she found people to help her transport them.

Transport them where? A lump formed in her throat. Where could she go now? The uncertainty choked her as she moved one trunk after the other to a place between two hedges, manipulating the leaves and loose branches to hide them as best as she could.

When her work was done, she set off toward the walking path that would lead her to the Lovell's house, keeping her smallest valise in hand. Going to Matthew now was too embarrassing. He had enough to occupy his mind with finding Margaret a place to work. Should Louisa seek work as a governess too? Was that the best option for her now? Her thoughts spun without pause for her entire walk, stopping only when she realized she was lost.

"Drat. Drat, drat, drat." Louisa turned one way, then another, examining the fork in the path. The branches from the trees above her cast shadows on the ground, the leaves rustling with the light breeze. She didn't quite remember the path being so wooded. Had she already taken a wrong turn?

Her lower lip began to quiver. What a disaster the last day had been. Could anything else go wrong? A tear slipped from her eye, then another. Her stomach growled furiously.

She sat down in the shade, tucking her knees to her chest and resting her face between them.

"Everything will be all right. Not to worry," she reassured herself as one might reassure a child to stop them from crying. But the tears came anyway. She let them soak into her skirts.

A twig snapped nearby, and Louisa looked up, heart pounding.

Two sets of toes peeked out from the hem of a dress, which was quickly lowered to hide them. The young lady who was walking barefoot through the woods carried a basket slung over one arm. Her eyes were brown like a doe, her ginger hair tied up loosely with a ribbon. She gasped when she saw Louisa.

"Oh, horse feathers," she muttered, pressing a hand to her chest. "I didn't see you there." The woman laughed softly, tipping her head to one side with concern. "Are you all right?"

Louisa nodded, using the nearby tree to help her weak body stand. "I am a bit lost, that is all." Her vision flashed black and white. She blinked hard to clear it.

"You must allow me to help you," the woman said, her voice gentle. She took Louisa's arm. "You look keen to faint."

"It would not come as a surprise if I did." Louisa's voice was slurred. She sniffed, remembering how she had been crying. Her face must have been covered in red spots.

"Oh, dear. Take small steps and hold fast to my arm. We are only a minute or two from my house. We have a very suitable fainting couch. Perhaps you are too hot. Are you in need of water?"

Louisa nodded, unable to refuse the woman's assistance. A fainting couch sounded quite comfortable. Much more comfortable than the bed she had tried to sleep on the night before. If she could have a moment to gather her wits about her, then perhaps she could think of a better solution than traipsing to the Lovells' house in the heat alone.

"Only a few more steps." The woman holding onto Louisa's arm smelled of flowers, and her voice was gentle enough to put Louisa's worry at ease. She seemed to be even more optimistic than Louisa in saying that there were only a few more steps. If it was the house Louisa thought it was, looming in the distance, then there were at least two hundred more steps before they would reach the front gate.

Louisa fought the dizziness in her head, placing one foot in front of the other. She blinked fast to keep her vision clear. She had certainly been on the wrong path. She hadn't passed this estate before.

The young woman led Louisa by the arm across the smooth stone path, a tall iron gate looming ahead of them. Vines covered the spokes at the top of the gate, soft orange flowers blooming amid the leaves. Red brick and a row of hedges flanked the gate, creating the perfect walkway toward the stately house beyond it.

After what felt like an eternity, they walked through the front doors of the house. The grandeur reminded Louisa of Larkhall, but on a smaller scale. The ceilings were tall, the furnishings in the current fashion. A pair of maids followed behind them with fans as Louisa was led to the fainting couch in the drawing room.

Louisa tried to sit up, embarrassed by the scene she was

making. A sharp pain dug behind one her eyes, and her dizziness intensified. She finally succumbed to the young woman's coddling, leaning back on the fainting couch. She had been through a great deal of distress over the last day between the horrific-events-which-shall-not-be-mentioned from the night before, her hunger, thirst, and wandering outside in the heat after having no sleep the night before. She had earned a moment or two of weakness.

A tray of food and a tall cup of water were brought out within minutes, and Louisa tried to mind her manners as best she could as she swallowed the slice of warm bread in two bites. Or less. She moved to the sliced pears, chewing more slowly when she noticed the young lady with the ginger hair watching her.

Already, her fatigue had lessened, and her dizziness had begun to subside. She gulped down the entire cup of water, wiping her lips before murmuring a quiet, "Thank you. You are too kind to have offered me your food and water. I am very sorry to have stopped you from your walk." Louisa eyed the maids beside her who waved their fans in her direction. A third maid appeared, placing a cool cloth around the back of Louisa's neck. As Louisa's face moved with her chewing and speaking, she could feel the dried tears on her cheeks. How embarrassing. She was a complete disaster.

"You must not apologize." The woman smiled, patting Louisa's knee. "Everyone is a little lost every now and then."

"That is true, indeed." Louisa managed a small smile before a laugh escaped her. "Some more often than others."

The woman's eyes widened as she nodded in agreement. "Well, there is only one way to avoid ever getting lost—having no destination to seek. It is better to have one, is it not?"

Louisa watched the way the young woman's eyes danced with intelligence and deep thought, a smile hovering on her lips. Finally Louisa had met an amiable person. Louisa laughed, eating the last of her food. "I must agree, yes." All Louisa needed to do now was figure out what exactly her next destination was. A lofty task, to be sure. But this woman seemed eager to help in any way she could.

"My manners have entirely escaped me today. My name is Miss Louisa Rosemeyer. What is your name?" Louisa asked.

The young woman gave a warm smile. "Miss Cassandra Warwick."

CHAPTER 10

"W-warwick?" Louisa stiffened, her smile freezing on her cheeks.

"Yes."

Louisa looked around the room, her brow furrowing. "*Miss* Warwick, you said?"

"Indeed...my name is Cassandra Warwick." She paused. "Are you still unwell?"

"Oh, no, I am well enough." Louisa forced a smile. Given the woman's apparent age, likely in her late twenties, and the fact that she was a miss and shared Jack Warwick's surname, she could only have been his sister.

Before Louisa could say another word, the drawing room door burst open. A tall woman with ginger hair much like Miss Warwick's came bustling in, eyes wide. Her eyes, a mixture between blue and grey, were instantly familiar. Mr. Warwick had the same eyes. The woman could only be his—

"Mama!" Cassandra stood, waving her mother forward. "This is Miss Louisa Rosemeyer. I found her all alone in the woods on my way to visit Jack."

Louisa's ears perked.

"She was on the cusp of fainting, so I brought her in and she is now recovering quite well." Cassandra smiled, adjusting the wildflower that was tucked behind her ear. "Miss Rosemeyer, this is my mother, Mrs. Warwick."

Louisa tried to stand to properly greet the woman, but Cassandra stopped her. "You must rest."

"Oh, poor girl." Mrs. Warwick touched a hand to her heart. "I am glad Cassandra was passing by."

"As am I." Louisa looked down, suddenly shy from all the attention. "I am most grateful."

"Are you new to town? I am not familiar with the name Rosemeyer," Mrs. Warwick said.

"Yes, I am new."

Both women stared down at her, as if expecting her to elaborate.

"I am only visiting," Louisa added in a quick voice. "I am visiting my friends, the Lovells." It wasn't a complete lie.

Mrs. Warwick pursed her lips. "I'm afraid I have not been acquainted with them either." It didn't surprise Louisa, considering the difference in their current social standings. "I suppose you will have to introduce me to them," Mrs. Warwick added with a cajoling smile.

With so kind a sister and mother, why would Mr. Warwick have left his family behind? The Lovells had told

Louisa that he was unwelcome in his childhood home. It didn't surprise her that he could have behaved in a matter that warranted such circumstances, but Louisa wouldn't have expected Mrs. Warwick or Cassandra to be at the center of any familial discord.

"It will be wonderful to have a new friend in town for a while," Mrs. Warwick continued. "How long will you be visiting?"

Louisa's eyes stung again, but she fought the sudden bout of tears. What had come over her? She had always been quite skilled at keeping her emotions at bay. Mrs. Warwick's eyes were looking down at her with too much kindness, which Louisa found humorous considering they were almost identical to Mr. Warwick's eyes. "I'm afraid I don't know," Louisa said. "That is yet to be decided."

"I see." Mrs. Warwick exchanged a look of concern with her daughter.

"Did you come here alone?" Cassandra asked. "Why were you wandering through the woods by yourself? I gathered that you were quite hungry and thirsty." She eyed the empty tray on Louisa's lap.

A disobedient tear escaped her eye, then another. Louisa tightened her lips to keep them from quivering. Blast her lack of sleep. It always made her far too emotional. "I had a very long day yesterday."

Mrs. Warwick touched a hand to her heart again, her features flooding with concern. "Oh, dear Miss Rosemeyer. We are here to help you now. What might we do to help you feel better?"

"You have already done much to help me, and I thank you very much." *Much more than your son*, Louisa added in her mind. Why had he wanted her to go back to his house? Had that been his way of helping her? She shook him from her mind. Mrs. Warwick and Cassandra were very amiable, but Louisa felt far too uncomfortable trespassing on their hospitality a moment longer. If only they knew what had happened the night before. She gulped. The more the story spread, even the innocent version, the more Louisa's reputation would suffer.

"There must be something more we can do," Mrs. Warwick said. "May we provide your transportation to the Lovell residence? I should hate to have you walk again."

Louisa gave a grateful smile, her worry subsiding for a moment. "That would be wonderful, thank you."

After a few minutes, Mrs. Warwick and Cassandra had made the arrangements for Louisa, and she was on her way again. From the coach window, Louisa waved, hoping her expressions of gratitude had been enough. She would likely never see them again. Unless she found work as a governess nearby, she would have to leave Yorkshire. Her stomach twisted as she thought of all the time and money Matthew had invested into this trip for her. She should have simply let him fund a season for her. Maybe then she would have found a match and been taken care of without burdening Matthew further.

She leaned her head back against the seat, watching the hills pass by. She would still need to return to Mrs. Irwin's house to fetch her hidden trunks, but for now, she had her valise on her lap. Opening the clasp, she withdrew Mr. Warwick's letter that he had left at her door that morning. What a strange man. Selfish and arrogant. He must have given his sweet mother and sister a great deal of trouble. Certainly they were as happy to be rid of him as Louisa was. She read over his words again, her eyes settling on the line at the end. *Do refrain from hiding in men's wardrobes in the future; it is a disagreeable habit to have, you know.*

She found herself staring at the words, not at what they meant, but at the formation of each line. He had terrible penmanship.

Her eyes narrowed. Where had she seen that dreadful hand before?

Her heart picked up speed as she rifled through her valise to withdraw the crumpled letter Mrs. Irwin had denied she had written.

Dear Miss Louisa,

Do come as soon as you wish. I will be most eagerly anticipating your arrival.

Sincerely,

Mrs. Irwin

Louisa's jaw dropped as she looked down at the two letters. There was no doubt they had been written by the same person.

Jack had received many threats in his life, but never had he received one from a lady. He crossed his arms, casting his coachman a look of disbelief.

"That's wha' she said, master. Ye must know I don't mince words."

Jack had difficulty believing that Miss Rosemeyer had used the exact wording that his coachman, Giles, had used, but the idea was amusing to say the least.

"I think ye ought not to pursue her any longer. She didn't seem interested."

Jack frowned. "Pursue her?" He scoffed. "I was simply trying to help her. But it seems she does not want my help."

"No, indeed." Giles chuckled. "She wants nothin' to do with ye."

Jack's frown only deepened. Why did that vex him so greatly? He touched a hand to his nose—the swelling had only decreased a little. Were his looks all he had? He shook his head in an effort to clear it. He shouldn't be caring one bit about what Miss Rosemeyer thought of him. But given the situation with his housekeeper and the rumors she was sure to spread, Jack felt some measure of responsibility to ensure Miss Rosemeyer hadn't been impacted too severely.

"Where did you leave her?" Jack asked.

"Mrs. Irwin's house. She 'ad three trunks to carry, so I 'spect she'd still be there."

Jack squinted up at the sky. It was a hot day to be

outside for such a long time. He strode to the stables, taking the first horse that could be saddled. He mounted, starting in the direction of Mrs. Irwin's new house. Before he made it far, he stopped, circling back. He dismounted and ran to the kitchen, remembering how hungry Miss Rosemeyer had been the night before. He packed a basket of fruit, ham, and bread. He doubted she had dared go to his kitchens that morning. Based on the coachman's description of where he had left Miss Rosemeyer—outside, Jack knew his prediction had been correct. Mrs. Irwin hadn't been willing to take her in.

He let out a sigh as his horse sprang into action, trotting faster along the road. Jack's conscience had been bothering him all morning; less now that Miss Rosemeyer had refused to take the coach back to his house so he could offer her further assistance. What had he done to deserve her dislike? She had been the one to break into *his* house. Had she found that *Matthew* whom she had spoken of to help her instead?

He spotted a coach up ahead, its path about to intersect with his own. He urged his horse along faster. Was that his family's coach? His heart pounded. He recognized the horses as well as the conveyance. Cassandra preferred to walk everywhere she went, and his mother rarely left the house during the day. Could it be his father? Jack's throat went dry as he watched the horses' approach where he had stopped. He was in their way, but he didn't want to move until he glimpsed who was inside.

As it drew closer, he tipped his head to see into the window.

Two round brown eyes peeked out from beneath the brim of a bonnet, staring at him with shock through the glass. Miss Rosemeyer?

Jack must have hit his head harder than he had first thought the night before. He closed his eyes for a moment before opening them again. It was indeed her.

"Aye!" He called to the coachman, waving his hands wildly above his head. "Stop!"

The coachman would recognize Jack as heir to the estate he worked at, so he wouldn't question his request. The moment the man saw him, he pulled the horses to a stop. Jack led his horse close to the window, staring into it for long enough to make Miss Rosemeyer uncomfortable enough as to open it.

Unobscured by the glass, he could see the hint of color on her cheeks.

"Mr. Warwick." She lowered her head in greeting, eyes remaining wide with shock.

"Miss Rosemeyer, I see you have found…an alternative method of transportation."

Her thick lashes hid her eyes from his view. She cleared her throat. "I met your sister Cassandra when I was passing through the woods. She and your mother kindly offered to convey me to my destination."

What were the odds of that? He shook the surprise from his face. "Is that so? As I recall from what my coachman told me, you have two legs perfectly capable of walking. There was something else they were capable of as well, but I cannot quite recall…" he tapped his chin, "did it involve kicking, perhaps?"

Her cheeks darkened yet another shade.

Jack concealed his smile. She was very endearing when she blushed.

He paused, examining the furrow in her brow and the tightness of her jaw. Oh. It seemed that anger was the cause of the color on her cheeks, not embarrassment.

In one swift motion, she lifted her hand out the window, extending a paper to him. "Did you write this?"

He frowned, reading over the words. "This is signed from Mrs. Irwin."

"She denied writing it, and when I compared the note you left me this morning, the writing looked the same." Louisa handed him another letter, gesturing for him to compare them side by side. He held the reins tight in one hand, fanning the two letters out in his other. He couldn't deny that the writing looked eerily similar.

"It would explain everything," Miss Rosemeyer said, her voice quiet as always, but firm. "That is why Mrs. Irwin doesn't recall inviting me here. That is why I arrived at the wrong address. You sent me that letter, pretending to be my aunt." She let out a huffed breath. "The only question that remains is why on earth you would have done such a thing."

Jack shook his head, scowling down at the paper. A faint memory burned in the back of his mind, but he couldn't quite grasp onto it. "I don't recall writing this. I—"

He rubbed a hand over his face. "I suppose it is possible that I could have been—er—drinking at the time."

Miss Rosemeyer's nostrils flared. "That is a disagreeable habit to have, you know."

His defenses rose. "So is kicking a man where he does not wish to be kicked."

She gasped, her cheeks turning red. "That is *not* how I phrased it."

"As I said before, so is hiding in wardrobes in the middle of the night."

"Something that only occurred because you sent me this letter and invited me to come to your house."

She did have a point. Jack's stomach twisted with guilt. It was all his fault. It could have been any number of evenings when he was drunk as a wheelbarrow and the letter from Miss Rosemeyer was handed to him. Now that she mentioned it and he was holding the letter in his hand, he did vaguely recall writing a letter that, at the time, seemed vastly amusing to him. He groaned. What had he done?

The fire in her eyes had extinguished, leaving a look of empty defeat in its place. "If not for you, I would never have taken this long journey and my reputation would not be ruined." She exhaled sharply, rubbing her forehead. "Now your housekeeper is spreading rumors around town. The gossip of servants never takes long to spread. I have no place to go."

Jack knew better than anyone how people could blather falsehoods. Especially servants. No man in town would be willing to marry Miss Rosemeyer once they heard the rumors. Just like no one in town would ever invite Jack to a party again after the things Evan Whitby had said about him and his uncle's death. His stomach turned over with guilt. It was his fault Miss Rosemeyer was here at all, and it was his fault she had been turned away by Mrs. Irwin. The entire mess was his responsibility to clean up.

A sinking sensation started in Jack's chest, followed by one sobering, yet intriguing thought.

He bit the inside of his cheek, tipping his head to one side as he let the idea sink into his mind. There was only one thing he could offer to make Miss Rosemeyer's situation better, and his honor, what little of it he had left, bound him to it.

He dismounted in one sudden motion, handing the reins to the waiting coachman to hold. Miss Rosemeyer's brow furrowed, and he thought she might shriek in terror again as he tugged open the carriage door and stepped inside.

The entire contraption rocked from his sudden movements, and Miss Rosemeyer cowered in the corner of the coach like a frightened mouse.

He removed his hat, sitting on the seat across from her, leaning his elbows onto his knees. He snapped the door closed behind him.

Miss Rosemeyer finally found her voice, and it cracked. "What on earth are you doing?"

He ought to act quickly before she began searching for the coach pistol. He met her gaze, putting on an expression of complete sincerity. He had never planned on doing this, but at the moment, it seemed like the correct course of action. If he thought too much about things, he often convinced his mind to change.

He took a deep breath. "I am offering you a place to go. It is my fault you are in this plight, so I will help you out of it. If you will accept my offer." He cringed inwardly. He had never rehearsed how he would phrase something like this.

"Your offer?" Her eyes flew open wider.

"Yes." He cleared his throat. "I am offering to marry you."

CHAPTER 11

Louisa didn't know whether to laugh or gasp. The latter would show her surprise, but the former would show how completely ridiculous she thought Mr. Warwick was to even suggest such a thing. The resulting sound was something of a snort. "Marry?" Louisa choked. She studied his face. He was quite serious.

Even as she repeated the word *marry* back to him, his face went white. "It was the honorable thing to extend the offer to you. If your situation is as desperate as you make it appear, then you will accept without question. You were at my family's estate today. I am still heir to it, whether my father likes that fact or not." Mr. Warwick met her gaze again. "I offer you a home. A fine one. In truth, my family would be quite pleased if I married. I might not be so despised if I had a wife."

Louisa's heart raced. This was not how she had imagined a man might propose to her one day. Not in the slightest. She glared at the floor of the carriage, unwilling to look at his face.

Mr. Warwick spoke again, his voice tentative. "Unless...I suppose...the one who despises me *is* my wife."

"I will never be your wife," Louisa said in a resolute voice. Her pulse rushed past her ears. "I-I thank you for your offer, but I must—"

"Consider it." Mr. Warwick raised both eyebrows. "You must consider it longer than a few seconds. This is a very important decision, and you must not be hasty either way." He pressed his lips together, his blue eyes boring into hers. "Although I was quite hasty in extending the offer, I promise I will not retract it."

How could she possibly agree to spend her life with a man who was so...so...

What was Mr. Warwick exactly? Infuriating. Ridiculous. Hated by his family for reasons she didn't know and couldn't possibly uncover before giving him her answer. He drank far too much. He gambled. He was handsome, she would give him that, even despite his crooked nose. As she stared at his stoic face, she realized she hardly knew him at all.

And the way he had said it...*I am offering to marry you.* It made her heart sting with protest.

Louisa had always dreamed that a man would *want* her to marry him. He would *ask* her to marry him—and he would be willing to beg if he had to, but of course he wouldn't have to because she would love him just as ardently as he loved her. Her heart pinched again as sorrow flooded it. Were her romantic fancies simply another dream she would have to bury?

She had been silent for far too long. Mr. Warwick opened the carriage door, stepping down before turning to face her again. "Take as much time as you wish." His throat bobbed with a swallow, and he rubbed one side of his face. He seemed just as surprised by the proposal as she was. He stared at her from his place beyond the carriage doorway, his eyes searching her face. What was he looking for?

When he finally looked away, she could breathe normally again.

"Was my family kind to you?" he asked suddenly, speaking more to the ground than to her.

Louisa nodded before realizing he couldn't see it. "Your mother and sister were very kind indeed."

"And my father?" The words were blunt.

"I didn't meet him."

Mr. Warwick looked up. "I see." He was silent for a long moment before his face lit up with realization. "Oh, I nearly forgot." He walked to his horse, and when he turned around, he was holding a small basket. He handed it to Louisa through the door. "I daresay this will put you in an agreeable mood." His lips curled into a smile before he closed the carriage door, leaning closer to the window. "I will leave you to be on your way. I should hate to stop you, as my coachman has informed me of the consequence should I try."

Louisa's face grew hot, and she scowled at him as he backed away from the carriage, chuckling.

The coach began rolling forward again, and Louisa closed the window, cutting off the sound of Jack Warwick's chuckling. How could he laugh at a time like this? Louisa's stomach felt like one great knot, her lungs tight and almost incapable of expanding. She looked down at the basket Mr. Warwick had handed her. With two fingers, she carefully pinched the cloth and removed it.

Bread, cheese, ham, and various dried and fresh fruits filled the inside of the basket. She glanced out the back window, watching Mr. Warwick's back as he rode away. Without warning, he turned his head back, catching her watching him. A sly smile pulled on his lips again.

She whirled around, brushing her hair from her eyes with a huffed breath. The tassels hanging from the carriage interior swung as the coach picked up speed. She looked down at the food again.

That was awfully kind of him, even if it was overdue.

She shook her head hard. A basket of food couldn't erase all the harm he had done. If marriage was the only path for her to take now, could she not meet a few other eligible men in town before deciding to accept Mr. Warwick's proposal? She laughed under her breath. It would do little good now that the rumors were spreading. At any rate, she had no money to entice a man to marry her so quickly.

Mr. Warwick's proposal could very well be the only one she would ever receive.

Just a year ago she and her sister Alice had been willing to marry almost anyone to secure a future for themselves, but after seeing Alice and then Bridget marry for love, Louisa had set her aspirations too high. Mr. Warwick was generous in his offer. It was honorable of him to even make one at all. Louisa and Margaret had assumed he would only ever marry a bottle of brandy.

Louisa put her face in her hands. How had so much changed in one day?

Mr. Warwick was right, as much as she hated to admit it. She could not make this decision rashly. Perhaps Margaret would talk her out of it.

If she didn't, Matthew surely would.

∼

"It will only hurt for a moment," a gruff voice said from above Jack's head. Jack held his breath as the physician pinched his nose between his hands. "One…two…three."

Pain shot through Jack's entire skull, tears springing to his eyes. He let out a deep grunt, rolling to one side. The physician continued pressing on the side of Jack's nose, forcing it back into place.

"There. Your nose should heal in the proper position now, although it had already begun to mend itself in the wrong one, so it may heal with a slight tilt." The physician seemed unaffected by Jack's reaction to his procedure.

Jack sat up straighter, taking several deep breaths. He ought to have thanked the man, but at the moment, he didn't feel much gratitude. At least his nose wouldn't be quite as crooked as it had been earlier that day. He checked his reflection on the silver tray on the tea table. It was only slightly better. He held a handkerchief to his nostrils as they began bleeding again.

Once the physician was gone, Jack sat alone in his drawing room, listening to the clock ticking. Without a housekeeper, his house would soon be in complete disarray. The servants that remained went about their business, but they needed to be guided, and there certainly needed to be more of them. The best course of action would be to hire a steward so he did not have to manage any of it.

He took a deep breath, surprised by his sudden determination to get the house in order.

Perhaps it was because he might soon have a wife.

He stared at all the empty seats of the drawing room, tapping his foot on the rug. He had been very generous offering to marry Miss Rosemeyer. Very generous, indeed. He hadn't done it for selfish reasons.

Had he?

It was true that his family would respect him more if he were married. Society would as well, even if their good opinion seemed so far out of reach. And he could not deny that Miss Rosemeyer was different than other women he had met in his life. She intrigued him. She made him smile.

He chuckled to himself. On the contrary, he made her scowl.

But what a charming scowl it was.

Jack was likely out of his mind for extending an offer of marriage to her, but it had felt like the right thing to do.

The guilt he felt over being the cause of her current circumstances was reminiscent of the guilt he had felt for the last five years. There was nothing worse than guilt, shame, or regret. In the moment, the only thing he could think of to alleviate his guilt was offering to marry her.

At any rate, he doubted she would accept his offer.

All he could do was wait and try to get the house in order perchance she did. Summoning his strength, Jack stood, walking out the drawing room door. He was surprised to find his butler standing at the open door, inviting a visitor inside.

Jack stopped, striding toward them. The man standing beside his butler was tall, with dark hair and a rather severe expression. Young, likely around the age of thirty. Completely unfamiliar.

"Good day," Jack's voice echoed, startling the butler, but not the man beside him. The strange visitor turned his gaze to Jack, a scowl forming on his brow. Jack stopped a few paces away. "Have we met?"

The man shook his head, eyeing Jack with misgiving before his deep voice said, "No, I don't believe so. Are you a relative of Mrs. Irwin's? I'm here to see my friend Miss Rosemeyer."

Jack let out a heavy exhale. "I'm afraid there has been a mistake," Jack said. "My name is Jack Warwick. And you are?"

"Matthew Northcott."

Ah. So this must have been the *Matthew* that Miss Rosemeyer had mentioned. He didn't give any further explanation, so Jack continued. "I am no relative of Mrs. Irwin's, but I am the new tenant of this house."

Mr. Northcott's eyes flashed with worry. "Louisa isn't here?"

Jack studied the man. Why was he using Miss Rosemeyer's Christian name? They must have been very dear friends indeed. "Before I continue, may I ask your relation to Miss Rosemeyer?" Jack inquired.

"I am the only guardian she has at the moment, though it is not legal. She was the companion of my sister, a friend to our family."

"I see." Jack could easily see how Miss Rosemeyer continuing to live with Mr. Northcott could be viewed as scandalous. It was no wonder she had been coming to try to live with her aunt instead. "Miss Rosemeyer is not here. She left this morning."

Mr. Northcott froze. "This morning? Did she not recognize the mistake of the wrong address yesterday?"

Jack really didn't enjoy the thought of having a fist thrown at his face again, so he would choose how he relayed the story carefully. "I was not home yesterday evening when Miss Rosemeyer arrived. My housekeeper mistook her for the new maid. When I returned home, Miss Rosemeyer was frightened and hid in my wardrobe. I found her there by accident." Jack paused, debating about including various other details. "And, well, considering the hour and the—er—situation, my housekeeper was, well, upset, when she saw us and so she quit her position and returned to work for Mrs. Irwin. She has already begun spreading false rumors about what she witnessed yesterday, and Mrs. Irwin refuses to take Miss Rosemeyer in now." Jack drew a heavy breath, rubbing one side of his face. "I am concerned for Miss Rosemeyer's reputation."

Mr. Northcott stared at him, his jaw tight. He was silent for a long moment. "Why are you letting this property?"

Jack frowned. That was a bit off the subject at hand. "I sought distance from my family until it comes time for me to inherit. My father and I have had our disagreements, and that is why I moved away."

"You are heir to an estate?"

"Yes."

"Is it thriving? Is income high?"

"Yes, indeed." Jack raised one eyebrow, surprised by the authority the man exuded with his personal questions.

Mr. Northcott stared at Jack again, his eyes boring into his soul, it seemed. Jack shifted uncomfortably.

"I know a broken nose when I see one. How did that happen?"

Jack felt as though he were being interviewed for an inquest all over again. "I was at a party yesterday before coming home. A man there said something I did not like, and so I showed him just how I felt about what he said." Jack cleared his throat. "His face did look worse than mine."

A slight smile passed through Mr. Northcott's facade. "Ah, well I cannot fault you for that. I have been in similar situations myself."

"There are times when a man simply needs a facer. He was begging me for it."

Mr. Northcott laughed, crossing his arms over his chest. "I am glad you obliged him."

Jack chuckled. "As am I, even if I have this as a result." He gestured at his nose.

Mr. Northcott laughed, but soon his smile faded as he sat up straighter, back to the business at hand. "I assume you are not yet well-acquainted with Miss Rosemeyer, but I assure you, she is a most amiable young woman. She does not deserve the hand fate has dealt her. She needs a place to live without the risk of scandal. She needs someone to look after her, and I prefer that it is a man of good humor and kindness and a reliable income. It has always been my stance that she should marry."

It was obvious what Mr. Northcott was hinting at, so Jack stopped him. "I agree that marriage is the course she should pursue. That is why I have made her an offer." Even as he said it, his stomach twisted. What the devil had come over him to make an offer of marriage to a woman he had known for one day? *One day.* He was a lunatic, that much was certain.

Mr. Northcott's eyebrows rose. "Already?"

"Yes, this afternoon."

Mr. Northcott paused. "Did she accept?"

"Not yet." Jack swallowed, rubbing one side of his face. "I may not have made the most favorable impression on her, so that has caused her to hesitate."

"You are a good man to do the honorable thing," Mr.

Northcott said. "And Miss Louisa is a good young woman. You will have to work hard to deserve her, you know."

A good man. Jack's brow furrowed. He had never thought of himself as a good man, not since he had even been old enough to be called a man. He was the reason his uncle was dead, the reason his family was torn apart and ruined to society. How could someone like that be a good man?

"Miss Rosemeyer deserves better than someone like me," Jack said, his voice quiet. "I should not have made an offer. I am a complete and utter disaster." Jack didn't know why he felt the need to tell Mr. Northcott that, but he couldn't keep it inside any longer. "I have many faults. They far exceed my virtues." He shook his head. "If you would rather, I will help you find a more suitable husband for Miss Rosemeyer." Regret had begun pouring through his chest. He could barely take care of himself…how could he take care of Miss Rosemeyer? Why had he even wanted to try? He didn't know the answers.

Mr. Northcott watched him with a somber expression before a slight smile pulled on the corners of his mouth. "I think you give yourself too little credit. It seems to me that you have a desire to become better. You recognize the areas in which you need to improve." Mr. Northcott shrugged. "That is much more than many of us have done."

There was one thing wrong with Mr. Northcott's philosophy. Jack could not undo the past. His uncle's death was a permanent dark stain on Jack, and like a droplet of ink when it touches clean parchment, it had spread. It had consumed him. How would Miss Rosemeyer feel if she knew what he had done? She already seemed terrified enough at the thought of marrying him.

"I know Louisa well," Mr. Northcott said. "And I don't think there is a more suitable husband for her, no matter how far we search."

Jack looked down at the floor. How could Mr. Northcott have so much confidence in him? "It will not be easy to win Miss Rosemeyer's good opinion. I daresay she does not like me very much." Jack gave a half smile.

"I will speak with her," Mr. Northcott said, "although she does not always take my advice. She is quiet, but I think she hides a fierce character behind it. In fact, when I first saw your face I wondered if it was Louisa who had broken your nose."

Jack tipped his head back with a laugh. "She would have taken great pleasure in it." He thought of how she had cleaned the blood from his face rather than running away the night before. She must have had a good heart to do such a thing.

Mr. Northcott continued chuckling as he turned toward the door. "Well, shall we go find Louisa? I have a suspicion as to where she might have gone."

Jack's stomach flipped. Why was he suddenly so nervous to see her? Why did it matter to him whether she accepted or rejected his proposal? Calming the turmoil inside his stomach, he gave a stiff nod and followed Mr. Northcott out the door.

CHAPTER 12

"Marry?" Margaret nearly dropped the spoon she was using to stir the pot of stew. Her eyes rounded. "You cannot be serious. I thought we agreed he would only ever marry a bottle of brandy."

"I don't know what to do," Louisa whispered. She hadn't mentioned Mr. Warwick's proposal to anyone but Margaret. "Do you think I should reject him?"

Margaret blew a puff of air up to the blonde hairs that stuck to her forehead. "I would say that depends entirely on your opinion of him."

Louisa had told Margaret about the events of the evening before, but had left out some of the details. It was too embarrassing to relay, and speaking of it made her face grow hot with mortification. "I have hardly known him long enough to form an opinion," Louisa said. "That is what terrifies me. All I know is that he is entirely too vexing. He enjoys making me uncomfortable."

"That does not sound promising." Margaret continued stirring the pot, pressing her lips together. "Hmm. I think you must decide if you would rather be married to someone you dislike, but live a life of comfort, or if you would rather live a life like mine." She glanced up, meeting Louisa's gaze. "A life of uncertainty."

Louisa's heart sank as that reality crashed over her. She did like Mr. Warwick's mother and sister. But how far did their squabble with Mr. Warwick extend? If she were to marry him, would she no longer be their friend? Even if Cassandra and Mrs. Warwick were no longer kind to Louisa, it wouldn't be so very bad living in Folkswich if Margaret and her family were nearby. Louisa would hardly have to see her husband if she didn't wish to. And Haslington estate was beautiful. She had always dreamed of being the mistress of such a beautiful house. But Louisa's heart was still bitter toward Mr. Warwick. He had stolen her opportunity to seek a love match. "Oh, Margaret." Louisa let out a sigh. "Perhaps you and I should work in a household together. We might find handsome footmen to marry instead."

Margaret laughed, the steam from the pot making her face pink. "I have a better idea. You marry Mr. Warwick, and I will work in *your* household. Since we are friends, you will provide me with the very best room and food and ensure only the most handsome of all the footmen are permitted to work in that house."

Louisa's laughter bubbled out, lightening the weight on her shoulders. "That may be the best idea yet. Although I still hope that you can find a position as a governess." Louisa studied her friend's slumping posture. "It would be more respectable. Then you might still marry a gentleman."

Margaret gave a half smile. "I have long since given up any dreams of wealth or prestige. Lord Blackwell did his worst on my family."

"Lord Blackwell?"

Margaret held a finger to her lips dramatically. "Do take care uttering that name around this house. It is as wicked as a curse word."

"Oh." Louisa clamped her mouth shut. "Who is he? What did he do?"

She and Margaret were close enough friends now that Margaret seemed comfortable confiding in her, especially since Louisa had just confided in her about Mr. Warwick's proposal. Margaret shook her head with disgust. "Lord Blackwell is a viscount who occupies the grandest estate in Yorkshire. His father and my father were dear friends since childhood. My father's entire income depended on his business relationship with Lord Blackwell's father. But when Lord Blackwell's father died, he cut my father off, leaving him and our family with nothing." Margaret's voice was heavy with bitterness. "That was when my family was forced to move here, and when I found my position at Larkhall."

Louisa's heart stung for her friend. "How cruel. Has he done nothing to improve your family's situation?"

"Nothing at all." Margaret's jaw tightened. "The man is

incapable of goodwill. He is greedy and selfish and proud." With each word, she stirred the pot vigorously. She took a deep breath. "He would make Mr. Warwick look like a gentleman of the most agreeable sort."

"How awful." Louisa hadn't known Margaret's family's situation had been caused by one man. By the way Margaret was stirring the pot with stiff motions, Louisa could see that she still harbored hatred for Lord Blackwell.

As though Margaret had read her thoughts, she looked up, meeting Louisa's gaze. Oh, dear. Was Louisa not even allowed to *think* the name Lord Blackwell in that house?

"Mr. Warwick is quite disagreeable himself," Margaret said after a moment of silence. "All I have heard about him has been negative. But I must question all I have heard now that he has offered for you. If he were truly disagreeable, he would not have done the honorable thing. He would have evaded all responsibility."

"I suppose that is true." Louisa swallowed. "But is it wise to marry a man who is known to be so disagreeable? His own reputation is not favorable at all."

"That is true. But he has money. And there is no question that he is handsome. Those two things don't often come together." Margaret chuckled. "These are matters that you must consider."

Louisa frowned, wringing her hands together. "But he is vexing! He drinks far too much. He is despised by his family and seems to be a man of many secrets." She paused, watching Margaret's smile. "You are supposed to be convincing me not to accept his proposal."

Margaret laughed. "It seems you are convincing yourself already."

"At least we can trust Matthew to caution me. He will surely advise me not to marry such a—" Louisa's gaze caught on something beyond the nearby window. She squinted. "*No.*"

"What is it?" Margaret stepped away from her cooking. "Are my brothers misbehaving outside again?"

It couldn't be. Two men, Matthew and Mr. Warwick, were walking toward the cottage. Together. Were they—were they…laughing? Louisa stepped closer to the glass, appalled at the way Matthew tipped his head back with what certainly appeared to be a boisterous laugh at something Mr. Warwick said. When her attention shifted back to Mr. Warwick, her gaze met his through the window. One of his eyebrows lifted, and the same side of his mouth rose in a smile, one far too flirtatious to be meant for Matthew. She ducked out of sight, brushing her hair back from her eyes. "Drat. He saw me."

"And it appears he quite liked what he saw," Margaret said.

Louisa tugged on Margaret's sleeve, pulling her away from the window. "Why are they together? And why are they behaving as if they are…" she swallowed, "*friends.*"

Margaret shook her head, seemingly just as surprised as Louisa was. "I daresay I have never even seen Mr. Northcott smile so much."

"Perhaps Mr. Warwick has been sharing some of his brandy." Louisa smoothed her skirts, hurrying to push back the loose pieces of her hair. Just as she finished, a knock sounded at the door. Being such a small cottage, the door was only a few feet away from where Louisa stood. She jumped back.

Margaret walked toward the entrance. Her parents weren't home and her brothers were all outside, so Louisa and Margaret were the only ones to receive these unexpected guests. Margaret chuckled as she glanced back at Louisa. "By your reaction it would seem there is a wild animal scratching at the door."

"Some might venture to call him that," Louisa muttered just before Margaret pulled the latch.

Louisa took a step back as the door swung open. She clasped her hands in front of her so tightly her fingers went numb. The two men walked inside, but Louisa only watched their boots. As she studied both sets of feet, she determined by the excessive shine of his boots that Matthew was the one on the right—the only one safe to look at. She glanced up, meeting his gaze, keeping it focused on him and not on Mr. Warwick, whose smirk she could see from the corner of her eye. How much did Matthew already know about the situation? Surely he couldn't know everything, otherwise he would not be acting so friendly toward Mr. Warwick.

Matthew greeted Margaret before stepping closer to Louisa, a deep furrow of concern in his brow. Where he stood, he blocked Mr. Warwick from view, so Louisa could finally breathe. "How did you know I was here?" she asked in a quiet voice.

"It was a good guess." Matthew gave a pained smile. "Mr. Warwick told me about the misunderstanding."

That was a gentle way of putting it. Louisa preferred to call it a *disaster*. Before Matthew could continue, Mr. Warwick stepped up beside him. Louisa's muscles tensed, her legs becoming stiffer than two trees. She gave a short bow in greeting, avoiding his gaze. "Mr. Warwick."

"Miss Rosemeyer."

Her eyes flickered to his face briefly, without permission. Even if his mouth was not grinning, his eyes certainly were. Did the mere sight of her discomfort amuse him so greatly? She had been known to be shy at times, but she had never felt so shy as this in her life. There was a proposal of marriage hanging between them, and it felt as thick and heavy as a brick wall.

"I'm glad to see my family's coach conveyed you here safely," Mr. Warwick said.

She nodded, not knowing what else to say. Her tongue was tied as she glanced between Matthew and Mr. Warwick. If only she could read Matthew's expression. He did appear concerned, but he also seemed entirely too fond of Mr. Warwick's company.

Louisa watched as Mr. Warwick's gaze shifted to the squat wooden table in the kitchen. The basket he had given her still sat there, the food inside awaiting the boys who were still playing in the small yard. "Were you not hungry?" he asked when he caught Louisa staring at the basket as well.

She looked up. "I'm certain the Lovell boys are much

hungrier than I am." She paused. "Your mother and sister gave me something to eat before you crossed my path this afternoon."

"I see." Mr. Warwick cleared his throat. "I apologize for not offering you something to eat sooner."

At the word *offering*, she was reminded of his other offer. Her stomach twisted, and she looked down at the floor. Silence fell between them for a long moment until Matthew finally spoke again. "Louisa, will you come outside with me for a moment?"

She nodded, eager to escape the stifling air of the cottage and Mr. Warwick's direct gaze. As she followed Matthew out the door, her arm brushed against Mr. Warwick's jacket, causing her stomach to plummet once again. With the door closed behind them, Matthew turned to face her from where they stood on the grass. Margaret's two brothers tossed a ball back and forth nearby, too distracted to eavesdrop.

"Mr. Warwick told me about his proposal," Matthew said. He crossed his arms, tipping his head down to look at her. "I know you do not always listen to my opinion or my advice, but I am still going to offer it."

"Matthew—" Louisa began shaking her head.

"I think you should accept it."

Those were the words she had most dreaded. Despite how much she liked to disobey Matthew's unwanted advice, she still respected his opinion. Her heart sank, and she looked down at her hands, wringing her fingers together. "I am afraid," she whispered. "I hardly know him."

Matthew sighed. "I know it is not ideal, but I respect him for doing the honorable thing. I am not always right in my assessment of people, but in the short time I have known Mr. Warwick, I see a great deal of…potential in him. I think he is a good man."

Louisa pressed her lips together to keep herself from refuting the words. In his short acquaintance with him, how could Matthew determine that Mr. Warwick was a good man? Another thought followed, crashing down on the first. In her short acquaintance with him, how could she determine that he was *not* a good man? She couldn't. There was much more to a person than a first impression, or even a second impression. And there was certainly much more to people than the rumors that circled around town.

Louisa took a deep breath. "I suppose I should not expect a better offer to come my way. It is more than I should have hoped for."

Matthew's face drooped a little, a sadness washing over his features. "There is nothing wrong with hoping and dreaming. But we should also be willing to accept a good thing when it is presented to us."

Louisa gave a resolute nod. *A good thing.* But why could she not see this as a good thing? Her heart hammered in her chest. There was something about Mr. Warwick that frightened her and thrilled her all at once. How could she marry someone who was such a mystery?

Matthew sighed. "I will not make your decision for

you, but I wanted you to know my opinion. It would be wise to accept his offer."

Louisa laughed under her breath. "It is easy for you to say that. You do not believe in love." Louisa had heard countless times from Bridget of her brother's aversion to marriage and love in general.

Matthew's eyes narrowed in thought. "You are mistaken. I do *believe* in love. But I do not trust it." Remnants of a broken heart still showed in his eyes when the subject of love was brought up. Louisa had seen it several times. Love had always been the only thing Louisa *could* trust. It had been her dream, her anchor, her hope. She had known, deep in her bones, that one day a man would fall in love with her and then marry her. But now that word—*love*...it lay dead and crushed at her feet.

"I suppose I should not trust it either," Louisa said in a dry voice. "I have believed in it my whole life, but it has disappointed me."

A slight smile lifted Matthew's lips. "It hasn't disappointed you yet."

Louisa frowned as Matthew began walking toward the door. What did he mean by that? Before she could question him, he opened the door. She started to follow him, but stopped when she saw his hand wave someone forward. Matthew glanced back before opening the door wider, making room for Mr. Warwick to come outside in his place. Louisa's heart leaped as Matthew stepped inside, closing the door behind him, leaving her alone with Mr. Warwick.

The sun was well on its way to setting, leaving orange streaks in the sky. A light breeze threatened to displace Louisa's bonnet a second time. She held onto the ribbons, hoping they would provide her with a little stability. Mr. Warwick walked forward, stopping several feet away. The silence was too much to bear. Louisa had to say something.

"Your nose," she blurted. "It looks better." It was not quite as crooked as it had been the last time she had seen it.

"Was that a compliment?" he asked, a grin lighting up his face.

Her stomach gave an unwelcome flutter. Margaret was right, at least he was handsome. "No. It was an…observation."

His smile only grew. "Ah. I wonder what other observations you have of me. How many of them are the cause of your hesitation to accept my proposal?" One of his eyebrows rose to accompany his smile.

"Are you asking me to tell you why I hesitate?" Louisa's heart pounded with nervousness.

"I confess, I am curious." He shrugged. "Although I might be able to guess at a few of your reasons."

Her own curiosity piqued. She wouldn't have guessed that Mr. Warwick was humble enough to recognize his own shortcomings. From the first moment she had met him he had struck her as pompous. "What would you guess?"

He tapped his chin in apparent thought, but there was still a gleam of mischief in his eyes. "I would guess that a large part of your hesitation comes from your fear that I will have a crooked nose forever. You might also hesitate because your attraction to me persists even despite it, and you are embarrassed to be drawn to such a disfigured man."

Louisa scoffed, grateful for the falling sun to conceal some of the color on her cheeks. How could she have thought for one second that he would take her question seriously? She marched forward, intent to pass him and walk back inside. Her emotions were spiraling, and tears stung behind her eyes. Could he not see how terrified she was?

Mr. Warwick grabbed her arm as she passed, stopping her. Her feet planted themselves in the grass as chills ran from her shoulder to the tips of her fingers. His hand loosened almost instantly. "Wait—Miss Rosemeyer." He sighed, a hint of frustration in his gaze. "I should not tease you at a time like this."

"No, you should not." She fought the lump in her throat, replacing her fear with confidence. "If I am to marry you, I have three stipulations."

His expression grew more serious, his brow furrowing. "Stipulations?"

"Yes." Louisa pulled her arm away, clasping her hands together as she took two steps back. She could think more clearly with a greater distance between them.

Mr. Warwick was silent for a long moment before chuckling, shaking his head. "I believe by offering to marry you to save your reputation, *I* am the one who should be setting these stipulations. I'm afraid you are the one with more to lose in this situation."

The sardonic tone of his voice set Louisa's blood boiling. It was true—she was certainly testing her luck, but she wasn't afraid. "If you wish to marry me, you must agree to my stipulations."

"I never said I wished to marry you. I *offered* to marry you."

Her eyes narrowed. "Very well then." She turned away from him, marching back to the house.

"Very well then…?"

She glanced back at him. "No."

"No?"

"That is my answer."

He looked taken aback, giving a hard laugh of disbelief. "You are rejecting my proposal?"

Louisa shrugged, her heart pounding. "I'm afraid so." What had she done? She had gone against Matthew's advice, and against her own common sense simply because he had vexed her. But she couldn't back down now—especially not now that she saw the disappointment in his eyes. She had wounded his pride, that much was certain. "Why should I accept the proposal of a man who will not even listen to a few small requests that I have?" Her stipulations were more than small, but he didn't know that yet. "In that case, I would be much happier on my own."

Mr. Warwick stared at her with the same disbelief as before as she turned away, taking the final few steps to the door and walking inside. Matthew sat on the sagging couch, and Margaret stood over her pot in the kitchen again. Both looked at her expectantly as she entered the cottage. She looked down like a guilty child. What had come over her? She had been prepared to accept Mr. Warwick's proposal, but she hadn't been able to bring herself to elevate his pride.

Louisa took a deep breath, walking past Matthew without meeting his gaze. "How may I help with dinner?" Louisa asked Margaret. As she walked into the kitchen, she caught sight of Mr. Warwick outside. He was turning away from the cottage. The sun only offered a faint glow as it descended, but it was enough to see the slump in his broad shoulders as he dragged the toe of his boot over the dirt. Was he frustrated…or disappointed? If what he had said was true…that he did not wish to marry her, then he would not be disappointed at all. He would be relieved.

"What happened?" Margaret asked in a hushed voice.

Louisa could feel Matthew's gaze on the side of her face, so she turned away from his view. She sighed. "I made a mistake."

Louisa looked out the window again, her heart pounding as Mr. Warwick walked away. She watched his back until he was out of sight.

CHAPTER 13

Jack's thoughts distracted him for too long. Before he could stop it, a slender hand snatched the bottle from the table in front of him. He grabbed at the air, missing the bottle as Cassandra threw it out the nearby window and onto the ground below. Jack cringed as he heard it shatter.

"What the devil—" he grumbled.

"You should not have picked it up in the first place." His sister brushed her hands over her skirts, a proud smirk on her lips. "If you are going to invite me here, you must know that I will do all I can to stop you from drinking." She raised one eyebrow.

Jack sighed. Why he had even invited Cassandra to his house that day was a mystery. But little did she know that he had already drank plenty the night before after returning from his conversation with Miss Rosemeyer. She had rejected him. He traced his finger over the grain of wood on the dining table. Could he blame her? His pride had caused him to speak out of line. The flirting…that he couldn't help, even if he knew she didn't like it.

Cassandra sat down on the chair beside him. "What is the matter?"

"Nothing." Jack shook his head. He had been a fool to invite Cassandra here. All she did was steal his drinks and try to read his mind. But he had wanted a woman's perspective to help him understand what he was feeling—what Miss Rosemeyer was feeling. Jack had been ready to prove himself, to do the right thing, and she had not even accepted his charity. Why it vexed him so much was a mystery.

Cassandra brushed her ginger hair from her eyes. She had a new set of flowers in her hair that day, arranged like a crown on her head. She squinted at him with scrutiny. "Tell me."

Jack sighed. What did he have to lose? With a deep breath, he started from the beginning, telling her everything from his mistake with writing the letter to the events Mrs. Chamberlain had witnessed, and finally to the rejection he had received the night before.

When he finished speaking, Cassandra stood from the table, pointing an accusatory finger at him. "You are the reason poor Miss Rosemeyer was wandering the woods alone. She was like a frightened kitten because of you. It is no wonder she would reject your proposal."

Jack frowned, his defenses rising. "She wandered the woods of her own accord."

"She was trying escape you. What made you believe she would want to spend her life married to you?" Cassandra laughed. "The idea is preposterous."

Jack flared his nostrils, but said nothing.

Cassandra covered her mouth, hiding her laughter when she saw his face. "Oh, dear. You *are* truly disappointed."

"I'm not," he said in a firm voice. "I'm simply confused."

"Have I made anything clearer for you? I cannot blame Miss Rosemeyer for being wary about marrying you. She has already seen you at your worst."

Jack bit the inside of his cheek, exhaling slowly. "Yes, she has. I—I wanted the chance to have her see me at my best." As the words came out, he realized how true they were. He had not had a reason to try his best in a long time. "She was demanding that I agree to three stipulations before she would accept my offer." He shook his head, scoffing.

"What were her stipulations?"

"I didn't ask. I was shocked that she would even suggest it. I didn't *have* to offer to marry her. She acts as though she is doing me a service by accepting my hand."

"Oh, that she certainly is," Cassandra said. "You would be much more tolerable with a pleasant, kind wife at your side." His sister paced in front of the table, a broad smile on her cheeks. "There is only one thing left for you to do."

"What is that?" Jack asked in a weak voice.

"Beg for her mercy."

His jaw dropped. "I will not do that."

Cassandra leveled him with a scolding glare. "Yes, you must. At least ask what her stipulations include. A woman does not like a man who will not listen to her."

Jack grumbled under his breath. "I refuse."

With an exasperated sigh, Cassandra planted both hands on the table, looking him squarely in the eye. "You are making a mistake." She paused. "I have heard Mother and Father talking. Father thinks you will never marry. And I know how you like to prove him wrong."

Jack crossed his arms. At every mention of his father, he felt smaller. Less significant. He felt the distance between where he was and where he wanted to be like a river, one that moved far too fast for him to cross safely.

Jack opened his mouth to speak, but was interrupted by a footman at the door.

There was a guest awaiting him in the drawing room. Jack's brow furrowed as he stood. Cassandra followed him all the way to the drawing room door. Before walking inside, he glanced through the doorway. Miss Rosemeyer sat on the nearest sofa, her hands linked in her lap, the toes of her shoes tapping on the carpet. He exchanged a glance with Cassandra, who wore a mischievous expression.

"Stay out here," he whispered.

His sister nodded, but something told him she would not venture far from the door. In fact, she would probably have her ear pressed against it the entire time.

What was Miss Rosemeyer doing here? Did she regret rejecting him? The questions coursed through his mind as he walked through the doorway. He willed a bit of confidence into his stride. She looked up from her lap, her brown eyes just as wide as usual. She had a way of appearing surprised at all times…even seeing him now in his own house. "Mr. Warwick." She stood and offered a curtsy in greeting.

He bowed. "Miss Rosemeyer. I thought you would never wish to set foot in this house again." His voice was more curt than he had intended.

"Well, now that your dreadful housekeeper is gone, it isn't so very bad."

Was that a smile he saw on her lips? The moment he observed her smile, it vanished.

"I have you to thank for finally driving her away," Jack said, raising one eyebrow.

"That is right. In which case you owe me a favor." Her soft, careful voice was endearing, and paired with the sincerity in her eyes, he couldn't look away from her face.

Both his eyebrows lifted this time, but he didn't protest. Cassandra was right. He was entirely at her mercy. How could he deny her any request that she had? "Do I now? Is marrying you not enough?"

"I did reject your proposal last night, as you know. I have come today to…make an alteration to my decision."

Jack rubbed his jaw. "Hmm. I'm not certain I should allow that." He fought against the smile that pulled at his mouth. She was so very serious, wasn't she? Each word she spoke seemed to have been meticulously planned, and she wasn't very skilled at hiding that fact.

A crease formed on her brow. "You said you would not retract your proposal."

"I am not retracting it, but perhaps I should alter it as well."

"Alter your proposal?" She frowned.

"If you are allowed to alter your decision, then I should be allowed to alter my proposal as well." Jack took a step closer.

"How so?" Genuine curiosity shone in her eyes, even though he could tell she was trying to hide it.

"I have come to realize that my proposal was not at all…traditional. It was not phrased in a manner that is pleasing to a woman's ear."

Miss Rosemeyer pressed her lips together, nodding. "I suppose it could have been better." Her voice was shy again, just a quiet squeak.

Jack drew closer again, surprised by the way his heart stalled in his chest when her gaze met his. That was a new sensation. He cleared his throat. "I revise my proposal as follows." He gazed into her eyes, noting small gold flecks around the edges of her irises. The centers of her cheeks had turned slightly pink. "Miss Louisa Rosemeyer," he began in a slow voice, enjoying the way her face deepened in color even more. "I know our acquaintance has been brief, but it has been quite eventful." He threw her a half-smile as he took her hand in his. Her fingers were stiff. "I have been the cause of your most recent misfortune, but I make you a promise today. If you marry me, I will do all I can to ensure no more misfortune falls upon you at my hand. I will do all I can to make you happy, comfortable, and safe. I will spend my days in the hopes that I can mend what I have ruined. I am far from perfect, but I hope you will accept me as your husband. You had your stipulations. If you wish to tell me, I will listen." Jack swallowed.

She looked at him with those round eyes, the shock still evident in them. She was silent for several seconds. "I did not plan to marry a stranger."

"I did not plan to marry at all."

She studied his face for a long moment, slipping her hand away from his. She brushed the hair away from her forehead, looking down at the floor. He had made her flustered, that much was certain. He grinned to himself until she looked up again.

"I do like your altered proposal better."

"Does that mean you will accept it?"

Miss Rosemeyer hesitated for a few seconds, circling away and putting more distance between them. "Not until you agree to my stipulations."

"I thought you had altered your decision?"

"I had, but then you offered to listen to my requests."

Jack exhaled slowly, turning to face her. He should have left that part out. "That I did."

She spoke in the same professional manner as before, the one he found far too endearing. "My first request is that you give me my own room, removed from yours." She looked down at the floor.

Jack nodded, grinning at the discomfort in her expression. He had expected nothing less from her. There would be no affection of any sort between them while she was so frightened of him. He hoped that one day that could change, but for now, he understood her reservations.

"The second is that you stop drinking to excess. I find you quite frightening when you are drunk."

Jack raised his eyebrows. That one would be a little more difficult.

"The third is that you take me to visit your family often. I wish to come to know your sister, mother, and father."

He laughed under his breath. "That third one I cannot promise."

"Why not?"

He shook his head, keeping silent. How could he explain the situation? His stomach twisted with guilt as he thought of all that Miss Rosemeyer didn't know about him. What would she think if he knew why his father resented him? What would she think if she knew the stories society believed about him? "I cannot agree to it. Not entirely. My mother and sister will wish to know you, and I will invite them here, but I am not welcome there so long as my father is in that house."

Miss Rosemeyer stared up at him for a long moment, her gaze boring into his. Could she see all his flaws? His secrets? "If you wish, you may replace your third stipulation with something else." He spoke in a direct voice.

"Very well." She paused for only a short moment. "If my friend Margaret Lovell does not find employment, you must hire her to work in this household and give her the most comfortable quarters possible."

Jack nodded in agreement. If it was a comfort to Miss Rosemeyer to have a friend there, then he would hire anyone she asked for. "I accept your stipulations."

She drew a deep breath. "Then I accept your proposal."

When she said the words, Jack's stomach gave a nervous flop. He was an engaged man. Miss Rosemeyer stared up at him, her own features appearing just as nervous as he felt. He wanted to put her at ease somehow, but he also wanted to see her blush.

He tipped his head closer to her, giving a flirtatious smile. "You look lovely in blue."

As expected, her brow immediately furrowed.

He held up both hands in surrender, backing toward the door. "There is no need to be alarmed. It was an observation, not a compliment." He winked, tugging the door open.

As he stepped into the hallway, he saw Cassandra still standing nearby. By the grin on her face, he could only assume she had overheard the entire conversation. "I quite liked her stipulations," Cassandra said.

Jack grunted. "I did not."

Her smile widened, and she rose on her toes. "May I plan your wedding?"

His wedding. Jack gulped. He could use a drink at that moment, but he had just agreed to refrain from such actions. Devil take it, what had he just agreed to?

Cassandra slipped past him, hurrying to Miss Rosemeyer's side with a cheerful squeal. "I have always wanted a sister."

Jack watched as a full smile spread over Miss Rosemeyer's face, the sight causing a surge of envy to bloom in his chest. Why couldn't he earn a smile like that? Determination took hold of him. One day he would, no matter how hard he had to work for it.

She met his eyes from over Cassandra's shoulder, her gaze lingering on him for a moment. He turned toward the door, rubbing a circle on his chest as he walked away. That woman did strange things to his heart, and he couldn't decide if he liked it or not.

CHAPTER 14

Although Louisa had told Cassandra she did not want an elaborate wedding, she hadn't listened. "I haven't married, and I may never marry, so your wedding may be the only one I have the opportunity to plan," Cassandra had said. Louisa had been unable to argue with that, so she had allowed the celebration to be as complete as Cassandra dreamed it would be.

The guests were few. Matthew and the Lovells came, as well as Mr. Warwick's mother. Cassandra, of course, was there. And so was another man, one with dark hair speckled with grey. She assumed it was the elder Mr. Warwick, Jack's father.

A common license had been obtained, allowing them to marry in the parish just a few days after she had accepted Mr. Warwick's proposal. Louisa had been staying with the Lovells, and her back ached from sleeping on the sagging couch.

Louisa watched the cold greeting between father and son just before the wedding began. It wasn't Mr. Warwick who introduced her to his father, but Cassandra. The elder Mr. Warwick looked very similar to his son, aside from the eyes that had clearly been inherited from his mother.

"I never thought Jack would marry," The elder Mr. Warwick said to Louisa. His voice was just as gruff as his son's—perhaps even more so. But there was something more intimidating about it.

Louisa didn't know how to respond, so she simply nodded. Jack had been avoiding his family, and they seemed to have been avoiding him as well, only attending out of obligation. It seemed no one thought Mr. Warwick was fit for marriage. The thought was not comforting. Louisa's stomach had been writhing all day, threatening to dispel her breakfast. Only minutes remained before she would become Mrs. Warwick.

The rushed nature of their wedding was likely what exacerbated the elder Mr. Warwick's dismay. Also the way Louisa refused to look at her betrothed. From the moment she had walked into the church, she had avoided his gaze.

A hand touched her shoulder, sending a string of shivers over her arm. "May I have a moment with my bride?"

Louisa turned, glancing up at Mr. Warwick. His jaw was tight, his gaze fixed on his father's face.

The elder Mr. Warwick nodded, looking away from his son in an instant. Louisa could hardly breathe amid the tension between the two men. What had caused it? She should have found the answers before agreeing to marry Mr. Warwick, but now it was too late. Her heart leaped as he caught her staring up at him.

Her heart hammered in her chest. With his black jacket and white cravat, he was unjustly handsome. She narrowed her eyes, watching as he sauntered a step closer, extending his elbow to her. She paused, noting his unsteady gait.

Had he been drinking?

She took his arm, following him toward the waiting clergyman. Her pulse raced past her ears, her legs shaking beneath her as the ceremony began. It was short, and the clergyman's words were all muffled in her ears. She didn't look at Mr. Warwick again until he was pronounced her husband.

He didn't seem affected by the ceremony, a distant look in his eyes that made her wonder yet again if he had already broken her second stipulation. But whether he had or not didn't change the fact that they were now married. Jack Warwick was her husband, and she was his wife.

And the only person in the room who smiled was Cassandra.

The cart that would take them back to Jack's house was decorated with ribbons. Margaret threw Louisa an encouraging smile as she stepped up to her seat. Jack ascended behind her, settling onto the bench by her side. Louisa could not have been the only one to have noticed his unsteady movements. Hot anger was already rising in her chest. Just the day before he had promised not to drink in excess, yet here he was at their wedding, drunk as a wheelbarrow.

He was skilled at hiding it, but not skilled enough.

His leg pressed against hers in the narrow seat, his arm overlapping with her elbow as he took the reins. Matthew stood with his arms crossed, observing with a stoic face as he always did. Louisa found Cassandra in the group, who was watching Jack with a sudden scowl. Surely she noticed that he had been drinking. And by the furrow on her brow, it was clear that she disapproved just as much as Louisa.

Mr. Warwick leaned toward her ear. "Off we go, Mrs. Warwick."

Louisa ignored the heat that climbed her neck. That was her name now.

"Or may I call you Louisa?" As he asked the question, he waved at Matthew.

Louisa would have preferred to have him call her Miss Rosemeyer, but since that was no longer an option, and Mrs. Warwick was far more unsettling, she nodded. "Yes, I would prefer that."

"And you may call me Jack." He was leaning so close. Without permission, her stomach fluttered. Why did he have to be so blasted attractive? It would be much easier to be angry with him if he were not. Even so, when she smelled the brandy on his breath, she scooted away, as far to the opposite side of the cart as she could.

"I would prefer to call you Mr. Warwick," she said through gritted teeth. She had to be patient. Once the horses started moving and they were out of sight, only then could she scold him.

"There is no need for such formality toward your husband," he said, laughing. He led the horses forward abruptly, causing the cart to jerk into motion. Louisa instinctively gripped his arm to steady herself, pulling her hand away the instant she touched him.

Her heart pounded with dread as the cart raced away from the church and down the road that led to Jack's house. The road was uneven, causing her to bounce in her seat. With one hand, she held onto the crown of flowers Cassandra had made for her, pinning it against her head to prevent it from blowing away.

"Slow down," Louisa said, her voice panicked.

He didn't seem to hear her, continuing forward with his careless driving, flicking the reins as if urging the team of horses to move even faster. They turned the first corner, and the cart barely made the turn without colliding with the short rock wall on the right side of the path.

Mr. Warwick laughed, seemingly thrilled by the experience.

He was mad. She had been right all along. Or at least he was mad when he was drunk. Why had she never learned to drive a cart? If she knew, she could have taken the reins herself.

She held onto the side of the cart, no longer caring what happened to the flowers in her hair. "Please slow down," she said again, her voice weak. Her stomach had begun turning dangerously. She would cast up her accounts all over Mr. Warwick soon if he did not listen.

Mr. Warwick turned to face her, taking his gaze off the road. He flashed her a cajoling smile. "I cannot hear you."

She glared at him, vexation gripping in all of her muscles. "Stop! This is dangerous."

She turned her attention back to the road the same moment he did. Her stomach lurched, no longer able to contain its contents. She hinged at the waist, casting up her accounts all over Mr. Warwick's boots. He shouted something intelligible, and when Louisa looked up, they were approaching a sharp turn, one that Mr. Warwick had failed to prepare for. As the horses swung around the bend, the cart teetered on one wheel, tipping onto its side with a crash.

The air was knocked from Louisa's lungs as she hit the ground. She gasped for breath, rolling out of the way as the cart nearly fell on top of her. Mr. Warwick had fallen nearby, also barely evading the cart. Louisa's head spun, and she finally caught her breath enough to sit up. Her hands stung as she pulled them away from the rocky path. Every part of her timid nature had fled, knocked out of her like the air had been from her lungs. She turned toward Mr. Warwick, who was struggling to sit. His soiled boots were caught under the cart, but he pulled them free, groaning. He turned toward Louisa, half his face covered in dirt. "Are you all right?" He reached for her arm.

"No," she snarled with disgust, crawling away until she had room to stand. Her white dress was now spattered with dirt. "You're drunk. You could not go one day without drinking, could you? You put both of our lives in danger!" She stood in front of where he still lay on the ground. This time she would not help him. She would not clean his face or stay by his side until she knew he was well. He could get up, fix the cart, and clean her vomit off his own boots.

Louisa's legs still shook, her shoulder throbbing from where she had taken the initial fall. "You could have killed me! Do you realize that?"

His gaze grew heavy at those words, his jaw setting. "Louisa—" He staggered, trying to stand, but toppled over again.

She let out an exasperated sigh. Turning on her heel, she marched toward the house. Thankfully it was just over the hill. She touched her head. The flowers Cassandra had given her were gone, and the right sleeve of her dress had torn. Her hands stung, and when she looked down, she saw the tiny cuts the rocks had put in them when she tried to slow her fall. Not only was the groom not what she had imagined, but the wedding day itself was already far from what she had always dreamed of. She should have known Mr. Warwick would not listen to her stipulations. He hadn't vowed to keep them. He hadn't signed a paper or given his solemn word. A man like him simply could not be trusted.

Yes, he could provide her with a place to live and food on the table, and for that she would be grateful. But she would not allow herself to hope for anything else. With each step toward the house, she locked her heart up tighter.

When she reached the front doors, the butler watched with shock as she marched up the stairs. Her belongings had been moved to Benham Abbey the day before, so all she had to do was find which room had been prepared for her. After checking three different doors, she found one with her trunks on the floor. At least Mr. Warwick had listened to her first stipulation. This room was on the opposite end of the hall from his. Perfect.

Louisa rang the bellpull, hoping there was at least one maid in the sparsely staffed house who could come assist her. Mr. Warwick, however, was on his own. As she waited for the maid to arrive, she walked to the window. If she leaned far enough to the right, it afforded her the perfect view of Mr. Warwick as he untied the horses, one by one, walking them back to the stables. His gait was even more unsteady than it had been before. Perhaps he had injured his leg in the crash.

She watched as he enlisted the help of two grooms. With a huffed breath, she turned away from the window, examining the room more closely. She had a feeling these four walls would become very familiar. She was too angry with Mr. Warwick to have any wish to leave for the rest of the day. Perhaps for the rest of her life.

Jack stared at his reflection, sitting alone in front of the mirror in his bedchamber. His hair was mussed, his eyelids heavy. His nose was still slightly swollen, discoloration from the bruising spreading under both his eyes. He let out a long sigh, dragging his fingers down his face and neck as he looked up at the ceiling. He could hardly look at himself. Not because of the bruises, but for countless other reasons.

He stood, throwing the chair back into place. It had been one day and he had already lost his wife's trust. He had been so determined to follow her stipulations, but he had disregarded them that morning. When Cassandra had told him his father would be attending the wedding, he had started with one drink. And then it had turned into far more than that.

He hadn't even tried to face Louisa. He was too ashamed, and he knew with complete certainty that she was happier without him nearby. Her words had been echoing in his ears all day, slicing him to pieces. *You could have killed me.*

It could have been another deadly accident that was his fault. The outcome could have been so much worse. He had gotten away with a few scratches and a bruised ankle, but he still didn't know if Louisa was injured or not. She had been hiding in her room all day, and he couldn't blame her. He had almost reached for his bottle again that night, but he had refrained, hiding himself away in his own room instead. He was such a fool. Weak. Despicable.

He paced the border of his room, stopping by the wardrobe. He stared at it, remembering all the details of that night when Louisa had hidden inside. She had been so confused and frightened then, and she likely felt even more so now. Guilt drove its blade deeper into his heart. He needed to do something other than continue wallowing. He couldn't undo the past, but he could try to be better in the future. That was all he *could* do. Try.

The determination in his stride distracted him from the pain in his ankle as he marched to every cabinet in the house and kitchen, gathering up every purchase he had made at the gin shop. If he worked too slowly, he might change his mind. One by one, he did as Cassandra had done and disposed of them. When they were all emptied, Jack found a tray, instructing the cook to fill it with each of the courses she was preparing for dinner. He didn't suspect Louisa would care to join him in the dining room, so he would bring the food up to her room when it was ready. He would give her a chance to join him for dinner, but if she declined, then he was prepared.

When it came time for dinner, he paced the hallway three times before gathering the fortitude to knock on her door. He waited several seconds with no reply. He knocked again, listening to his own heartbeat as he waited.

"Louisa?" He was certain she was inside, even if she didn't answer. He leaned his forehead against the wood, closing his eyes. "Would you like to come to dinner?"

Silence.

He took a deep breath. "I—I understand if you do not. I'm sorry. I truly am." He waited a few more seconds. "Are you…injured? Are you alive? Please answer me so I know you are well. I will not walk away until you make a noise, even stomping your foot on the floor or cursing my name will suffice."

He listened to a slight rustle of fabric. It grew closer, and so did her quiet footfalls. He took a step away from the door. Was she going to let him in?

The door shifted as she slid the lock into place, the metal making a loud *screech* against the wood.

Ah. She was locking him out.

He fought the smile that tugged on his mouth. Louisa was far more stubborn than she appeared. It would take no small amount of effort to win her trust.

"Thank you," Jack said. "I am glad to hear you are alive and well."

CHAPTER 15

She may have been alive, but she was not well.

Louisa listened as Mr. Warwick's footfalls moved away from the door, her hand still gripping the edge of the lock. She had been surprised to hear the sincerity in his apology. Her heart pounded. She had been holding onto her anger all day, but now she felt it slipping out of her grip. Louisa had always struggled holding onto feelings of resentment, even when she wanted to. There was no good that came from it.

With a sigh, she sat down on the edge of her bed. But now her pride would not allow her to go downstairs for dinner. Her stomach growled. Did she really plan to hide in her room all day? When she considered the alternative, which was facing Mr. Warwick, she decided that yes—she would rather hide in her room, even if it meant she had to be hungry. The last time she had gone wandering that house in search of food had been the start of a disaster.

Louisa looked out the window as the sun set, watching the streaks of orange and blue disappear. A few minutes later, another knock sounded on her door. Louisa jumped a little before rising to her feet slowly.

"Louisa?"

It was Mr. Warwick's voice again. Her heart hammered. What could he want now? She eased her way closer to the door, biting her lip. Should she open it? Her hand hovered over the lock before a thought made her freeze. Mr. Warwick was her husband, and it was the night of their wedding. Surely he did not expect the proceedings of the evening to be…traditional. No. She shook her head even though he could not see her. No, no, no. She banished the idea from her head. Only a simpleton would have such expectations given their circumstances.

Well, Mr. Warwick *was* a simpleton at times.

"Louisa, I know you are there." His voice was low. "Please, open the door."

"Why?" Her voice was sharp.

He was silent for a long moment. "I'm afraid I cannot tell you." He paused again. "It is a surprise."

She frowned, taking a step away from the door. "I do not like being surprised."

He laughed under his breath. "You will like this surprise. I promise."

Misgiving flooded her chest, and she almost darted into the far corner of the room. "I had my share of surprises when I fell out of the cart today."

"Yes, well, I was surprised when you deposited the contents of your stomach on my boots."

She scoffed. "That was your fault."

She heard his deep inhale followed by a sigh. "Yes, the entire ordeal was my fault, and I offer my sincerest apology."

There was nothing flirtatious or remotely romantic about his voice or words, so she gathered the courage to move closer to the door again. With slow movements, she slid the lock, pulling the door open just enough to peek her head out.

Mr. Warwick held a large silver tray, every inch of the surface covered with bowls and plates, each piled high with meat, bread, soup, fruit, and even desserts. "My cook prepared a special meal for us this evening," he said. "I thought you might like to eat in your room. It would be a shame to miss such a meal." His eyes met hers, a wry smile pulling on his lips. "And I know what becomes of you when you are hungry."

Louisa stared at the feast in front of her, too shocked to speak. She glanced up at Mr. Warwick's face again, noting a certain shyness in his features. She had only seen the pompous smiles or the flirtatious ones. The only sign of vulnerability she had seen in his expression was that day, when she had accused him of nearly killing her. Now, as he looked down at her, he seemed to be searching for something. Was it forgiveness? Approval?

She opened the door wider, propping it open with her

leg as she took the tray. "Thank you," she managed in a quiet voice.

The tray was heavier than she had expected, and she struggled to balance it while keeping the door open with her back. In a swift movement, Mr. Warwick reached behind her, pressing his hand against the door, just above her shoulder. Her breath caught in her lungs, trapped between an inhale and an exhale.

The tray faltered in her hands, but she managed to steady the opposite edge of it against Mr. Warwick's chest. He tipped his head down to look at her, a small smile flitting across his lips. "That was a near disaster," he breathed. "May I remind you that you already spilled one meal on me today."

It took her a moment to catch his meaning, and her cheeks flamed with embarrassment. Surprisingly though, her anger had faded to a small spark, one she was having trouble igniting. He couldn't expect that a tray of food would mend a mistake like the one he made that day. "May I remind you that it was entirely your fault?"

He kept his hand planted on the door behind her, the tray wedged between them. He seemed to be leaning closer though, his eyes smiling directly into hers. His expression shifted to one that was much more serious. "May I remind you how very sorry I am?"

Louisa pursed her lips, looking down at the food. Why was her heart racing? She was unaccustomed to seeing him this serious. "If you were as sorry as you say, you might have procured me a pineapple for dinner."

He raised his eyebrows. "Such exotic fruits do not grow in England."

"When I lived at Larkhall, Mr. Northcott once had one imported. There was only one small piece of the fruit that was not rotten from the long journey, but it was the most delicious fruit I have ever eaten."

Mr. Warwick chuckled. "If I ever have the wealth to import a pineapple, I will personally carve out the portion that has not yet rotted and present it to you on a silver platter if it means you will forgive me."

Louisa held back her smile, but she feared Mr. Warwick caught a glimpse of it—at least based on the victory in his eyes. No. She could not let him have any victory yet.

She put on a stern expression. "I eagerly await that day. Only then will you have my forgiveness." Louisa pressed against the door, her skin flushing as she backed away from him. He had been standing so close. She hadn't noticed the ring of green around his irises, nor the dusting of freckles on his cheeks before that night.

His hand fell away from the door as she slipped inside her room. Just when she thought the door was going to close between them, he caught it by the handle, peeking his head inside. He wedged his shoulder inside as well, half his body in her room, half in the hallway. He didn't seem as though he would enter without permission, so she let her posture relax.

She raised her eyebrows. "What is it?"

"May I remind you that you are now my wife?" he said.

Her eyes rounded.

"And I am your husband?"

Louisa's throat dried up like an autumn leaf, and she gripped the tray tighter. "I suppose that is true."

"You realize that it is our wedding night, do you not?" His lips curved into a grin.

Where was the poker when she needed it? Perhaps if she threatened to stab him, he might fall into the hallway and she could lock the door again.

He continued in a slow voice. "Husbands and wives are expected to—"

Louisa cleared her throat in an effort to drown out his words. "How *dare*—"

"...expected to dine together on the night of their wedding," Mr. Warwick finished with an innocent smile. "Wouldn't you agree?"

Louisa glared at him as heat flooded her face yet again. He knew exactly what he was doing with his choice of words. He was teasing her relentlessly. A low chuckle escaped him as he observed her reaction from the doorway. "Oh...was there something else you thought I was implying?"

He was infuriating. And tremendously inappropriate.

"No."

His chuckling continued. "Did you think all that food was for you?"

She looked down at the tray, noticing for the first time that there were at least two servings of every item. She had been hungry enough to overlook that fact. She was *still* hungry enough to overlook it. And, at the moment, his laugh at her expense was entirely too vexing to tolerate.

She set the tray down on her bed, turning to face him again. She crossed her arms, speaking in a quick voice as she walked toward the door. "One would not expect a woman like myself to eat two servings of an elaborate meal like this, nor would they expect a woman to lock her husband out of her room on the night of their wedding, but my life has never gone according to expectation." Louisa gave a sweet and rather false smile, taking hold of the door handle.

Mr. Warwick still laughed as he stepped back in surrender. She tried not to notice the lines that stretched out from the corners of his eyes as he smiled. It would not do to let his endearing qualities overshadow his vexing ones.

"Thank you for the food," she said. "I will enjoy every last bite." With that, she closed the door between them, sliding the lock firmly into place.

She turned away with a content sigh. Her hands stung from holding onto the tray so tightly. She looked down at the cuts on both her palms. They had turned an angry red. The maid had cleaned the dirt from them earlier that day, but they still stung with every movement. Her shoulder carried a dull ache, and she had seen the start of a bruise forming on her hip…all because Mr. Warwick had been careless.

Yes, indeed, she would enjoy every bite of her meal. Not only that, but she would *thoroughly* enjoy every bite of his. Better yet, she wouldn't feel the slightest bit guilty for it.

She laughed softly to herself, the image of his shocked expression as she closed the door still floating through her mind. Pride surged in her chest. She had never known herself to be so bold, but Mr. Warwick had a way of bringing out the lion inside her, one that had been disguised as a lamb her entire life.

She could not be a lamb with Mr. Warwick or she would be eaten alive. The only way to deal with a lion was to become a lioness herself.

She ate the dessert first, enjoying the lack of social rules dictating which coarse she ate first. The sweet blueberry tart flooded her senses, the faint smell of cinnamon wafting up to her nose as she took the first bite. She chewed and swallowed, unsettled by the silence of the house.

Drat it all. She did feel a little guilty.

With careful steps, she walked to the door, peeking one eye between the crack.

Mr. Warwick was gone.

CHAPTER 16

A slow smile curved Jack's lips as he listened to the faint rustling in the hallway beyond the breakfast room the next morning. He had seen Louisa's maid enter her room earlier that morning, so he knew she was awake.

And she was sneaking through the hallway.

He pushed away from the table, careful not to make any noise as he walked toward the door. If Louisa was going to live there, she ought to feel welcome enough to walk normally, not moving about the house as if she were stalking prey. Unless, of course, he *was* the prey. He held back a laugh. Something told him she was avoiding him, not trying to sneak up on him.

Jack waited until the rustling was right outside the door. And then he threw it open, stepping out into the hall. "Good morning," he said in a cheerful voice.

Louisa gasped, nearly jumping out of her shoes. She pressed a hand to her chest, whirling to face him.

One dark curl fell over her eyebrow, and she brushed it away, looking down at the floor. Jack took her in with his gaze. He was discovering that there wasn't a color that didn't flatter her. Just when he thought white was the best, she wore a pink dress like the one she wore that day, the color matching the flush in her complexion that he found so blasted endearing. Was it a crime to be attracted to his wife? Certainly not. But it was unwise to dwell on her beauty when she wanted nothing more than to stay as far away from him as possible. Her lips pressed together momentarily, an expression he had learned usually preceded a scolding.

"You startled me," she said, taking a deep breath. Her brow furrowed. "And since you are smiling, I suspect you did it intentionally."

Jack grinned. "You may call it revenge. Now imagine that this room was dark and you thought you were alone in the house."

A slight smile lifted the corners of her mouth. "Do you think you still have to prove to me how frightened you were that night? Your scream was proof enough."

"Did I scream?" Jack leaned against the doorframe. "I am fairly certain that was you."

Louisa shook her head resolutely. "You screamed like a newborn infant."

He couldn't help but laugh. "Well, you chose to marry me despite that tendency. So long as you have abandoned your habit of hiding in wardrobes, you should never have to hear my scream again."

Louisa's eyes lifted to his before flitting away. Her smile was smug, as though she were proud of herself for making him scream the first time. "I'm afraid my habit is very difficult to abandon, especially with such a spacious wardrobe tempting me each time I pass your room. You ought to always be prepared to find me inside." Her face was serious enough that Jack might have not caught the hint of teasing in her voice. It shocked him...she had never done anything but scowl when he teased her. And now she was teasing him back?

He quite liked it.

"Is wielding a weapon part of this habit of yours?" he asked.

"Only if I am threatened."

"Or hungry?"

Her face broke into a smile, and she nodded. "Yes. It seems, for your own safety, you will have to sacrifice your dinner to me every night."

"Well, you do seem to be in an agreeable mood today, so perhaps I should." He studied her smiling face for a long moment, surprised at the way it tugged at his heartstrings. Her smile faded and she looked down, seemingly back to the shyness he was accustomed to. He tore his gaze away from her face, pulling the door open wider, gesturing inside. "While we are on the subject...breakfast is on the sidebar. Of all the staff that has deserted this house, at least the cook has remained."

Louisa walked past him, taking a plate tentatively. "In truth, I am still quite satisfied from my meal last night."

"Meal?" Jack raised one eyebrow.

She glanced at him from over her shoulder. "*Meals*."

He chuckled, watching as she took a small serving of fruit and sat at the table. Her eyes wandered the room, settling on everything but him as he sat in the chair across from her. "Are you going to begin hiring new staff for the other areas of the house?" she asked. "As I recall, the house has a need for maids."

"Indeed." Jack smiled. "I plan to hire a new steward who will manage it all for us." He clasped his hands together on the table.

"Once the house is fully staffed," she began in a quiet voice, "may we have guests? Surely you have friends in town, and I would like to make some friends of my own here as well." She looked down at her plate. "I still need to write to my sister and tell her that I am married. I daresay she will be very surprised." Louisa still appeared surprised herself. She pushed the blueberries around with her fork, but didn't eat a single one.

"I'm afraid you are wrong." Jack gave a weak smile. "I don't have friends in town. Not anymore." He had once called Lord Bridport his friend, but the man had believed every word Evan Whitby had said. Or rather, he had pretended to believe him in order to gain his favor. Jack's jaw tightened.

Louisa tipped her head to one side, suddenly far more interested in him than in her blueberries. "Not a single one?"

"I suppose if your friend Mr. Northcott remained in Yorkshire we would come to be friends."

Louisa nodded. "Matthew is very kind. He would be friends with anyone."

Jack raised one eyebrow. "Do you mean to say that I am one of these pitiful creatures he would befriend out of kindness?"

She didn't hesitate for a moment. "That is precisely what I mean."

Jack laughed, leaning back in his chair. She was in an agreeable mood indeed. Although her words were sharp, there was something in her eyes that he hadn't seen before. Amusement.

She glanced at him with curiosity. "I wonder how a man of your position could have so few friends."

His *position*. A gentleman, set to inherit an estate in town—that must have been what she meant. He blew out a long, slow exhale. "As I have said before, rumors can be the cause of upheaval, and reputations are more fragile than that blueberry." He pointed at her plate at the same moment she skewered a berry with her fork.

Her eyes widened.

"I am not admired by society...to put it kindly." He wasn't admired by anyone. Not even his family wished to claim him. His heart stung. He had thought his marriage might help gain his father's approval, but his father had seemed indifferent. Jack hadn't been exactly cordial toward him at the wedding. "Although, I suspect I will be more admired now with you at my side." He cast her what he thought to be a charming smile.

She didn't seem to agree. Her brow furrowed. She was silent for a long moment, her face reflecting deep thought. When she finally spoke, her words surprised him. "You must be very lonely."

The smile slipped from his face, and he cleared his throat. Her gentle voice struck him squarely in the chest, unstopping a pain he hadn't realized was there. He looked down at the table, certain the vulnerability showed in his eyes. He had become very skilled at hiding anything he felt, but he was fairly certain Louisa's large brown eyes were capable of seeing everything. "I suspect you have felt a similar loneliness," Jack said, avoiding confirming her words directly. There was so much he still didn't know about Louisa, but the fact that she had come here to live with an aunt she had never met told him her circumstances had been abnormal. He recalled what she had said the night she had tended to his broken nose. She had told him that she didn't belong anywhere.

Louisa's eyes were heavy and distant as she nodded. "Yes, but I have grown accustomed to it."

"As have I." Jack gave a small smile, meeting her gaze. Understanding passed between them with that one glance. Warmth filled his chest as she looked down at the table, fleeing back to her shyness as she always did.

"I suppose no one should ever become accustomed to being lonely," she said in a quiet voice.

"It is a good thing you married me then."

She glanced up at him from under her lashes, a conceding smile on her lips. She quickly erased the expression. It was cruel of her to only let him see it for a second or two.

Louisa may have felt like she didn't belong anywhere, but it was now Jack's objective to change that. He wanted her to love her home, her life, and eventually—if it were possible—to love him. He was beginning to discover that Louisa was far too easy to love. His blasted heart had already grown attached to her in a matter of days. He could only imagine what a lifetime would do. The notion scared him a little, if he were to be honest with himself. What if she never loved him in return?

Louisa ate the last of her fruit in silence, her eyes still wandering the room. He tucked away his unwelcome fears, packing them down and out of sight inside him.

"I imagine this is all very overwhelming for you," Jack said. "I have not lived here long, but I suspect I know a little more about the house and grounds than you do. Would you like a tour?" He waited, holding his breath. He had fully expected her to spend another day locked away in her room, but so far that day she had seemed very forgiving. Much more forgiving than he deserved.

"I suppose I should become acquainted with the place." She stood as a footman cleared her plate. "If only to prevent another *incident*. These halls are quite confusing in the dark."

Jack chuckled. "At least if we are seen alone together again, it will no longer be cause for distress."

"For the spectator, or for me?" Louisa raised one eyebrow.

She was relentless today. He could hardly tell whether or not she was teasing, because being alone with him did indeed seem to cause her distress. Only when he saw the faint smile touch her lips did he deem it appropriate to tease back. "For me. So long as I keep you well fed and the fire pokers hidden, I will be safe in your presence."

He started walking out the door of the breakfast room, glancing back as he held it open for her. He flashed her a teasing smile.

Her eyes narrowed as she passed him. "You are the one who put both our lives in danger yesterday."

Jack's stomach twisted with guilt. How had he been so foolish? "I know." He followed Louisa into the hall, moving ahead of her so he could see her face. "And I promise it will not happen again."

She eyed him, obviously skeptical. "Do you plan to teach me to steer the horses?"

"If you wish." He gave a soft smile. "But an even better solution would be for me to stop drinking to excess as you requested. That is why I have disposed of all my brandy, port, and sherry."

Her eyebrows rose. "All of it?"

Jack nodded. "Yes. Not a drop remains. I do not intend to ever break another promise I have made to you."

Her head tipped slightly to one side, lines of surprise still creasing her forehead. "Are you certain it wasn't Cassandra who disposed of it?"

"Yes, although she would have taken great pleasure in it. I suspect you would have as well."

Louisa shrugged. "Perhaps." The shock still lingered on her face. "I cannot believe you would dispose of it."

Jack could hardly believe it himself, yet here he was. "I'm beginning to realize there is little I would not do to gain your forgiveness." He had heard that forgiveness was won by action. Words of apology were only the seed from which it grew, although sometimes no amount of watering could make it grow. Ever since his uncle's death, Jack had been doing all he could to show his father he was sorry. He had blamed himself for so long, and that was a weight that was too heavy to lift off of his own back. All his father had done was add stones to his satchel.

Louisa stared up at him, hands interlocked behind her back. "I am glad to hear my forgiveness is more valuable than a bottle of brandy."

"Few things in life are." He smiled.

"I knew you would say so." She followed him as he began walking down the hall. "I did hear a rumor about you, but I wasn't certain if it was true," she said.

Jack's heart pounded and he turned to face her again. Had she heard about the hunting accident already?

"There was a rumor in town that if you were ever to marry, you would sooner wed a bottle of brandy than a woman."

A laugh burst from his chest. "Rumors are never to be believed, especially outrageous ones such as that. There are times I wonder who could have started such a ridiculous falsehood." He shook his head.

"I did."

He glanced up as Louisa began walking forward, a smug smile on her lips.

He froze, unable to stop his laugh of disbelief. "Is that so? Isn't it a bit counterproductive to have disproved your rumor so quickly by marrying me yourself?"

How could she walk so quickly? His strides could barely keep up with hers and he was several inches taller. As he caught up to her side, he realized what she was trying to hide in walking so quickly. Another smile. Each one felt like an unexpected prize, and he felt inclined to start a collection.

"I believed the rumor wholeheartedly. That was the most important reason for my hesitation in accepting your proposal."

"Are you certain it wasn't my nose?"

Louisa eyed him sidelong. "Fortunately the swelling will eventually subside."

He burst into laughter, melting her facade for a brief moment. She gave a shy smile, as if proud of her quips but too humble to relish in them.

"Well, before you can insult me further, shall be begin our tour?"

Louisa turned to face him, her eyes dancing with amusement. "It wasn't an insult. It was an observation." Her cheeks were flushed to match her dress, her lips pressed together to hide her smile. There were many other *observa-*

tions about her he could have made known in that moment, but he kept his mouth shut. She did not enjoy his compliments.

Jack extended his arm to her as they walked down the hall. At first, she pretended she didn't notice, focusing intently on the lofted ceilings. He waited, keeping his elbow outward until she finally placed her hand softly around his arm without looking at him.

Even with her reluctance, he would still call it a victory.

CHAPTER 17

Benham Abbey was much larger on the inside than it appeared on the outside. Perhaps it only felt larger because Mr. Warwick stopped at nearly every door, explaining the purpose behind each room. Based on the broad smile on his face, Louisa assumed he was inventing some of the information to make the tour more exciting. The dramatic gestures of his arms and the enthusiasm in his voice added to her amusement. She tried her hardest to focus on the information he was telling her, but most of her focus was captured by his voice and his mannerisms, his expressions and movements. She scolded herself each time she found herself distracted, but the distractions were becoming more and more frequent.

Had he truly disposed of all his drinks? She hadn't fully believed that he was remorseful until that morning when he had told her that. She was still cautious, but her confidence grew each moment she spent in his company. Her shyness was fading a little, at least when he was being so cheerful and welcoming. She was proud of herself for taking his teasing comments a little more lightly—and for giving him a quip or two in return. There was no harm in at least trying to be friends with her husband.

She was still worried he would break his promises, but for now, she enjoyed his company. He was entertaining to listen to and even more entertaining to watch. She followed silently for most of the house tour, asking questions only when necessary. Each time she smiled he seemed to pause, as if pocketing the expression for safekeeping. It took a great deal of effort to keep her smiles at bay, but she could not have him thinking she thought him as entertaining as she truly did.

She quite enjoyed seeing his efforts to win her favor.

She refused to believe they were working, even if her heart fluttered a little every now and then.

Mr. Warwick's eyes met hers as they walked outside, progressing to the tour of the grounds. In the sunlight, his eyes appeared even more blue. He was so much more amiable when he had not been drinking. It almost made her forget how much he had vexed her before. "What did you think of the house?" he asked. "Describe it in one word."

"Only one?"

"It's a test of your creativity," he said with a sideways smile.

Louisa glanced upward in thought. "Large."

His features flattened. "Is that all you could think of?"

"That is the first word that came to my mind." Louisa shrugged. She nearly laughed at his deflated expression. "If you would allow me more than one word, then I might describe it to your satisfaction."

"I will give you one more attempt."

She pursed her lips. "Undermanned."

He let out a grunt of dismay. "I already told you I plan to hire a steward and many other staff members soon. Do you know who you are beginning to sound like?" One of his eyebrows arched dangerously.

A laugh bubbled in her chest. She held it back, shaking her head. "Do not say it."

He drew a step closer. "*Mrs. Chamberlain.*"

Louisa glared at him, but she could only hold the expression for a few seconds. Mr. Warwick's face twitched, his shoulders shaking. Her laughter burst out, and she shook a finger at him as he started laughing as well. "Never, ever compare me to that woman again." She crossed her arms, walking a few paces away from him. He seemed far too proud of himself for making her laugh. His eyes were fixed on her, a triumphant grin on his face.

"Then you ought to think of a better word for the house, one that is not so offensive."

She sighed. "Why do you take such pride in a house that is not your inheritance?"

He looked down at the grass. They were walking aimlessly on the back lawn, circling the perimeter as they talked. When they approached the gardens, Mr. Warwick took a turn onto the row of stepping stones flanked by rose bushes, waving Louisa forward. "Perhaps one day I will be proud of Haslington, but for now, I resent it." His voice wasn't angry like she had expected. It was sad. A little broken.

One word hovered on her tongue, but she held it back. *Why?* That was all she wanted to ask, but she was afraid of ruining the tour for both of them. Mr. Warwick's quarrel with his father must have been caused by something more drastic than his drinking and gambling habits.

"I understand that," Louisa said. "I have no wish to return to the house I was raised in." She kicked a weed that had sprouted between a crack in the stone path. "My stepfather ruined that house for my sister and me."

Mr. Warwick's eyes met hers as they stopped by a stone bench under the shade of a tree. He gestured for her to sit before taking his place beside her. "How so?"

Louisa crossed her ankles under her skirts, staring up at the leaves as they twisted on their stems with the breeze. "After my mother died, he tried to arrange a marriage for my elder sister to one of his dreadful creditors. He threatened to send us to the workhouse if she did not marry him. Thankfully, the Northcotts invited us to Larkhall. As luck would have it, Alice, my sister, fell in love and married during our visit there. I stayed as a companion to Matthew's sister Bridget." Louisa smiled. "When she married, I felt…a bit out of place at Larkhall with Matthew. It was not proper for me to stay, so I wrote to my aunt." She glanced at him from the corner of her eye. "Or rather, I wrote to you. And now I am here, and my stepfather is in debtor's prison." She was silent for a long moment. "I will likely never see my childhood house again, and I have no wish to."

She could feel Mr. Warwick's gaze on the side of her face, so she gathered the courage to look at him. His eyes were heavy as they traced over her face. "And the events of your arrival here were yet another misfortune you did not anticipate." His voice was edged with frustration, and she could practically see the guilt that lined his face. She hated to be the cause of it. Guilt and regret were two of the most wicked emotions. They clung to a person without mercy, and were often impossible to remove. At least not without help.

"I would not call it a misfortune. I would call it a… surprise. Life, as we know, is full of unexpected things. In truth, I think your company today has proven much more agreeable than Mrs. Irwin's." Louisa avoided his gaze when she said that part, returning her attention to the leaves and not the satisfied smile on his lips.

Mr. Warwick's voice was gentle. "And I confess, despite your similarities, your company is slightly more agreeable than Mrs. Chamberlain's."

Louisa gasped, turning to face him. "Slightly?"

He chuckled. "The comparisons will continue unless you think of a better word to describe the house."

She sat back in surrender. "Very well. In one word…" She paused, tapping her chin. "Functional."

Mr. Warwick groaned, but his smile persisted. "You will not flatter me, will you?"

"I'm afraid not." She gave a quiet laugh. "You must confess that all three of my words accurately describe the house."

"Yes, they do." He crossed his arms. "However, your words of choice make it sound equal to the stables."

"I haven't yet seen the stables, but I imagine they are quite fascinating." Louisa kept her eyes fixed on the large yellow butterfly that flitted toward their bench. Her heart pounded. There was no reason behind it, but she had been afraid of butterflies for as long as she could remember. The little creatures seemed to have no fear of approaching people, but simply because they were beautiful did not mean they were welcome near *her*. One had once landed on her arm after she had fallen asleep outside, and she had awoken to the tickle of wings brushing against the hairs on her arms. Even at the memory, chills ran up and down her limbs.

"Fascinating?" Mr. Warwick cast her a look of dismay. "That should have been the word you used to describe the house."

"If you are so skilled at this game, I would like to hear you describe that butterfly in one word," Louisa said. It would be good to have another set of eyes on the wicked creature so it could not sneak up on her.

Jack followed her gaze, seemingly intent to accept the challenge. He studied the butterfly as it landed on a knot in the tree across from where they sat. "Curious."

Louisa raised her eyebrows.

"It is curious enough to investigate this corner of the

garden where we are sitting. I suppose it hopes to eavesdrop on our conversation."

She gave a weak laugh as she watched the creature balance on the tree.

"How would you describe it?" he asked.

"You will tease me for it," she said in a quiet voice.

Now Mr. Warwick seemed rather *curious* himself as he leaned forward, resting his elbows on his knees to look at her and not the butterfly.

She took a deep breath before revealing her word of choice. "Evil."

Mr. Warwick's face contorted in shock.

Her heart leaped as the creature took flight from the tree, moving straight toward them with alarming speed. She shrieked, grabbing hold of his arm without thinking. When her scream failed to startle the butterfly, she jumped up, running away from the bench and out of its way.

She could hear Mr. Warwick's laughter even beyond the frantic beating of her heart. She pressed a hand to her chest, her gaze darting around to see where it had gone.

The wicked little thing was on Mr. Warwick's knee, standing there like a queen on its throne, yellow and black wings moving slowly back and forth. He extended a finger toward it.

"Don't touch it!" Louisa said in a sharp whisper.

He chuckled, ignoring her warning. She knew her fear was irrational, but she could barely tolerate seeing the creature's prickly little legs crawl onto the tip of his finger. "Mr. Butterfly, it is a pleasure to make your acquaintance." His grin became more wicked, and he glanced at Louisa with one raised eyebrow. "Might I introduce you to my companion?" He made to stand, but Louisa was already running away.

She only made it out of the gardens and back onto the lawn before Mr. Warwick's chuckling was right behind her.

She squeezed her eyes shut, covering her face as he grabbed her arm.

"Mr. Butterfly, might I make known to you, my wife, Louisa."

She screamed into her hands when she thought she felt a tickle on her arm, thrusting her hand away from her face. Her fist struck Mr. Warwick's arm. She jumped back in horror. Where was the butterfly?

He rubbed his upper arm, backing away from her as he laughed. "I was only teasing," he managed through his laughter. "It flew away the moment you started running."

"Jack!" She glared at him, but his laughter was contagious. Her heart stopped racing for long enough for her to realize how ridiculous she must have appeared, running from a butterfly. A slow smile engulfed her glare. There was no sense in fighting it.

"You called me Jack." He stopped rubbing his arm, his laughter fading. "I thought you preferred to call me Mr. Warwick?"

Louisa's face grew hot. "Jack was the only name I could think of while scolding you. I would not call a child Mr. Warwick, and you were behaving much like one."

He chuckled again, taking a careful step toward her. "Are you going to strike me again?"

"Only if Mr. Butterfly is in your pocket." She eyed him with suspicion.

"I would never keep such a dangerous creature on my person. I am not so careless as that."

Louisa threw him another glare. "You do not realize how much they frighten me. Look." She held up her hands. "My hands are still shaking."

His brow furrowed with genuine concern, his laughter fading. He took her right hand, unfolding her fingers into his palm, exposing her own. The cuts from her fall from the cart the day before had been too difficult to bandage, so she had left them uncovered. He traced one finger over the edge of her palm, sending a jolt of warmth up her arm. "When did this happen?" His eyes met hers, serious and gentle.

"Yesterday." She swallowed, ignoring the way her heart picked up speed again. But this time it was Mr. *Warwick*, not Mr. Butterfly who was to blame.

Frustration filled his gaze again, and he looked down at her hand. "I'm sorry." He shook his head. "I should not have put you in danger. It was irresponsible and selfish. I will call the physician today."

Louisa's focus was captured by the way his hand felt around hers. He was capable of creating a lot of damage, but he was also capable of mending it. "The physician does not need to be called. And you don't need to keep apologizing," Louisa said, finally finding her voice. She inched her fingers away, offering a smile. She could breathe normally again. "The past is over and done with."

Jack released her hand. "I wish it were as simple as that. Because of my carelessness, you are hurt. Consequences live only to remind us of the past."

Louisa studied him for a long moment. "Well, we shouldn't live only to remind ourselves of our mistakes. We must live with the intention of not repeating them. That is all we can do."

Jack met her gaze, nodding. "You're right. And that is my intention." A soft smile touched his lips, and she had to tear her gaze away. Jack could be just like a butterfly. Fascinating to look at, seemingly innocent, but enough to send her running if he came too close. What was he hiding? She had told him about her past, but he didn't seem inclined to reveal anything about his own. He was obviously haunted by something that he wished to keep hidden. She would have to be patient. She already knew far more about him today than she had known the day before.

"Now, shall we go see these *fascinating* stables you spoke of?" His voice was lighter now. Louisa was much more comfortable with this side of him.

She nodded. "I would be delighted."

Walking across the lawn, they made their way to the southeast corner of the property. Louisa clasped her hands together in front of her so Jack would not try to extend his arm to her again. She did not abhor his company like she thought she would, but each time she touched him or came close to him, it did strange things to her heart. Aside from being handsome, Jack was charming. And that was what made her so nervous.

"Tell me, Louisa..." Jack began in a curious voice, "if you were to describe *me* in one word, what would it be?"

She threw him a sideways glance. "Are you certain you wish to continue playing this game?"

He chuckled. "I may regret it, but yes."

"But you don't like my words of choice."

"I will not criticize this one." He raised both hands in surrender before watching her intently. Waiting. "So long as it is not the same as the word you used to describe the butterfly." He paused. "Or the house."

She laughed, covering her mouth with one hand. "You do not care to be described as large and evil?"

"Not particularly."

There were so many words that came to mind, flooding her thoughts all at once. Confusing, infuriating, charming, vexing, ridiculous, frightening. Louisa could hardly pick just one. She fiddled with the ribbons of her bonnet, wrapping them around her finger and then unwinding them as she considered her answer carefully.

"Have you decided yet?" he asked.

She pursed her lips. "Yes. *Impatient*."

He laughed, dipping his head. "Although that is accurate, I don't think that's the word you would have chosen."

Louisa finally settled on her answer, feeling suddenly shy. Just the night before she would have chosen a much more insulting word. She still did not want to flatter him, so she chose a word that was perfectly in the middle, not meant to cause either offense or arrogance.

"Determined." She stole a quick look at his face. He didn't object, but walked silently, deep thought reflecting in his eyes.

"Why did you choose that word?" he asked finally.

Louisa shook her head. "I did not promise an explanation. I only promised one word."

He laughed under his breath.

They approached the stable doors, and he pushed them open. The smell of horses was strong—enough to make Louisa hold her breath for a moment as she adjusted to the unsavory scent. Particles of straw and dirt floated through the air, illuminated by the sunlight that filtered through the small windows.

"Is it my turn now?" Jack asked.

Louisa was distracted by a black horse in the first stall as it made eye contact with her. She smiled like one might coax an infant as she approached the animal. With a slow movement, she stroked the horse between the eyes. "Your turn?"

Jack came to stand beside her at the stall, leaning against the gate and crossing his arms. His eyes found hers. "To describe you with one word."

Louisa continued stroking the horse, hoping it would distract her from the twisting in her stomach. It felt like a hoard of butterflies had made their way to her stomach, fluttering their wings with all their might. The sensation was rather disconcerting, especially since it was associated with Jack. And with butterflies.

"I suppose you may make an attempt...if you would like." Louisa cringed at the way her voice stuttered. She could usually speak clearly, but not when Jack was standing that close.

She stared into the horse's eyes. She could see Jack's reflection in them.

Silence filled the space between them, making her understand why Jack had been so impatient with her. Anticipation flooded her senses, and she nearly shouted at him to hurry and choose. All the while, she recognized that she was the subject of his deep, prolonged musing, and it made her heart pound.

"Must I only choose one?" he asked.

Louisa released the breath she had been holding. "This is *your* game, not mine. A game which only has one rule—that you may only use one word."

"It is my game, which means I can make new rules."

"No." Louisa laughed, turning to face him. "That isn't fair." She quickly turned back to the horse.

Jack let out a long sigh. "There are simply so many things I could describe. Your manner, your voice, your appearance, your character."

"Describe my character," Louisa said, although curiosity tugged at her to request a word from each category. "That is the category I chose to describe you."

"That does narrow it down a little." He rubbed one side of his face, still seeming to agonize over the decision. She focused on the horse's hair, letting each bristle unfold under her finger as she traced it up the horse's head, then down.

"I have it," he said.

She glanced up, feigning nonchalance. "What is it?"

"Hopeful." He searched her face. "Despite all the misfortune you have endured, you do not seem to live life expecting the worst to happen. You seem to be always hoping for the best. It is an attribute I deeply admire and envy." He gave a half smile, one that made her heart nearly leap from her chest.

What was wrong with her? She looked down. "Being hopeful doesn't come without its disappointments," Louisa admitted in a shy voice. His praise had made her nervous. Perhaps it was the heat of the stables that had caused her pulse to speed up. She could not allow herself to be drawn in by his face. His handsome, *handsome* face. That was an easy mistake to make, so she needed to be aware of the possibility. If her heart became attached, he could easily break it.

"That is the risk of hope, is it not?" Jack's voice was close to her ear as he leaned toward the horse, rubbing its muzzle with his palm. "That is why so many people are afraid of it. They have been beaten down by disappointment so much, they wish to protect themselves from it."

"Is that what you do?" Louisa asked.

He shrugged. "I have been guilty of that at times."

Louisa met his eyes quickly before looking away. "As have I." She hadn't been willing to hope that her marriage to Jack could result in something happy or good. Even now, she was still afraid to hope that the ease she had experienced with him that day would remain. He was hiding something from her. So long as he was, she would hide her heart from him. It was the only way to keep it safe.

"There is much I am learning about you today, Louisa." His voice took on a lighter tone, and he moved back a step. "You see, this is what is called a courtship."

She laughed at the certainty in his voice. "I thought the courtship came before the marriage."

"Traditionally, yes."

Louisa dared a look at his eyes, which danced with amusement. "There is nothing traditional about this, is there?"

He chuckled. "Nothing at all."

Louisa would not have found the situation humorous in the slightest the day before, but now it did seem rather amusing.

After seeing all the horses, Jack led her on a walk around the front of the property. The grounds were lovely in the summer, with bright flowers and vibrant green leaves at every turn. Her first task would be to meet other young women in town to befriend. She did quite enjoy Cassandra's company, and perhaps she had friends Louisa could meet. Margaret was still nearby, and Louisa was eager for her to see the house and grounds of Benham Abbey.

As she walked beside Jack, her worries began to subside a little. Perhaps it wouldn't be so very bad being married to him. That day they seemed to have come to understand one another better. The purpose of a courtship was for a man and woman to become better acquainted with one another—to determine whether they were compatible or not. Once that determination was made, the two would decide whether or not to marry.

In Louisa's case, the outcome of their compatibility would not change the result. They were already married.

She listened to Jack's explanation of the flowers that had been planted unevenly on the front lawn, watching his smile and expressive eyebrows. Her heart pounded as she realized that this version of Jack could steal her heart just as easily as he had picked up her bonnet that first day in town.

And he seemed rather determined to do so.

CHAPTER 18

Finding a suitable steward was more work than Jack had anticipated. There were many men willing to pursue the job, but only one had seemed qualified to manage a household the size of Benham Abbey. Over the last week, Jack had been traveling to town and back every day, as well as gathering recommendations from the servants that remained in his house. He had hired two scullery maids on his own, as well as three new footmen. With each new arrival, he had ensured Louisa approved of his choices.

"I'm not certain about the footmen," she had said, chewing her fingernail.

"What are they lacking?" He had thought all three young men were suitable for the job.

"If, perchance, my friend Margaret comes to work here, I did promise…" the pause that followed had lasted at least ten seconds. "I promised that they would be very handsome."

Jack chuckled at the memory from a few days before as he rode his phaeton back home. Louisa had eventually agreed that Margaret would be content with the appearance of at least one of the three footmen. He had hardly stopped laughing about the conversation since it had occurred. There were many things about Louisa that kept him smiling throughout the day, even when they were not together. He found himself eager to see her again at dinner each night, and when he returned from town and she wasn't home, often visiting the Lovells, he found himself waiting near the door until he saw her.

He was like a deuced puppy.

After dinner each night, she retired early to her bedchamber, sliding the lock into place on her door. He had done all he could to ensure she felt safe, but she still felt the need to lock herself away. It puzzled him, but he was determined to solve it.

That day, when he walked through the doors, she was already home, sitting in the drawing room, the door halfway open. He had heard her voice from the entry hall, but then he heard another voice. A man's voice.

He walked through the drawing room door, removing his hat. Mr. Northcott sat on the sofa across from her, and she poured him a cup of tea before glancing up. A shy smile crossed her lips, and the tea dripped onto the saucer. She looked down, jumping as the hot liquid touched her hand. The teapot clattered to the tray, and she quickly wiped the tea off her hand with her skirts. Her face flamed. "I'm sorry," she muttered to Mr. Northcott. Her eyes met Jack's again, and she gave a quiet laugh. "I didn't know when you would be coming home."

Jack walked forward, unable to stop the smile from climbing his own face. "Are you all right?" he whispered. "Did you burn your hand?"

"I'm perfectly fine," she said, pursing her lips as she focused on pouring a second cup of tea.

Jack studied her profile, chuckling at the way she avoided looking at him with Mr. Northcott watching.

Mr. Northcott stood to greet him, his gaze shifting between Louisa and Jack with deep curiosity.

"I didn't know you would still be in town," Jack said. "I am glad to see you have found Yorkshire so appealing."

Mr. Northcott smiled, glancing at Louisa again. "In truth, I stayed to ensure Louisa was settled. As soon as I help Miss Lovell find work, I will be on my way back to Larkhall. My brother is managing it while I am away."

"Is your brother trustworthy?"

"Indeed," Mr. Northcott said, the end of the word raising like a question.

"Then you might stay here a little longer than you planned. I haven't yet introduced you to my sister, Cassandra. You both came to the wedding, but I failed to make proper introductions." It wasn't often that men as amiable and wealthy as Mr. Northcott came into their area of town. Jack had never tried playing the role of matchmaker, but if he could help his sister meet an eligible gentleman who he approved of, he would try his best.

Louisa caught Jack's gaze, shaking her head subtly. He frowned. Why would she oppose the match?

Mr. Northcott cleared his throat, taking a step back. "I will be quite busy while I am here. I have limited time for social calls. In fact, I ought to be leaving soon." He offered a friendly smile. "It was a pleasure to see you both, and I am glad to hear Louisa is comfortable here."

Jack nodded in farewell, watching with confusion as Mr. Northcott took his leave of the room.

Louisa shook her head with a *tsk*. "You should not have said that."

"What did I say wrong?" Jack chuckled, sitting on the sofa beside her.

"Matthew does not take well to matchmakers, although he has attempted to be a matchmaker himself."

Jack frowned, picking up the cup of tea Louisa had poured for him. "It isn't as though I said I wanted him to court my sister. All I said was that I hoped they could become acquainted while he was here."

"That is like putting a snake in front of a horse and expecting it not be spooked." Louisa raised one eyebrow, shaking her head. "Matthew will never marry. I have been told as much many times."

Jack laughed, crossing his arms as he settled into the cushion behind him. "That is the same thing Cassandra says."

"Really?" Louisa's eyes widened. She looked far too

enchanting that day, with her hair piled high atop her head and her lips pressed together in surprise. For a moment, he found himself distracted from the conversation at hand, memorizing each of her features instead.

Oh, yes. She had asked him a question.

He nodded. "My sister also claims she doesn't wish to marry," he said, "but I believe she only says so as a way to hide her disappointment. She does not expect at her age that she will find a match." Jack's guilt stabbed at his chest. The disrepute he had brought upon their family had not helped her situation.

Louisa's eyes grew heavy. "Any man would be very fortunate indeed to marry Cassandra. As for Matthew, he has given up. He had his heart badly broken years ago. I do not know the details, for he refuses to speak of it, but it was enough to stop him from considering marriage at all. I do believe he considered it again when my sister was visiting Larkhall, but unfortunately she injured his delicate heart again."

Mr. Northcott had not struck Jack as the sort of man with a *delicate* heart. If he did have such a heart, he disguised it well.

Louisa turned her gaze to Jack, her eyes wide and thoughtful. The simple glance made his heart melt to a puddle. Blast it, had his own heart become just as delicate at Mr. Northcott's? "I wish we could help them," she said. "Matthew has been very kind to me, and Cassandra has been very kind to you."

His sister had been the only one to continue reaching

out to him. His mother likely feared overstepping his father's wishes, but Cassandra feared nothing when it came to ensuring others felt loved and included. Even though she liked to start arguments with him and throw his brandy out the window, he still wanted her to be happy.

Jack grinned. "If only we had willing participants, I suspect you and I could be very skilled matchmakers."

Louisa took a sip from her teacup, the corners of her mouth curving upward. Her eyes peeked at him mischievously from over the rim. "We would indeed." When she set the teacup down, he found his gaze drawn to her lips. He tried to focus on his own words, but it was becoming increasingly difficult when watching her speak was so much more captivating.

"Well," he said with a sigh. "I already know you are trying to find the perfect footman for your friend Margaret." He leaned slightly closer to Louisa on the sofa. Even the slight change in the distance between them made his heart pick up speed.

"You were not as helpful as you should have been," she said, her voice suddenly serious and pensive. "The three you hired did not have the appearance that Margaret prefers."

He laughed. "I apologize that I did not consider asking. Hiring footmen is not like planning a menu for a dinner party."

That earned a smile from Louisa, one that made a crease appear in her cheek. The laugh that followed sounded more like an embarrassed giggle. "Matchmakers must consider these things. For instance, Margaret has a preference for men with light hair. She is not opposed to men with dark hair, but she does have a preference that I had to consider."

Jack chuckled, thoroughly enjoying the way Louisa wriggled uncomfortably while offering that explanation. It was cruel of him, but he would make her squirm a little longer. "And you? Are you opposed to men with dark hair?" He raised one eyebrow, throwing her a grin.

She scooted away from him, laughing. "Yes. I am thoroughly opposed."

He moved closer, trapping her against the right arm of the sofa. "You should have told me as much before agreeing to marry me. Are there any other preferences I should be aware of?"

The sound of her quiet giggling was far too contagious. The pure delight on her face made his heart skip a beat—or several—as he awaited her response.

Her features grew serious for a brief moment as she examined his face. "I have always preferred straight noses. Perfectly straight."

His jaw dropped as her laughter intensified.

"You are vicious today," he said, shaking his head. And yet he still wanted to kiss her as thoroughly as she had just insulted him. His leg was pressed against hers on the sofa, her back against the edge. If he moved his arm just a few inches, he could wrap it around her waist and pull her the rest of the way to him. The temptation swirled through his mind relentlessly as she tipped her head back, giggling at his expense.

When her laughter finally subsided, her gaze returned to his face. The moment her eyes met his, he caught her gaze flicker to his mouth before falling to her lap. He smiled as he watched a hint of color creep over her neck and ear. Her eyes flickered back to his, a hint of curiosity behind them. Her smile was shy as she examined his face. "In truth, I think it suits you quite well."

It took Jack a moment to recall what they had been speaking of. "My nose?"

"Yes," she said through a laugh. "It was far too perfect before."

"There is nothing perfect about me," Jack said with a smile. "Now my nose reflects that." He paused. "Does that mean you noticed how perfect my nose appeared before it was broken?"

"No," she stammered. The guilty tone of her voice belied her answer.

Jack grinned. "You did."

"I did not." Though she glared at him, laughter still hovered in her voice.

It was his turn to be relentless. "There is something else I saw you noticing about my face just now."

Louisa scoffed with disbelief. "And what is that?"

"My lips."

She gasped and turned her face from him, likely to conceal the color. "I did not."

His stomach ached from his laughter. Teasing Louisa like this was not the way to entice her to kiss him, but he couldn't help himself. She had been thinking what it might be like to kiss him, and she knew it.

"Is it so ridiculous to think your husband has a fine set of lips?"

"Stop!" She covered her face with her hands, laughing enough to make the sofa shake.

He obeyed, waiting silently until she uncovered her face, just enough to peek through her fingers. "Why do you take such pleasure in embarrassing me?"

"I only take as much pleasure in it as you take in insulting me."

His gaze caught on a strand of hair that had fallen over her eyebrow. He leaned closer, lifting his hand to brush it away from her eyes. His heart hammered in his chest as she gazed up at him. Her eyes were wide, filled with caution and curiosity at once. His throat went dry, his lungs leaden and weak.

Louisa shifted, looking down at her lap. Jack pulled his hand away. He had to be careful not to frighten her. Every glance they shared, every brief touch was like putting a serpent in front of a horse, just as she had described Mr. Northcott. Louisa could be easily spooked if he wasn't careful.

"Well..." Louisa began, as if searching for something to break the silence. "If we already failed to find Margaret a good match, perhaps we should return our efforts to Matthew and Cassandra." She sat up straighter, reaching for her teacup. Jack noticed a slight tremor in her hand as she lifted the cup to her lips. She sipped, then swallowed.

"However, I do think Matthew's nature might be too reserved for Cassandra. I suspect she needs a man with a little more freedom and vigor in his spirit."

Jack chuckled, pretending he hadn't noticed the abrupt change in subject. "I wouldn't approve of my sister marrying a man who chooses to walk the grounds barefoot if that is what you mean."

"Well, it is not *your* approval she would be seeking." Louisa said. "Your father would be the one to deem the man worthy of her."

At the mention of his father, Jack stiffened. Louisa sipped from her teacup, watching him out of the corner of her eye. It was the first time she had casually brought his father into a conversation. She was likely hunting for a reaction from him, something that might give her insight into his relationship with his father and why it had suffered. Jack had almost told her what had happened when they were in the gardens nearly one week before, but he had been too afraid. How differently would she look at him if she knew he had been the cause of his uncle's death? Would she agree with his father? His heart stung at the thought of Louisa looking at him the way his father did.

He pulled his thoughts back to her question. Rubbing his jaw, he nodded. "I think my father would approve even of a barefooted man if it meant Cassandra was happy." Jack set his teacup down on the table, the cup clattering louder against the saucer than he had intended. "He adores her."

It was true. His father loved Cassandra far more than he loved Jack. She was the eldest child, but she was a daughter, not a son, and therefore Jack was the one who would inherit the estate, much to his father's dismay.

Louisa shifted in her seat, curiosity burning in her eyes. "Does he? I wish I had become better acquainted with your father, but I'm afraid I hardly had the opportunity to speak with him at the wedding." She fiddled with her skirts, something he had noticed she did when she was nervous. "I should like to visit your family again and have the opportunity to learn more about your parents. May we go to—"

"No." Jack shook his head.

Louisa shrunk back in the sofa, her eyes wide.

Guilt immediately flooded his chest, and he tried to soften his interruption. "I—I do not think it is wise for me to try to visit them." He leaned his elbows onto his knees. "I am not welcome there. I have been told many times." His jaw tightened, and he looked down at the floor.

"Are you certain there is nothing that could change that?" Louisa asked. Her voice was gentle, unraveling the emotions that had begun building inside him.

"I will always be inadequate." He sighed. "We can live with the intention of never repeating our mistakes, but we still cannot erase the past." He shook his head, avoiding her intent gaze. "I live each day wishing I could."

Louisa said nothing for several seconds, not moving. Then, suddenly, her hand touched his arm. The simple gesture brought a surge of emotion to his throat, and his heart picked up speed. He met her eyes, and she looked down at her hand rather than holding his gaze. "What happened?" she asked in a hesitant voice. "What caused this discord in your family?"

He stared at her downcast lashes until she finally looked up at him. *Hopeful* was indeed the perfect word to describe her. She had too much faith in him. She hoped that the man she married was good and noble. How could he disappoint her? If she knew what he had done, she would never look at him the same way again. He felt like he was beginning to make progress with her, and telling her about his family and his past would only drive them apart again. Louisa would regret who she had agreed to marry. She would be afraid of him.

She had already told him that she thought he was careless. If she knew what his carelessness had cost five years ago, she would never believe that he could change. Even if she knew it was an accident and not a murder as Evan Whitby believed, it would still change her opinion of him. And her opinion of him was the only one that mattered. It was all he truly cared about. He wanted to impress her, to make her happy, and to give her a place to belong. But who would want to belong with a monster?

Jack swallowed hard. "That is a tale for another day," he said. "I'm sorry."

Disappointment flickered across her features, and she moved her hand away from his arm. Her brow was furrowed as she picked up her teacup and took a sip, avoiding looking at him.

Within a few seconds, she stood from her place beside him on the sofa. She always seemed to find a reason to leave shortly after he joined her in the drawing room each day. Today, he did not blame her. Withholding the truth from her would keep her from becoming close to him, but so would telling her the truth. There was no way to escape her disappointment in him either way.

"I think I will go visit Margaret today," Louisa said with a false smile as she walked toward the door.

He watched her go, his heart sinking in his chest.

CHAPTER 19

"Does Jack know you're here?" Cassandra poured a drop of cream into her own teacup, then into Louisa's.

"I confess, I did not think it wise to tell him." Louisa smoothed her hands over her skirts. Why was she so nervous? Mrs. Warwick and Cassandra were both far too kind to make her uneasy. This was a simple social call, and any woman had the right to visit her mother-in-law and sister-in-law for afternoon tea, especially when they lived so close by.

"I think you are right," Mrs. Warwick said with a sigh. "He and my husband do not always see eye to eye." It was still so astonishing how much her eyes looked like Jack's. The first time she had met Mrs. Warwick, Louisa had noticed the kindness in her eyes, assuming it was what set Mrs. Warwick's eyes apart from Jack's. But now, Louisa realized it was one of their greatest similarities. Jack had a kindness about him that she hadn't noticed at first, but now that she had noticed, it was one of her favorite things about him.

Louisa bit her lip. She felt guilty visiting Jack's family without his permission, but they were her family now too. She missed having a motherly figure to converse with, and without her sister Alice nearby, she needed a sister as well. Although important, those were not the only reasons she was there.

Ever since her conversation with Jack two days before when she had tried to mention his father, he had been more distant. She blamed it on his hard work in training the new members of the household, but part of his distance from her seemed deliberate. She had made it obvious that she was curious about his family. Did that mean he was avoiding her so he would not have to answer her questions?

Louisa took a deep breath, planning her words carefully. "Do you miss him?" Louisa asked, turning toward Mrs. Warwick. "Do you miss Jack?"

Her eyes immediately flooded with tears. Drat. Louisa hadn't meant to make her cry. Mrs. Warwick blinked fast, clearing them as she took a sip of tea. "Yes. It is a difficult situation." She looked like she wanted to say more, but she clamped her mouth closed.

Cassandra drummed her fingers in her lap, adding creases to her pale green skirts. "It does upset my father when he discovers that I have been visiting Jack. If it were up to him, we would separate ourselves from him entirely."

Cassandra's voice was quiet. "I refuse to do that." She didn't look at her mother, which led Louisa to believe that Mrs. Warwick was a little more compliant, and that was why she hadn't come to visit Jack.

"Would he—would your husband be upset to know that I am here visiting you today?" Louisa didn't wish to drive even more distance between Jack and his father by upsetting him.

Cassandra exchanged a quick glance with her mother. "It might upset him a little, but I doubt he would forbid your presence here."

Louisa nodded in understanding, filing through the questions in her mind, deciding which to pose next. There were so many. "Do you have other friends in town? I feel that I have hardly met anyone. I thought you might be able to help me. Are there any other young ladies who I might have the opportunity to meet and befriend?"

The two women exchanged yet another glance. This time it was filled with even more obvious concern. "I'm afraid there are not many young ladies who wish to connect themselves with our family," Mrs. Warwick said. "Nor young men." She eyed Cassandra, whose brows drew together in apparent irritation.

"That is not entirely Jack's fault," Cassandra said in a defensive voice.

"Your father disagrees." Mrs. Warwick added another cube of sugar to her tea, shifting uncomfortably.

Silence filled the room for several seconds before Mrs. Warwick cleared her throat noisily. "Forgive me, Louisa. I am not accustomed to visitors here. It still astonishes me that you married my son. It may take me a few months to fully comprehend it." Her eyes welled with tears again. "It is my hope that eventually our...situation can be different."

Louisa nodded. "It is my hope as well." She didn't know what else to say. Disappointment fell heavy in her stomach. She had hoped that coming there would give her answers, but both women seemed just as secretive as Jack.

The conversation turned to lighter things, but Louisa's mind was elsewhere. She tried her best to answer their questions about her time at Larkhall, but she found it odd how Mrs. Warwick avoided speaking of her own son. Cassandra was silent most of the time, watching Louisa carefully. When it came time for Louisa to leave, Cassandra offered to walk with her.

As Louisa tied her bonnet ribbons under her chin, Cassandra stepped into the sunlight without anything covering her curls. She likely planned to gather a few wildflowers on the way to put in her hair. Louisa smiled at her sister-in-law, grateful for the company. "I'm sorry to have made your mother so uncomfortable by visiting today," Louisa said. "I am just...a bit frustrated that Jack seems to be keeping secrets from me." The words spilled out. Even though she was Jack's sister, Louisa needed to confide in someone.

Cassandra was rarely seen without a smile, but in that moment her expression was somber. "There are events that Jack does not like speaking of. None of us do." She sighed.

"It is not my place to tell you. I wish I could." She cast Louisa an apologetic look. "I do believe Jack will confide in you eventually. Give him time."

Louisa nodded. Patience was not one of her virtues.

"There are other secrets of his that I am willing to share," Cassandra said, eyebrows wiggling.

Louisa's spirits lifted. "Now I am very intrigued."

Cassandra laughed. "The day you first rejected his proposal, he was quite distraught."

The butterflies found their way to Louisa's stomach once again. Why did the idea of Jack being distraught over her in any way cause her stomach to flutter? "How so?"

"I think he has been smitten with you from the first moment he saw you. He pretended his intentions for marrying you were all noble, but I suspect it injured his heart, not only his pride, when you first refused." Cassandra's grin grew wider.

Louisa tightened her lips to keep from smiling. "He hardly knows me, and he especially did not know me when he first proposed."

"He was intrigued by you." Cassandra stopped to pluck a small yellow flower from the side of the hill. Rather than tucking it in her own hair, she pushed the stem between Louisa's ear and her bonnet, embedding it in her hair. "Soon enough he'll love you. You shouldn't have any fear that he won't."

Louisa's stomach flipped, her heart following suit. A hard laugh escaped her, and she tugged on the tips of her gloves. She searched her mind for something to say, but she came up blank.

"Do you think you could ever love him?" Cassandra prodded with a mischievous smile.

Louisa cast her a scolding glance, to which Cassandra only laughed. "You two are quite alike in your attempts to embarrass me."

Cassandra did not seem to actually expect an answer, because she turned toward the hillside, laughing as she collected more flowers for her own hair.

A few minutes later, they reached the edge of Benham Abbey's property, and Cassandra bid her farewell, still wearing her sneaky smile as she walked back toward the path.

Making her way toward the house, Louisa still felt a slight flush on her cheeks, and she couldn't only blame the summer heat. Why did it flatter her so much to think that Jack's feelings, no matter how slight at the time, could have influenced him to propose? She hadn't ever given much meaning to his flirtations, but each moment now stood out in her mind. When he had teased her two days before about noticing his lips, she had nearly burst into flames with the embarrassment of it all. Because yes, she had in fact been noticing his lips far too much of late.

Louisa started toward the front doors, willing her cheeks to cool. She didn't know whether or not Jack was home or not, but she certainly didn't want him to see her while she was blushing. When she got close to the door, something caught her eye from below a tree around the back of the house. She squinted, walking closer.

Was it…?

Jack?

She moved slowly, examining the odd scene in front of her. A discarded pad of paper sat on the ground, face down on the grass. Jack was also laying prostrate on the grass, his head nestled into his elbow. Her heart picked up speed as she approached, her feet moving faster. Was he all right?

As she came within the shade of the tree he was under, a loud sound startled her, making her jump back a step. She paused, listening as the sound repeated itself, joining the chorus of birds in the tree above.

He was snoring.

She covered her mouth with one hand, careful not to laugh and wake him. From the discarded pencil and paper, it seemed he had been attempting to draw before opting to nap instead. Crossing her ankles, she carefully lowered herself to the ground, scooting closer to him on the grass. The last time she had been this close to him while he was unaware had been when she had cleaned the blood from his face.

She would have to be very quiet so as to not wake him this time. With the loud birds singing up in the trees, any sounds she accidentally made would likely be drowned out. She assessed his profile, smiling to herself at the way his cheek was squished against his arm. The bruising on his nose had almost faded completely, leaving just a few traces, and of course, the slight crookedness that would likely never change.

Her smile grew as she noticed the thick lashes that shadowed his cheekbone, and the freckles that the sun had brought out on his nose and cheek. Without a devilish smile on his face, he appeared tranquil and innocent. If she were an artist, she would have picked up the nearby paper and created a likeness of him in that moment so she could remember it forever.

Her heart thudded as he stirred. She held her breath, watching him with wide eyes until he went still again. The snoring continued, transforming into a whistling sound. She bit her lip to keep from laughing. She didn't care if he would be embarrassed that she was watching him. If he took pleasure in embarrassing her, why should she not take pleasure in embarrassing him?

Plucking the flower out of her hair, she raised it carefully above his head, sliding it amongst the thickest part of the hair at the front of his forehead. Thankfully, he slept through it. She grinned as she looked down at him, imagining how appalled he would be to find the flower in his hair when he finally awoke.

An even better idea struck her, and she reached for the pencil and art book. A blank sheet of foolscap was already folded over the back. Louisa turned it over, poising the pencil over the paper while looking at Jack with one eye closed. Working as quickly as she could, she drew him sleeping with the flower in his hair. The work appeared to have been done by a child. As soon as she filled in the final lines, she signed her name at the bottom. She pressed her lips together, nearly losing control of her laughter as she set the book beside him on the grass.

Just as she was about to walk away, she caught sight of the corner of the page behind her own drawing. Curiosity tugged at her, so insistent that she couldn't help but return to the book. Stooping down, she checked Jack's face to ensure she wasn't caught as she slid her drawing aside enough to see the one below it.

Her heart leaped as the picture came into view.

The woman in the drawing was unmistakably her.

Louisa's brow furrowed as her chest flooded with warmth. Had Jack drawn it that very day? She had been thinking he was avoiding her, that perhaps he didn't care for her like she had dared to hope that he did, but if he had drawn this…he must have cared at least a little. Her stomach fluttered with those blasted butterflies again, but this time she didn't banish them. In the drawing, she was smiling. He had somehow depicted her with impressive accuracy without even being near her during the process. She scowled at him, even as he slept with the ridiculous flower in his hair. Why hadn't he told her he was such a skilled artist? Did he even realize that it was a talent of his?

She could hardly believe that she had ever thought him prideful. If anything, he was not proud enough. He saw only his faults, and he disguised his disappointment with himself by pretending to be arrogant and confident.

A flood of understanding washed over her, and she

found herself staring at his face again as he slept. She needed to leave before he saw her.

Carefully positioning her own drawing at the top of the art book, she slid it even closer to his face before walking away. A laugh bubbled out of her chest as she made it safely around the side of the house and out of sight. Her heart swelled with emotion as she walked through the halls of the house. The things she felt were new and thrilling, and she could hardly make sense of them. When she finally found the morning room, she slipped inside, kneeling in front of the window that overlooked Jack and her drawing.

And then she stared at him a little longer.

~

"What the devil…" Jack rolled over on the grass, rubbing his blurry eyes. The creature that stared up at him from the art book could not have been his own work. He studied the drawing, blinking the sleep from his eyes. It looked like a man with a flower in his hair, sprawled on his stomach under a tree. As he studied the hasty lines, he could only conclude that it was the work of a child.

His brow furrowed, and he tipped the paper to one side. The man in the picture did look oddly similar to him. His stomach flipped. The prospect of a strange, unknown child watching him sleep for long enough to draw this picture was unnerving to say the least. His eyes darted from side to side. Were they still watching him?

He staggered to his feet, wiping the grass from his trousers.

How long had he been asleep? Judging by the position of the sun, he would guess at least a few hours had passed since he had set his drawing down to take a *short nap*. Jack flipped the drawing over, relieved to see that his own work was still there. His drawing of Louisa wasn't as polished as he would have liked it, and there were certainly parts of her face that weren't quite accurate since she hadn't been there in front of him while he worked. But next to the strange drawing that had been beside him when he awoke, he would call his own work a masterpiece.

He flipped back to the page with the childlike drawing. As he walked back to the house, he caught sight of the initials that had been signed at the bottom in minuscule letters.

L.W.

He stopped walking, shaking his head as a smile climbed his face.

He chuckled under his breath. Despite the horror of the drawing, a sense of achievement flooded his chest. He could picture Louisa sneaking around him while he was asleep, stopping to draw that ridiculous picture. If it had been anyone else, he might have been mortified—or perhaps a bit disturbed—but instead he felt flattered. His smile grew impossibly wider as he marched inside the house, searching around every hall for Louisa. Where had she gone?

"Louisa!" he called, a laugh hovering in his voice.

He checked all the rooms on the ground floor, moving up to the first. "You aren't in my wardrobe, are you?"

"I'm down here," the quiet voice carried up the stairs, floating up to him with a hint of amusement.

He turned around. Louisa stood at the base of the staircase, a broad smile across her cheeks. Her nose scrunched as she tried to conceal her laughter. "Is something the matter?" She took one step up the stairs, then two.

Jack met her in the middle, stopping two stairs above her. He leaned against the banister, holding out the drawing she had done of him. "Does this look familiar?"

She tapped her chin, the corners of her eyes creasing as she pretended to study every corner of the paper. "Hmm. It does look like something I witnessed today. There was a man sleeping beneath a tree. He wore a flower in his hair and snored like a hog."

Jack's jaw dropped as Louisa's laughter intensified.

No.

Her eyes were focused on something at the top of his head.

He locked her gaze in his, shaking his head. With one slow movement, he reached up to the front of his hair. He closed his eyes as his fingers wrapped around a flower. He exhaled slowly, a laugh bursting out of his mouth. "You—" his voice cut off as he lunged down the final two stairs toward her, dropping his art book at his feet.

She let out a sound that was half shriek, half laughter, turning to run away. But he was too quick, lunging down an extra stair and stopping on the one just below her instead, blocking her path. When she tried to turn and run up the staircase, he caught her by the waist, whirling her back around to face him.

Jack reined in his laughter for long enough to catch his breath. Louisa pushed her palms flat against his chest, trying to wriggle free as she laughed. When her eyes met his, she stopped, her laughter fading. From where he stood on the stair below her, his eyes were level with hers. His grip around her waist was firm, but she no longer fought against it. A surge of longing tore through his chest, and nearly kissed her, right then and there.

"I wonder...was it you or Cassandra who put that flower in my hair?" His voice came out weaker than he intended.

Louisa's face was flushed as she looked down at her hands, still pressing against his chest. "That is a secret." A smile still lingered in her eyes. "One you shall never know," Louisa finished in a breathless voice. In one swift motion, she twisted, ducking around his arms and darting up the stairs.

Jack caught his breath, laughing as she stumbled over her skirts. She caught herself with the banister, turning to face him at the top of the staircase. "You forgot to offer your compliments to the artist."

He chuckled. "I will not compliment an artist who says I snore like a hog." He paused. "That isn't true, is it?" He had never been told that he snored, so he suspected Louisa had invented the insult.

"Unfortunately, yes, it is true. I first noticed when you fainted after I jumped out of your wardrobe."

What a relentless woman. He would have chased her up the stairs again, but his head was still reeling from the first time he had caught her in his arms. "Do you think it could be the change in the structure of my nose that caused it?" He laughed at the notion before realizing that it was very possible.

Louisa tipped her head back with a laugh. "That would be my first suspicion."

He held onto the banister with one hand as he picked up the art book. Now that he knew Louisa had drawn it, the picture was becoming even more humorous. "You are a dreadful artist."

"You are a very skilled one," she said in an accusatory voice. "I did not know you had such a gift."

His brow furrowed as he glanced down at his art book. Had she looked at his other drawing? His drawing of her? He had meant for it to be a surprise. When he lifted his gaze back to the top of the stairs, she threw him a shy smile before slipping around the corner and out of sight.

CHAPTER 20

It was rather shocking how much Jack now smiled when he was alone. It had started shortly after he had married Louisa, and the longer he knew her, the more often he thought of her when they were apart. Thinking of her was what caused the frequent smiles, and they were nearly impossible to remove from his face, even as he rode his horse into town the next day.

He was celebrating a small victory. Each night when he went to bed, he listened to Louisa down the hall as she walked into her room. She had formed a habit of locking her door each night, the screeching metal reminding him of her apparent fear of him. But the night before, after she had drawn that horrendous picture of him, she had gone to bed, bidding him a cheerful, "Goodnight," and closing the door.

But she hadn't locked it.

He smiled at the achievement, patting his horse on the neck. "We are making progress, aren't we?"

He had been meeting with his man of business in town, working through the challenges that came with the task of importing a pineapple from South America. The price was rather absurd, but so was Louisa's request. Jack couldn't help but try, especially as he imagined her surprise if the pineapple actually arrived in one piece.

He dismounted near the man's office, tying his horse to a post before starting toward the doors.

"Warwick, is that you?"

Jack stopped, his fists tightening at his sides. His limbs went cold as he turned toward the familiar voice.

Lord Bridport stood in all his finery, walking stick in hand, top hat perched far too high on his head. Beside him, Mr. Evan Whitby stood nearby, looking every bit as smug as Jack had last seen him. Today, however, his eyes appeared darker, rimmed with darkness that was directed straight at Jack. Only when his mouth spread into a sneer did Jack fully understand why.

Two of his teeth were missing.

Jack swallowed, grimacing. Had that been his doing?

Lord Bridport stared at Jack for a long moment, as if unsure whether he should greet him in a friendly manner as he once had, or take to ignoring him. Jack's teeth gritted when he recalled the way his friend had tossed him out of his house in favor of the nodcock who stood beside him now, sneering and flexing his hands at his sides. Jack was itching to plant another facer on the man as well.

"Have you already forgotten what I look like?" Jack asked Bridport, raising his eyebrows. "I'm surprised you remembered my name."

"You do look a little different with the…" Whitby gestured at his nose.

Jack rolled his shoulders back, keeping his arms loose, though his muscles tightened with each word from the pair of them. "I thought people were meant to be finished losing teeth by the time they reached your age." Jack tipped his head to one side.

As if sensing the tension of the conversation, people on the streets stopped to watch, pausing their errands as they whispered from the street corners, eyes fixed on Jack and his company.

He took a deep breath to calm the irritation that raged in his chest. He didn't want to cause a scene. Turning on his heel, he walked toward the office door.

"Does your wife know she married a murderer? Or have you murdered her already too?" Whitby's voice grated on him, digging underneath his skin just as it had that night at the gambling party.

Jack's jaw tightened. He breathed deeply through his nose, lifting his fingers from the door handle. Lord Bridport stood in silence, watching Evan Whitby as he gathered a crowd with his words about murder. How had Jack once called that man his friend? Because Bridport wished to maintain Whitby's good favor, he stood by and watched without interfering. The spectators around the streets had become even more focused on the scene, some watching with concern, others with fascination. What gossip could they take home that day? Whose misfortune could provide them with entertainment? It was all a game to them.

"I didn't know my marriage was common knowledge," Jack said.

"Oh, yes, and so is the fact that you ruined her before taking her to the marriage noose. Was that the only way you could convince a woman to marry you?"

Jack tried to keep his fists at his sides, but it was becoming increasingly difficult. Whitby's teeth were uneven. Perhaps Jack could straighten them for him.

He wouldn't even try to deny the accusations Whitby threw at him. It wasn't worth his time. Hot anger pulsed through his veins. If the man pushed him hard enough he might burst. "I think your own success in finding a wife should be of greater concern to you, especially with the state of your missing teeth."

Whitby's broad shoulders raised as his own hands curled into fists. Jack did not want to fight him. Not here. He backed toward the door. Whitby laughed, kicking the dirt beneath his feet. Lord Bridport motioned for Whitby to walk away as well, but he wasn't finished. "You never answered my question," he called. "Does she know you're a murderer?" The volume of his voice grew, as if he wanted everyone in town to hear it. "If she did, I suspect she would rather annul the marriage and live a life of ruin than spend another second as your wife." He laughed, spitting on the dirt as his face grew redder, his anger seeming to catch up to him.

It took every drop of willpower at his disposal, but Jack managed to walk away rather than knock another tooth or two from Evan Whitby's head. He stepped through the door of the office, leaning against the door frame as he caught his breath. Whitby's first attack on him at the gambling party hadn't been personal. But now that Jack had disfigured his face, he seemed to have revenge on his mind.

His heart pounded as Whitby's words clattered through his mind over and over again. *Does your wife know she married a murderer?* His jaw tightened. Was that what he was? He knew in his heart that he had not fired the gun intentionally. But if everyone else doubted him, how could he defend himself? His guilt over his uncle's death had already consumed him, even knowing that his gun fired against his knowledge. Would Louisa believe them too? His heart broke at the thought of her regretting her choice to marry him. And it broke even more at the thought of her choosing a life of ruin over him. He was ashamed every day of his life, and he would never wish the same feeling upon Louisa.

A lump formed in his throat, but he pushed it away. The emptiness in his chest spread, hollowing out all the hope and merriment he had felt on his ride there. Although he had an appointment with his man of business, he walked outside instead, pushing past the crowd and finding his horse. He rode blindly, rage and frustration and guilt building in his chest until he could hardly breathe. He needed to bury it somehow.

∼

The sun had already set by the time Louisa saw Jack's horse in the distance. She could barely decipher his form in the dim light. The moon had already risen, claiming its place in the sky above where he rode toward the house.

She smiled as she watched him from the window, turning toward the mirror in her bedchamber. Her hair was a complete mess, but she did not have time to call the maid to fix it for her. She fiddled with a few curls, making them more presentable before making her way toward the staircase. She had been sitting in her room worrying over why Jack hadn't returned home yet. He had missed dinner, and so she had eaten alone. She had taken the opportunity to practice the pianoforte after the meal, but her mind had been wandering. She had even debated walking into town to look for him. It was too much to hope that the reason for his delay was a visit to his family, so she hadn't allowed herself to consider that option.

Then what had delayed him?

She made her way quietly to the drawing room, sitting near the bookcase and choosing the first book she saw, opening it on her lap. She couldn't have him thinking she had been waiting for him to return home all evening. The only sounds she heard were the ticking of the long case clock in the corner and the tapping of her own foot on the floor. If he came inside now, he wouldn't know where to find her. She was being too quiet.

Her gaze caught on the pianoforte. Yes, that was a much better plan.

Sweeping her skirts underneath her, she hurried to the bench and began playing the liveliest tune of her repertoire, pressing a little harder than usual on the keys. She didn't hear the front door open, nor did she hear the drawing room door open. Her heart thudded when she saw Jack sit down on the sofa from the corner of her eye.

She stopped playing, rotating on the bench until she faced him. The smile fell from her cheeks when she noticed his slumped posture. His elbows were leaned over on his knees, his hands buried in his hair.

"Jack?" Louisa rose hesitantly. "Are you all right?"

He moved his head, throwing her a lazy glance. His face was dull, hardly any expression showing in his features. When he sat up straighter, the movement was slow and unsteady.

She narrowed her eyes.

"I'm as well as I'm able," he muttered, chuckling under his breath. "Nearly fell off my horse."

Her teeth gritted, and the concern she had felt moments before vanished. "You have been drinking, haven't you?" She glared at him.

He hardly seemed aware of her question, stretching out his legs in front of him as he stared at her. "Whitby was right." The laughter in his voice faded, his brows drawing together as he closed his eyes. "You think I'm a murderer."

Louisa's stomach twisted. What on earth was he talking about? She was no longer afraid of him in his drunk state, but simply angry with him. Rage boiled in her chest at his disregard for her request that he not drink to excess. She knew habits such as this were not easy to break, but he had done well for more than a week. He had seemed so determined to change. She searched within herself for a shred of pity, but all she could find was more disappointment.

"You are afraid of me, are you not?" he asked, opening his eyes. "You have already come to regret marrying me." His voice was slow and quiet, as if piecing the words together in his brain came with a delay. He scrunched his brow. "You do not care for me like I care for you. I knew he was right."

Louisa's heart hammered. Had he just confessed that he cared for her? Any words he spoke in his current state couldn't be taken seriously, yet her heart still skipped. He seemed to be speaking more to himself than to her. He had not been *this* incoherently drunk the day of their wedding. What had driven him to drink while he was in town? Who was this man he was speaking about?

"I should have knocked out what remained of his teeth."

Louisa froze, eyes rounding as she sat down on the chair opposite him. "You knocked out a man's teeth?"

"And then he broke my nose." Jack started laughing again, his eyes opening to slits as his gaze swept over her. He seemed to be surprised that she was no longer glaring at him. It wouldn't do to scold him while he was drunk…he wouldn't remember it the next day. She would save her admonishing for when he was fully aware.

She sat back, crossing her arms. So it seemed he had met that same man in town again that day. Either that, or he was reminiscing on the day their fight had first occurred. But the other things he had said…about Louisa being afraid of him, or wondering if he was a murderer…none of it made sense.

"Well, are you a murderer?" Louisa asked in a hesitant voice. Her heart picked up speed when Jack stopped laughing. He was silent for a long moment, staring at her with a weighted sadness in his gaze.

"No." He shook his head with a resigned sigh. "But I knew you would not believe me."

Louisa frowned, watching with deep concern as he closed his eyes again. Moisture gathered at the outer corners of his eyes. She had never seen such a vulnerable side of him, and she was certain he wouldn't allow her to see it if he were aware of what he was doing. His emotions played out of his face, unshielded by confident smiles and teasing words. "You are too good for me," he muttered. "Too beautiful and kind and innocent."

Her legs stiffened, the air catching in her lungs.

"You are more than I could ever deserve," he mumbled. "You shouldn't have married me." His voice cracked, a furrow marking his brow. "You should've married someone like Mr. Northcott, even—even if he says he won't marry, I'm certain he'd marry you if you asked. Any man would be a fool not to love you and want you. Even Whitby wants you, that must be why he tries to fight me. He's envious." A pained smile crossed Jack's lips. Shortly after, a snore escaped him, and the furrows cleared on his forehead.

Louisa stared, unblinking. She nearly started laughing, but the sound was stuck in her chest. Warmth flooded her limbs as she watched him sleep. Even drunk as a wheelbarrow, she couldn't look away. She swallowed, digging for the anger she had felt when he had first walked into the room. It was gone, dried up in a desert of compassion. That was all she could manage to feel as she watched him sleep. *Do not take his words seriously*, she demanded to her heart. He wouldn't remember them the next day, and neither should she.

After taking a quick walk to the first floor, she found a blanket, bringing it down to the drawing room and draping it over him. She paused as she stood above him, listening to that whistling snore that came repeatedly from his nose. What a ridiculous man. What a confusing, infuriating, troubled man. If only she knew what was troubling him. If he told her, she could help him. She wanted to help him, to understand what had shaped him into the man he was today, crumpled and broken on the sofa. Her heart ached as she brushed her fingers lightly over his hair. She tucked the blanket around his back, her heart still warm from the things he had said about her, coherent or not.

Her throat tightened as a single tear slipped down her cheek. "Oh, Jack. You are difficult, aren't you?"

The complicated emotions in her heart had been taken on a chaotic ride, much like when Jack had driven the cart the day of their wedding. Had Jack been given to her so she could learn to be patient? It was a fault of hers to be unwilling to wait for things. There were other things she wished she could slow down, such as the rate of her heart when he was near her, and the rate at which her feelings for him had grown. It had happened slowly at first, but watching him now, she felt as though all the defenses around her heart had just been trampled.

Even so, that would not stop her from giving him a thorough scolding the next day.

CHAPTER 21

Sunlight crept through Jack's eyelids. He rolled over with a groan, squinting toward the source of the light. His eyes shot open wide. Where was he?

The details of the room came into focus. The pianoforte, the heavy drapes on the window, and the writing desk near the fireplace. He had a vague memory of falling asleep on that sofa the night before, but the blanket draped over him was a mystery. He sat up straight, the quick motion causing his head to spin. A sharp pain cut between his eyes, and he leaned forward until the sensation subsided. Staring at the bench of the pianoforte brought another memory to his muddled mind. Louisa had been sitting there the night before. She had been glaring at him.

His heart pounded as guilt poured over his shoulders. What had he done? He thrust his fist into the cushion beside him, gritting his teeth. How had he been so foolish? He had been so determined to remain true to his promise to keep Louisa's stipulations, but he had already failed. All it had taken was a few words from Evan Whitby to throw him over the edge. Old habits had driven him to the tavern he had once frequented, and he had obviously drunk far too much. As much as he had tried not to take Whitby's words seriously, Jack had failed. Fear had been planted in his chest, enough that he had done the very thing he had promised Louisa he would not do.

His legs shook as he stood, folding the blanket in a neat square. Had Louisa put that blanket on him? The entire evening was blurry in his memory, and he could only grasp onto brief moments. He did recall seeing Louisa, poised and pretty as always, even if she had been scowling. Anguish cut across his heart as he thought of how disappointed she must have been in him.

Raking a hand through his hair, he started toward the staircase. He needed to change his clothes and become cleaner before he saw Louisa. The apology he was about to offer would need to be presented properly, and not from the same man she had seen the night before.

Working as quickly as possible, he had a bath drawn and clean clothes selected. His valet helped shave the overgrown hair from his face, and Jack even combed his hair enough to keep it from falling over his forehead. He took a deep breath, shaking out his hands at his sides as he looked in the mirror. He had risen early, so breakfast would be being served at that very moment.

Once he made his way downstairs, he stopped by the breakfast room door. His heart pounded with dread.

"I can see your boot from here," Louisa's voice flitted through the doorway from inside.

Jack swallowed, stepping into the room.

Louisa sat at the table, a plate of eggs in front of her. The light from the nearby window illuminated her hair, bringing out auburn tones he had never seen before in the dark strands. She held her fork poised above her plate, one eyebrow raised. "I trust you slept well?"

He approached her with cautious steps. "Louisa—" he sighed, struggling to complete his thoughts. "I'm sorry. There is no excuse for my behavior." His jaw clenched as he looked down at his boots. The shame he felt was potent, enveloping every part of his being. The feeling brought a sense of panic to his soul—it was a familiar sensation of helplessness. He couldn't change what he had done. He couldn't undo the damage, and he couldn't bring back what was lost. What he felt now was only a small fraction of the anguish he had felt when his uncle died, but even that small fraction was large enough to span all of England.

He heard her chair move, but he didn't look up until she was standing right beside him. "Next time you feel inclined to drink, please come to me instead." Her eyes searched his. "I wish I knew what had caused you to be so troubled. You can confide in me anytime you wish to." Her voice was quiet.

Jack nodded, swallowing hard. He couldn't recall the last time someone had spoken to him so gently, even when he had done so much wrong. He wasn't accustomed to it.

Wasn't she angry? He searched her gaze, but all he could find was concern. Despite the softness of her expression, it struck him down, filling him with weakness and strength at once.

"Thank you," Jack said, his voice hoarse. "I-I will try harder. I'm relieved I didn't cause any damage this time."

A slight smile touched her lips. "You did say a thing or two that you might have wished to keep hidden."

His stomach flipped, horror clutching the back of his neck. "What did I say?"

Louisa shrugged, her lips pinching to hide her smile as she walked back to the table. "I don't think you would wish for your words to be repeated."

He couldn't believe it, but his own face grew hot. He laughed at her smug grin, willing his face to cool. "Are you now wishing that I'll continue to drink so you can have more entertainment?"

She flashed him a warning glance, taking a bite from her fork. "You would do well to remember that if you are ever drunk again, I will ask you as many questions as I like while you are too incoherent to withhold your answers from me." She grinned. "Yesterday evening was already quite educational."

What the devil had he told her?

Louisa seemed quite content with herself as she finished her breakfast, brushing past him with a secretive smile. He would never know.

Before she could leave the room, a footman entered, extending a letter to him.

Louisa turned at the doorway, casting him a curious look. "What is that?"

"An invitation." He frowned at the name, signed with a flourish at the bottom. Lord Bridport. His skin prickled with distaste.

With Louisa peeking over his shoulder, they both read the words carefully.

"We are invited to a ball?" Louisa jumped back, hope igniting in her features. "The only balls I have attended I went as my friend Bridget's companion. I spent most of my time at those balls helping her drive away the suitors Matthew had chosen for her." Louisa took the invitation from his hand, tracing the corners lovingly. "Shall we go?"

Jack eyed the invitation with suspicion. The timing was a bit unsettling. Why would Bridport invite him to a ball the day after their encounter in town? Was this his way of trying to make amends? Perhaps he had finally seen what a boor Evan Whitby was and felt some remorse for how he had treated Jack. As much as he would have liked to believe it, he couldn't. There was something sinister about the timing of it all.

He returned his attention to Louisa, who still looked up at him expectantly. As always, he found it difficult to refuse with her looking at him in that way. He let out a sigh. "I'm not certain we should go."

The excitement in her features deflated, and it stabbed at his heart. "Why not?"

"Lord Bridport and I...well, we are not on polite terms

at the moment. The last time I was at his estate, he instructed a pair of footmen to throw me out."

Louisa gaped at him. "Then why would he invite you to a ball?"

He found it amusing that she didn't even inquire as to *why* he had been thrown out. She didn't even seem surprised that he had been thrown out of an earl's estate at all. "That is my question," he said. "I do not entirely trust him at the moment."

"This may be his attempt at reconciliation." She offered a hopeful smile. "He could be seeking your forgiveness."

Jack gave a slow nod, the idea making more sense when she offered it.

"May we please go?" Louisa begged with her eyes.

There was no possible way he could refuse—especially not when he had behaved so poorly the night before. She had been so quick to forgive him and to offer him exactly what he wanted: a second chance. A third chance, or whatever number he had reached now. All Louisa asked of him was to go to a ball.

He cursed himself for being so submissive, but her large brown eyes could convince him to do anything, even invest an absurd amount of money to have a pineapple imported to England. With her lips quirked in a cajoling smile, dark curls framing her face, and her brows drawn together, he could scarcely think clearly for long enough to phrase his answer.

"Very well, but I do have three stipulations." He tossed her a mischievous smile.

A light laugh escaped her, deep interest flashing across her face. "Is that so?"

He was relieved that they could return to teasing and laughing, even when he had been so afraid that she would hate him for his actions the night before. "You must agree to all three, or I'm afraid we cannot attend."

She raised one eyebrow, her curiosity obvious. "I will not promise my cooperation until I have heard what these stipulations entail."

He chuckled, rubbing his jaw in thought. "First, you must allow me to order you a new ballgown and slippers. It may be as elaborate as you choose."

The spark of excitement returned to her eyes, a wide smile spreading over her cheeks. "Do you realize how dangerous that offer is? If I were not such a sensible woman, I might spend your entire fortune."

"It is a dangerous offer indeed, but not nearly so dangerous as my next one."

She stared at him with eager anticipation.

He paused, building the suspense. "My second stipulation is that you must eat a hearty meal before attending the ball, so as to ensure you are in an agreeable mood among the other guests."

She covered her mouth with a laugh. "I suppose I can manage that."

Jack took a step closer, no longer surprised at the way her closeness affected him. The weakness, the strength, the overwhelming longing, all battling for dominance inside him. Being near Louisa lit a fire in the pit of his stomach. It wasn't only his longing to touch her, to kiss her, to remain near her much longer than she would let him. It was a fire that burned his desire to be a better man—to be the sort of husband she deserved, and not the sort she would come to resent.

Her chest rose and fell with a heavy breath. He could see that his closeness affected her too. "And the third…" he began with a smile, "is that you must promise me your first three dances."

"Three?" Her eyebrows shot up, a shy smile on her lips. "That is a bit scandalous, you know."

"Nothing is considered scandalous between husband and wife. No one could hold it against us."

There were times he forgot that they were married. The fact that he could kiss her now in the middle of the breakfast room without consequence was a tempting notion. He banished the thought, forcing his mind to remain focused.

"I suppose you are right," she said, looking down at the floor. "I will promise to fulfill all three of your stipulations."

Jack feigned a deep sigh of relief. "Good. I was certain you would refuse the last one."

She put on a thoughtful expression, one that he could tell was false. "I must confess, it was the least enticing of the three."

He laughed, no longer surprised by her sharp tongue. He could only hope that her insults toward him were her best attempt at flirtation.

"If your dress is to be ready on time, we ought to order

it today." The ball was in one week. Under normal circumstances the invitation would have arrived much sooner, and that was what made Jack suspicious. It seemed his invitation to the ball had been an afterthought, perhaps an idea that had sprung up after Jack's encounter with Bridport the day before. He shook away his concerns, focusing instead on the excitement on Louisa's face.

"How do you expect me to make a decision on all the fabrics in one day?"

"I will help you." Jack grinned. "I may not be skilled at many things, but one of my strongest skills involves selecting fabrics."

She ducked her head with a laugh. "I would sooner wear a sheet to the ball than trust you to choose the fabrics for me."

He chuckled, holding the door open for her. "If you insist on wearing a sheet, then at least add a little embroidery and ribbons."

"Will you be doing the needlework as well?" she asked. "Is that another hidden skill of yours besides drawing?"

"You've uncovered my secret."

He followed her into the hall, and she turned to face him, one eyebrow raised. She seemed to hesitate before speaking, her voice taking on a curious tone. "You do have many of those. I am glad to have uncovered at least one."

Jack didn't deny her words, the familiar unease beginning to spread in his stomach. He didn't want moments like this to end. It had been a long while since he had felt like a person and not a disgrace. He couldn't bear the thought of Louisa's smiles becoming infrequent, or her laughter becoming a mere memory. He needed her.

The realization made his legs weak, and his heart beat hard in his chest. He had been lost for so long, alone in his disgrace, that he had forgotten what it felt like to need anyone. He had never experienced needing someone so much, more than he needed food or water or air. He survived on Louisa's voice and smiles and teasing. Since she had come to live in that house, he hadn't dreaded waking up each morning. If she were ever gone, he would be nothing but an empty shell.

He swallowed, taking a deep breath. Louisa was right—he did have many secrets, one of which he hadn't fully faced until that moment. He had lost his heart to her, day by day, hour by hour—and he was helpless to ever retrieve it.

∼

The mantua-maker was a short woman, even shorter than Louisa. She bustled in a circle, gathering up bolts of fabric to present to Louisa as she stood in the center of the shop. For how small the woman was, she was certainly strong. The fabrics she held up for Louisa's inspection were heavy brocades and silks, wound tightly around bolts. The dress Louisa envisioned wearing to the ball was much like one she had once seen her friend Bridget wear. The gold fabric had flattered Bridget beautifully, and the neckline and hem had been exquisite.

Keeping the same shape of the dress in mind, she wanted to choose a different color for the fabric, and perhaps a few different details in the beadwork and trim. This ballgown would be the product of all her childhood dreams, if only she could justify the cost. She asked Jack for what must have been the third time, biting her lip hesitantly, "are you certain the expense will not be too great?" She knew the rush they had put on the order would come at an additional cost.

He shook his head with an exasperated sigh. "It will not. If you ask again, I will assume you are failing to comply with my stipulations."

She hid her grin, turning back to the fabric selection like a scavenging bird. She picked up the corner of each piece, excitement surging in her heart as the buttery soft fabric slipped across her fingers. Perhaps she shouldn't have teased Jack about being unable to help her make a decision. She didn't trust herself to choose on her own.

"Is there a certain color you prefer?" Louisa asked.

Jack met her gaze, walking forward. The mantua-maker had bustled back behind her desk, gathering a few varieties of ribbon.

"I thought you didn't trust me with such a feminine task?" He flashed her a grin.

"At the moment, I do not trust myself." She sighed. "They are all so very beautiful."

His eyes lingered on her face before he turned to study the fabrics. After a few seconds, his gaze settled on her again. Louisa peeked up at him from beneath the brim of her bonnet, suddenly self-conscious under his scrutiny. "There isn't a single color that wouldn't suit you," he said finally, his voice soft. "I'm afraid I'm at a loss."

Her chest flooded with warmth, and so did her cheeks. "There must be one that you prefer." She found herself unable to look at him, too unnerved by the look in his eyes. He had never looked so adoringly at her before. It made her heart pound wildly.

"The decision is yours," Jack said with a wink. His voice grew lower. "I will be smitten when I see you in the dress no matter which you choose."

The mantua-maker looked up from her place behind the desk. Jack spoke quietly enough that she likely hadn't heard his words, but it was the quiet tone of his voice so close to her ear that made Louisa's insides go up in flames.

She turned away from him, nearly stumbling as she walked closer to the bolt of fabric the color of a bluebell. She could no longer scowl at him when he said such flirtatious things. In truth, she quite liked it. "I believe the word you meant to use was 'bewitched.'"

He chuckled, likely remembering his past description of her, long before she had welcomed his compliments. Her heart thudded as she sorted through the decision in her mind. Jack had thoroughly distracted her. He was far more captivating than any of the beautiful fabrics in the room.

"I think I will select this one." She pointed at the fabric that had first caught her eye upon entering the shop. It was a pale blue, and she could easily envision it with the deep neckline, intricate beading, and corded trim she had seen on Bridget's dress. It had been so long since she had had a new dress to wear. Most of her dresses were old, handed down to her from Alice or Bridget. Many of them had also begun to wear at the seams. Louisa could hardly contain her excitement, rising on her toes and squeezing her hands together. "It is perfect."

She stole a quick glance at Jack, her heart leaping when she found the same admiration in his gaze again.

The mantua-maker rejoined them at the center of the room, taking Louisa's measurements swiftly, darting back to her desk to make note of what she found and all of Louisa's preferences for the dress. Jack sat on a stool nearby, seeming to be thoroughly enjoying himself as he watched the ordeal.

Louisa tried her hardest to focus, but she felt like a spectacle as the mantua maker stuck pins all around her waist, draping her body with fabrics, Jack watching all the while with a grin on his absurdly handsome face. She had tried, *oh*, she had tried, but it had been impossible to stay angry with him. He was too blasted charming and kind. She was far too aware of every movement he made as he watched her from across the room. His arms folding across his chest, his eyes blinking, each smile that curled his lips—

He could entertain her for hours by simply existing.

When the mantua-maker's work was finally done, Louisa followed Jack out of the shop and back into the streets. Several people stared at them as they walked through the crowd, many of whom were servants sent on errands. How many of them had heard the rumors about

Louisa? If they recognized Jack, they would know that she was his new wife. From the Lovells' description of Jack, it seemed he was somewhat famous in the area, and he was likely even more so now that gossip had spread about how his marriage had come to be. Louisa ignored the unease that spread through her stomach, focusing instead on her excitement for the ball.

A couple rode by in a curricle, the woman holding the reins as the man instructed her. Louisa threw Jack a cajoling smile. "Will you teach me to lead a team of horses?"

Jack tipped his head to one side. "I'm surprised you would be willing to ever enter a wheeled contraption with me again after what occurred the last time."

"That is why I wish to learn," she said with a smug smile. "So I may be the one to drive from now on."

Jack's lips twisted into a grin. "I suppose that is fair, so long as you do not vomit on my boots again. I have just had them shined, you know."

She threw him a half-hearted glare. "You did deserve it. If I were to do it again, I would ensure I soiled your buckskin breeches and waistcoat as well."

Jack dipped his chin in surrender, and Louisa couldn't help but laugh. He cocked one eyebrow at her. "Perhaps we should not embark on these driving lessons."

"Please." She eyed him carefully, watching his resolve unravel, just as it had when she had asked if they could go to the ball.

The corners of his mouth lifted. "If it will give me the

opportunity to spend more time with you, I will gladly teach you."

Her heart skipped, hammering hard against her ribs as it had been doing recently when he looked at her in that flirtatious way.

"We shall begin our lessons tomorrow."

CHAPTER 22

Leading a team of horses required more skill than Louisa had anticipated. It required a deft hand, a strong memory, and impeccable focus. The last area was where she struggled most.

It could have had much to do with the fact that Jack was her instructor.

Each time he took her hands in his, adjusting her hold on the reins, her mind went blank. He had taken to sitting much closer to her on the seat than was necessary, his thigh pressing against hers or his elbow brushing her side. Every encouraging smile he tossed her way made her arms weak.

These distractions infuriated her, as they kept her from progressing. However, as she dressed for their lessons each morning, she found that those *distractions* were what she most anticipated.

Her time in the curricle with Jack was her favorite part of each day. She had abandoned her efforts to pull his secrets from him, turning her efforts instead to coming to know more about him. The happy things. The light things. She wanted to know what had caused the wrinkles around his eyes when he smiled. During their rides, they spoke of both their childhoods and all the good they had experienced, long before they knew that both their lives would eventually take dreadful turns.

Louisa told him what she remembered of her late mother and father. She had hardly known her father, but her mother had been all that was good and kind, and she had raised Louisa to strive to be the same. Jack spoke of his childhood with similar joy, but he didn't mention his father at all. Louisa was learning that it was a sure way to keep Jack in a cheerful mood—keeping the topic of their conversation far away from the elder Mr. Warwick.

Their daily rides were a time to laugh, and at the end of each one, Louisa's stomach and cheeks ached. As strange as it was, Jack had become her friend. Her dearest friend. *Love*, that thing Louisa thought had died, that hope and dream, was stirring. Each time Jack looked at her, she felt it move, coming back to life. When he teased her, she wanted to kiss his grinning lips, no matter how smug.

There were many times when they were on their rides together when she caught him looking at her lips. Jack did not strike her as the sort of man who would be afraid to kiss a woman, especially his own wife. She hardly knew what he was waiting for. Did he think she wouldn't welcome his kiss? She supposed she *had* forcefully demanded that she have a separate room as part of her stipulations. It wasn't ridiculous to think that that could have taken part in Jack's reluctance to show any affection. She couldn't deny that the notion did frighten her a little. Louisa had been so cautious, but she was now prepared to throw caution straight into the river Derwent.

Two days before the ball, they walked into town to see the progress of her ballgown. The mantua-maker promised that her seamstresses would have it completed by the next morning, the day of the ball. As usual, while they were in town, Louisa didn't fail to notice the attention they drew from the other people who surrounded the streets.

"Why do you suppose they are staring at us?" Louisa asked, holding tighter to Jack's arm. The lingering glances from each passerby were not pleasant. They seemed to be appraising her, scrutinizing each step she took as Jack led her over the cobblestone street.

"I think they are questioning how on earth I managed to convince you to marry me."

Louisa shook her head. "I think it is quite the contrary. If they heard the story Mrs. Irwin heard, they are likely wondering why you would have sacrificed your bachelor life for me."

A nearby woman covered her mouth with her hand, whispering to her companion as she stared at them. Jack lifted his chin. "If Evan Whitby had anything to do with it, they are gossiping about something else entirely," his voice was edged in anger.

Louisa looked up at him with alarm. *Whitby*. That had

been the name he had said repeatedly while he was incoherently drunk, hadn't it?

The moment they were back on the quiet path toward Benham Abbey, Louisa released the reins on her curiosity. "Is Evan Whitby the man who broke your nose?"

Jack nodded, his jaw tight.

"You never did tell me why you fought him that night." Her heart pounded as she watched the signs of distress in his profile. A muscle jumped in his clenched jaw.

"He was accusing me of something I didn't do. He was perpetuating the rumors my family has been desperate to escape." His voice was weak, almost…defeated. "It's the reason my father has come to despise me, and Whitby treated it like a piece of entertainment for the entire party."

Once again, Louisa was tempted to ask what the rumors were. There was so much Jack was keeping from her, but each time she pried for more information, he grew more distant. *Have patience,* she reminded herself. But it was becoming arduous to keep her questions less intrusive. "Are you certain your father despises you?" Louisa found it difficult to believe that anyone could despise Jack. And why would his father have attended the wedding if he despised his son? Louisa's heart cracked a little to see the loss of hope in Jack's eyes. "Is there nothing that can resolve the discord between you?" she asked.

Jack's throat bobbed with a swallow, his arm becoming stiffer against her hand. "For years, I lived with him refusing to look at me or speak to me. He hasn't forgiven me, and I don't believe he ever will."

Again, she was tempted to ask what he needed forgiveness for. She bit her tongue, holding back her curiosity. Not only did she think it unwise to ask while he was so distraught, but she was also afraid of the answer. He could tell her in his own time, without any pressure from her. All she could do now was try to help him, to offer some words of advice. "Well, have you ever *asked* for his forgiveness?"

Jack met her gaze. The top half of his face was shadowed from the afternoon sunlight by the brim of his hat, creating a line between light and dark. He took several steps in silence. "Not in such plain words, no."

She cast him a thoughtful glance. "People are often more willing than you would expect to give things, so long as they know what you want from them. All you have to do is ask."

His eyes reflected deep thought as he looked down at her. "I don't think it's quite as simple as that." His jaw tightened again.

She gave a hopeful smile. "How do you expect to have what you want if you will not ask for it?"

The deep pondering in his eyes gave wings to the hope inside her. If he would consider having a conversation with his father, then he might finally have the weight lifted from his shoulders.

She hadn't known Jack to be so quiet and thoughtful, but he hardly said another word for the rest of the walk back to Benham Abbey. And when they walked inside, he went straight to his room.

Louisa told herself not to fret. He was likely overwhelmed. Still, she couldn't rid herself of the worry that she had said something to upset him.

When Jack's silence persisted through dinner, her worries intensified. He was acting differently, his thoughts seeming to be far away from the present. Many times throughout the meal, she caught him watching her as if he were trying to solve a puzzle of some sort. Each time she caught his gaze, he looked away.

After the food was cleared from the table, he excused himself abruptly, leaving her alone at the table.

Louisa fought the sudden tears that burned behind her eyes. What had she done to upset him? She shunned her emotions as she walked to the drawing room. Jack wasn't anywhere to be seen in the dim hallways, and when she opened the drawing room door, she found it empty as well. She let out a huffed breath. She had been so forgiving toward him for his drinking earlier that week, simply because she cared about him. Did he not care for her enough to forgive a few unwelcome words of advice?

A tear slid down her cheek as she sat on the bench at the pianoforte. She wiped it away in one angry swipe, spreading out the sheets of music she had been practicing. It was a piece from Haydn, one that she had been struggling to learn because of its difficulty. The notes were quick, the turbulent tune reflective of her mood. It was one of the only sonatas Louisa had encountered from Haydn in a minor key. The notes were blurred through her tears as she tried to regain her composure. *Focus,* she demanded to herself. She tried to practice the most difficult measures of the song, but her patience was wearing thin, in more ways than one. Another tear slipped from her eye, then another.

She swallowed hard, willing her hands to keep moving over the keys, even as she played several wrong notes. The song was already very turbulent, so each mistake she made seemed to blend into the music, reminding her just how accurately the piece mirrored her own feelings.

A movement caught her attention from across the room. Her heart leaped. Jack was walking toward the pianoforte. She could only see him from the corner of her eye, but she recognized his blue waistcoat and fitted black jacket. Her pulse raced past her ears as she sniffed, unsure whether to stop playing for long enough to wipe the tears from her cheeks, or to carry on playing as though nothing was wrong.

She prayed the tears would evaporate by the time Jack came close enough to see them. It had been silly of her to cry at all.

To her dismay, Jack sat down on the bench beside her when he reached the pianoforte. If she had thought being so near to Jack while driving a curricle was difficult, focusing on Haydn's sonata was even more of a challenge. Her fingers hit three wrong notes, one after the other. She gritted her teeth, attempting to play the measure once more. Another wrong note rang through the air, and her hands froze over the keys. She could feel Jack's gaze on the side of her face, and she could sense his concern without even looking.

He must have noticed her tears.

The notes on the sheets in front of her looked like a splatter of ink on a letter, dots and lines coming in and out of focus.

"Louisa—" Jack's voice was gentle, but it sliced through her composure. She sniffed again, fighting the tear that wobbled on her eyelid. "Louisa, what's wrong?"

She ordered her emotions to realign, clearing the lump in her throat with a hard swallow. "Nothing."

"No, something is obviously amiss." Jack angled toward her, but she remained focused on the music in front of her.

"Why should I tell you?" Louisa snapped. "Something has obviously been amiss with you this evening, and many times before, yet you will not tell me what it is." She glared down at the keys. "You hardly spoke to me after our conversation on our walk home today." Her voice cracked, and she sniffed again. Her tears had dried, her face growing hot. "I wish I understood you, but every time I try, I become more confused." She placed her hands on the keys again, trying to focus on the notes.

Jack touched her wrist, stopping her. "You gave me much to think on. I'm sorry if I've seemed distant today. It wasn't intentional. There are matters I must contend with on my own."

Louisa shook her head, daring a quick glance at his face. His eyes were down-turned at the corners, his mouth just as solemn. "No, Jack. No." Her voice was firm. "There is *no* matter that you should contend with alone. I cannot tell if you want me here or not, and that is what confuses me. If you are so determined to do everything on your own, then you should not have married me." Her face flamed at the realization of the things she was saying, but she couldn't stop. Her heart had been a bystander at first. It had been safe there. But now it was an active participant, fighting against her resolve to keep her feelings for Jack hidden.

She managed to focus on the first measures of the music. Poising her hands, she began playing, letting the music fill the silence her words had caused. Her focus slipped once or twice as she awaited Jack's reply. When he finally spoke, her heart joined the music like a drum, pounding hard against her ribs.

"How can you possibly doubt that I want you?"

Her stomach fluttered. That had not been her phrasing. She had said she didn't know whether or not he wanted her *here*. She was grateful for the pianoforte; it allowed her to pretend she was focused on something besides his last question. She shook her head at the keys, suddenly embarrassed for speaking her mind. "I wonder at times if you are simply being kind and honorable, trying to make me as comfortable here as possible."

He shifted on the bench, and she could sense his frustration building. He was turned completely toward her now, and it took all her concentration to continue the song. He seemed personally affronted by her words. "Are you mad?"

She glared at the keys as she played with renewed vigor. Her nostrils flared. "No."

"You are if you require more proof of my feelings." His voice was heavy with exasperation. "I have never known whether you hated my company or enjoyed it. I cannot tell you how many times I would have kissed you if you had allowed me to."

Her hands froze on the keys, her heart leaping to her throat. Her mind went blank, and the notes became mere dots and lines again. She could hardly breathe as silence pulsed between them. "You never asked." She swallowed, stealing a glance at his face.

His eyes locked on hers, his chest rising and falling with a heavy breath. Had she just done what she thought she had done?

Had she given him an invitation?

Her heart thudded frantically as she turned her gaze back to the music. Before she could play a single note, Jack took her face in his hands, turning her toward him. His mouth captured hers just as swiftly, his fingers burying into her hair. Louisa gasped, but Jack stole her breath with another kiss, informing her that if she had indeed extended an invitation, he had wholeheartedly accepted it.

His lips pleaded with hers, giving an invitation of his own as he kissed her without restraint. That stirring in her chest, that dormant dream of love was not only awake now, but it was on fire. She had never kissed a man before, but even in all her romantic fancies, nothing could have prepared her for this. Perhaps it was because she hadn't known Jack before.

She hadn't known love before.

She gave in to his unspoken persuading, kissing him with all the same intensity with which he kissed her. Her emotions were tempestuous, her heart beating wildly as her hands found his chest, sliding up to his neck and settling on the sides of his face. The stubble on his jaw was soft under her fingers, but rough as it rubbed the skin around her lips. His hands moved to her waist, and his knuckles flattened against her as he took a handful of the back of her dress, tugging her toward him on the bench.

She leaned against him, letting the thrill engulf her senses. She had never felt more wanted, more loved, in her entire life. His quickened breath brushed against her hair as he kissed the corner of her jaw, pausing to lean his forehead against her temple.

"I will only stop if you ask me to," he whispered, brushing a strand of hair away from her eyes. His breath came as quickly as hers. Her hands were still gripping his lapels. His fingers traced her cheek, and his thumb pressed against her lower lip.

She couldn't speak, especially not if it was in an attempt to stop him from kissing her. His hand cradled her face as his lips grazed over hers again, slow and taunting. She could sense his restraint. Fierce longing stole through her chest. Of all the secrets Jack kept from her, this was the one she had most wanted to know. He did want her. He might have even loved her too.

She had never felt so close to anyone, not in body or in soul. Although she felt that she had come to know Jack for who he truly was, the questions that remained in the back of her mind still taunted her, just like his soft, grazing lips. What was he hiding from her? Her heart ached with each kiss that he pressed along her cheek and hairline.

"Jack," she breathed, shaking her head. The movement was too subtle, too indecisive. Her eyes fluttered closed as his lips found hers again. She couldn't resist another kiss, not when she was already so weak. Her heart shuddered with the effort to keep itself at bay as his lips moved fervently with hers. Was it worth the effort? She could surrender to her heart with no consequence. This was her husband, after all, and he was no longer a stranger. But a voice whispered in the back of her mind, giving her pause.

Was he a stranger?

No matter what her mind demanded, her heart seemed intent to ignore it. Kissing Jack was far too enjoyable, and Louisa lacked the strength to stop, even as doubt climbed her spine, shadowing her certainty. It wasn't until her elbow leaned against the keys of the pianoforte that her mind was jarred back to life.

The assortment of mismatched notes rang through the air, making her jump. Her lips tore away from Jack, her face hot. Her arms were still draped around his neck, but she quickly unraveled them, wriggling out of his embrace just as quickly.

"Louisa—" he laughed breathlessly. "Where are you going?"

Her heart still thudded, her lips burning. "I—I am rather tired. I think I'll go to my room now." She emphasized the word *my*, if only to ensure he did not take another unspoken invitation and follow her. The uncertainty that had been prickling the back of her mind nipped at her heels as she walked out of the room, up the stairs, and behind her closed door. She pressed her fingers to her lips, melting against the inside of her door. She stared at the opposite wall, her heart still reeling.

She had just been kissed, quite thoroughly in fact, by the man she loved.

And she had run away from him.

Why *on earth* had she done that?

Instant regret poured through her veins, but she managed to resist the urge to go back down to the drawing room. She couldn't love Jack as she wanted to if she knew he didn't trust her. His secrets created an unseen barrier between them, and she feared that his feelings for her were only a distraction for his pain. She needed to know what caused it...the very root of his anguish. She sensed it wasn't linked only to his father's disapproval of him.

The true source of Jack's pain was buried deeper in his past. She was sure of it. And it still hurt that he didn't trust her to help him through it. She had made herself vulnerable that night in confessing her concerns, so now it was his turn to be vulnerable.

No matter how difficult it would be, she vowed to herself not to kiss him again until he did.

Her legs were weak as she walked to her bed, falling

into a heap on top of her blankets. Where was Mrs. Warwick's fainting couch when she needed it? She covered her face with both hands, forcing herself not to think of Jack a moment longer.

But by the time she finally rang for her maid, she was still thinking about his smile and breathless laugh when she had jumped away from the pianoforte.

When she climbed under her blankets, she was still thinking about how perfectly she had fit in his arms.

And when half the night had passed and her eyelids finally drooped closed, she was still thinking about how difficult it would be to keep her vow not to kiss him again.

CHAPTER 23

Blast the pianoforte.

Jack had been conflicted about his feelings toward the instrument all day. On one hand, it had been the place he and Louisa had first kissed. On the other, it had been the reason Louisa stopped.

At least, that had been his first theory. But the fact that she had been hiding in her room all day was beginning to give him doubts. She hadn't just run away from him because she was embarrassed, but because she was still upset with him. He sat on the sofa in the drawing room, tugging on his cravat as he scowled at the black and white keys. Louisa was rarely late for dinner. He checked his pocket watch, raking a hand over his hair. The ball was that night, and if she didn't come down to dinner, then she might not come to the ball either. He knew how eagerly she had been anticipating it.

He stood and paced to the window, no longer able to

sit still. Should he go knocking at her door? He tugged on his cravat again, loosening it from his throat. He had spent the last two weeks doubting that Louisa cared for him, but he had been hopeful the night before, at least until she ran away. He hadn't meant to act distant, but her words of advice to him on their walk home from town had been weighing heavily on his mind. The only reason he hadn't asked his father for forgiveness was because he didn't feel worthy of it. How could he be forgiven for such a horrendous thing? His uncle's life had been cut short at Jack's hand. Accident or not, Jack was the reason his father's brother had died. At times, Jack felt unworthy to live his own life after what he had done. How could he be worthy of forgiveness?

How could he be worthy of Louisa?

Realization settled into his bones as he paced the drawing room. His refusal to tell her the truth was hurting her, and that was no way to begin to deserve her. No matter how much it scared him, he needed to tell her tonight. He was now more certain of her feelings for him, and though doubt threatened to overthrow his certainty, he clung to hope, a practice he was unaccustomed to.

He took a deep breath. He would do all he could to ensure she enjoyed the ball, and then on their return home, he would tell her everything.

Tucking his plan away in his mind, he returned his attention to the most pressing matter. Louisa was nowhere to be found. They had planned Louisa's favorite dinner for that night, and by now, the roasted duck and boiled potatoes were likely growing cold.

He eyed the door again, hesitating. Should he go find her?

No.

Yes.

No.

He took a step forward, then a step back. *Be a man.*

With determined strides, he made his way out of the room and up the staircase. He couldn't allow his kissing her be what scared her away from enjoying the evening she had been looking forward to all week. Raising his fist, he struck it firmly against her bedchamber door.

"Louisa?" He swallowed, suddenly nervous to see her. "Dinner has been prepared. Do you—do you plan to dine with me?"

He strained his ears as he listened to a soft patter of feet from inside. He waited for what felt like an eternity before the door opened, just a crack. Louisa's large brown eyes peeked out at him. "My maid has been arranging my hair."

Was that the only reason for her delay? The shyness in her features reminded him of the first time he had met her. She could hardly look at his face.

A smile curled his lips. He needed to erase the creases of concern and nervousness from her brow. "I see. Well, you did agree to all three of my stipulations. A hearty meal was one of them. We mustn't have you in a disagreeable mood for your first ball."

She seemed to relax a little, though her eyes were still

focused on his cravat rather than his face. "This isn't my *very* first ball."

Jack nudged a finger under her chin, lifting her gaze back to his. His heart stuttered at the way it sent a flush across her cheeks. "It's your first ball with me."

She was still hidden behind the door, keeping it as a barrier between them. Reservation flashed across her face. "I will come down in a moment," she said in a quiet voice.

Jack nodded, stepping back as she closed the door again.

Rather than return to the drawing room, Jack went straight to the dining room. Only a few minutes passed before the door opened again, and Louisa walked into the room. He rose, turning toward her.

Louisa's hands were clasped together at her waist, her head tipped down as she greeted him with a shy smile. Jack's heart nearly escaped his chest. Her dark curls were piled on her head, ribbons and pearls threading through them. A pendant hung low on her exposed neck, the candlelight from the chandelier above the table leaving a warm glow over her skin. She wore the gown they had ordered for the ball, the satin fabric fitting perfectly over her curves. Her shy gaze fluttered to his as she hid behind her lashes. She seemed self-conscious with his staring, but he couldn't have looked away even if he tried.

"Should I have chosen the gold fabric instead?" the question blurted out of her mouth. He realized how long he had been staring at her without saying a word.

He laughed under his breath, moving to pull out her

chair. He gestured for her to sit. His heart was like a disobedient child, unwilling to sit still. He did not wish to frighten Louisa with too much flirting, but all he really wanted was to see another blush color her cheeks. He captured her gaze in his as she looked up at him from her seat. "You look beautiful."

A reluctant smile tugged at her lips, and she looked down at the table linens.

Jack returned to his chair adjacent to hers at the head of the table. "I have instructed the cook to prepare two servings for you, and one for me."

Louisa's eyes leaped to his, their shyness dissipating. "I cannot eat two portions of a meal as extravagant as this." A laugh escaped her as she shook her head. "My dress will tear open before we even reach the ball."

Though Jack would not have objected to such an occurrence, he kept his mouth shut on the matter. He clasped his hands together on the table. "If I 'snore like a hog,' then it is only fair that I encourage you to eat like one. We cannot possibly be compatible if only one of us is a hog."

It warmed his heart to hear her laughter again. He grinned, watching as she took her first bite. She glared at him from over her fork, but her laughter persisted. He joined her, chuckling until his stomach ached. His laughter was a balm to the fear that gnawed at his heart. By the end of the night, would she still laugh with him? He had faced the possibility of hanging before the inquest concerning his uncle's death, and even then Jack hadn't been this afraid. Louisa was the only person who still viewed him as a person and not a mistake, and he didn't want to lose that. He didn't want to lose her.

When it came time to go to the ball, a sense of foreboding flooded his chest. Despite his concerns, the pure excitement and joy on Louisa's face overshadowed them. As they walked to the carriage on the moonlit drive, Jack forced himself to remain calm. Extending his hand to her, he helped her into the carriage.

―――

Newton Hall was illuminated with hundreds of candles, the chandeliers burning as brightly as a yule log. Louisa's sister had often scolded her for gaping in awe at her surroundings, but she couldn't stop herself. Men and women gathered in the ballroom, each and every one of them dressed in their finest. Louisa looked down at her own skirts, smiling as the candlelight glistened off the satin fabric. Her hair was simple in comparison to many of the other guests' hair who wore turbans and feathers of every sort. As was becoming common in public places, many eyes lingered on Louisa and Jack as they made their way around the outskirts of the room.

Two pairs of eyes in particular were rather unsettling. Two men stood on the second floor balcony that overlooked the ballroom, champagne flutes in hand. Even when Louisa looked up at them, they didn't stop staring. She turned to tap Jack's arm, but he had already noticed.

A muscle jumped in his jaw as it tightened. He immediately pulled his gaze away from the two men when he caught her watching. His blue eyes met hers with a smile. "Are you enjoying yourself?"

Louisa nodded. "Very much."

Jack appeared pleased, his lips quirking upward. She was glad to feel comfortable around him again. They seemed to be carrying on as though the events of the night before had been erased. Even so, each time Jack looked at her, a fire was stoked in her chest. Try as she might, the past could not be erased, and now that she had kissed him, she was rather desperate to kiss him again. But her vow remained firm in her mind, schooling her heart into submission. Until Jack confided in her, she would remain politely distant. If only it weren't so torturous. Even throughout the carriage ride to the ball, her decision had been agonized each time his knee bumped against hers.

Louisa snapped herself out of her thoughts. "Are you… enjoying yourself?"

His attention seemed to be shifting back to the upper balcony and the two men who stared at them repeatedly. When she spoke, Jack tipped his head closer to hers. "Yes, but I will enjoy myself a great deal more once the dancing begins. You did promise me your first three."

Her heart flipped as another of his warm smiles wrinkled the corners of his eyes. Before she could reply, his gaze darted to the balcony again. A furrow marked his brow.

The two men were no longer there.

The ensemble began to play a quadrille. Jack's gloved fingers wrapped around hers, leading her toward the line of dancers. Her heart beat fast as she practiced the steps in her mind—she had been doing so all week. It was her ultimate goal not to embarrass Jack in front of all the guests with her clumsy dancing. There was no doubt that she would miss a step or two, but she was determined to at least perform most of them correctly.

Her nervousness faded as she met Jack's gaze from across the grouping. He cast her a reassuring smile as the steps began.

The lively music gave her a surge of energy. Her feet floated over the ballroom floor, her cheeks aching from smiling as she carried out the steps the dance demanded. Each time the dance led her back to Jack, his hands held hers, firm and strong, guiding her through each motion. His whispered compliments to her dancing abilities made her grin stretch wider, and by the time the dance was over, she and Jack were both laughing. The other dancers in their circle clapped for the ensemble, but all Louisa could do was hold Jack's gaze. He captured her without even trying.

They walked to the refreshment table between each dance, and by the end of the third, Louisa's forehead and neck were damp with perspiration. She let out a breathless sigh, nearly spinning with exhilaration as Jack led her by the hand back to the outskirts of the room. "I never knew I could like dancing so much," she said.

"Nor did I." Jack grinned, leaning close to her ear. "I've never had so lovely a partner."

Did he realize how his words affected her? Of course, he did. Those butterflies had formed a nest of sorts in her stomach, ever present when Jack was nearby. She gazed up at him, her pulse pounding in her neck.

"Would you like to take a turn about the gardens with me?" Jack brushed a curl away from her eyes before wrapping his fingers around hers.

A shiver ran over her skin at the pure adoration in his gaze, the secretive way in which he spoke to her. She had only ever dreamed of moments like this. She licked her lips, glancing around the ballroom to see if anyone else had noticed his rapt attention. A turn about the gardens sounded romantic enough to make her heart burst. And it certainly might if Jack continued looking at her in that same manner.

His thumb brushed over the back of her hand, tracing a circle as he awaited her reply.

She nodded, grinning up at him as he tugged her forward. Weaving their way through the other guests, Jack led her out the nearby exit, the music growing quieter as the door closed behind them. There were a number of other guests outside, laughing or whispering. Several other men and women walked hand in hand or with their arms linked together. The crowd was much sparser out here, away from the music, refreshment, and candlelight. The world was quiet, lit only by the natural glow of the moon and stars.

Jack led her to the narrow garden path, flanked by trees and hedges, much like the gardens at Benham Abbey. The deeper they walked into the gardens, the more alone they became, and soon the muffled music from the ballroom completely faded from her ears. All she could hear was her own heartbeat, the rustling of her skirts, and Jack's boots as they moved over the stone pathway. Her resolve to keep her distance from him was fading just like the music. It was becoming weak, a mere tap against the back of her skull rather than the drum it should have been.

They stopped by a tall hedge. Jack turned to face her. Both his hands interlocked with hers, and she dared a glance up at him. His eyes roamed her face, appearing a darker blue than usual, speaking without saying a word. He must have been thinking about their kiss too. Had it not left either of them alone? Her heart beat like a wild creature against her ribs, begging her to set it free—rather determined to escape if she did not. In the darkness, she could barely see the details of his face.

His head tipped closer to hers, and her disobedient toes lifted her closer to his height. With one hand cradling her neck, he brought her face to his, closing the gap between their lips. His kiss was heart-rending, slow and gentle. His arms pulled her behind the hedge, where he pressed her back against the dense leaves. She clung to his jacket, then buried her fingers in his soft hair. Her vow had not lasted long, but she didn't feel remorseful in the slightest. Every moment she spent with Jack made her feel alive, happy, and free, and that was how she had always wanted to live.

He paused to lean his forehead against hers, keeping her back pressed against the hedge. His hands caressed her face, and she felt his lips curl into a smile when she stole them in her own. She had already broken her vow, so she couldn't see a reason not to break it again. The ballroom felt so far away from their hidden corner of the gardens. Dancing was diverting, but this was more so. Louisa had half a mind to stay there all night.

She reminded herself that Jack still hadn't confided in her. It was too dangerous to lose even more of her heart to him before she knew what was truly in *his* heart. She wanted to know every piece, every part, every broken and battered bit of him, no matter how grave the truth could be. Why couldn't he see that?

She allowed herself a few more seconds, letting each kiss linger a moment longer than the last. And then she lowered her heels to the ground, pushing softly against his chest. "We're missing the fourth dance," Louisa said in a whisper. She didn't know why she felt the need to whisper at all, but the moment felt too intimate to speak any louder.

He brushed a curl away from the base of her neck, sending a new string of shivers over her body. "It must be at least the sixth by now." Jack's grin made her heart skip.

She laughed, feeling just as shy as she had the night before. Would she ever grow tired of kissing those grinning lips?

He took her hand in his again, wrapping it up and pressing a kiss to the back of her fingers. "I'm sorry that I haven't been honest with you," he said in a hoarse voice. "I wish to change that. I'll keep no secrets from you, Louisa. Never again, for as long as I live." He let out a long sigh. "I was afraid to tell you because I didn't want you to see me as society sees me."

With a slow movement, he wrapped her hand around his arm. They walked slowly in the direction of the ballroom. She watched the signs of unrest in his profile. "What are you so afraid to tell me?" Louisa had chosen not to dwell on the possibilities of what he could have been hiding. What if it was as unforgiveable as he thought it was? She had always been so optimistic, but there were certain things that would be difficult to overlook.

Even so, her heart whispered with conviction, calming her concerns. There was nothing in his past that could change her love for him. Her feelings were steady, as solid as the stone path beneath them. The foundation had been building layer upon layer, and she was confident in its strength.

Jack rubbed one side of his face with his free hand, exhaling sharply. "I don't want to lose you," he muttered.

"You won't lose me. You *cannot* lose me." She laughed softly, hoping to reassure him.

A gruff voice came from around the nearby tree, followed by at least two sets of heavy footfalls. "I wouldn't be so certain of that if I were you."

Jack stopped, gripping her arm as he turned toward the voice. Louisa followed his gaze. It was the two men who had been staring at them from the second floor balcony, and they were blocking their path out of the gardens.

CHAPTER 24

Evan Whitby and Lord Bridport walked out from the shadows of a nearby tree, interrupting the calmness Jack had begun to feel. He stepped in front of Louisa, blocking her partially from their view. She looked far too enchanting, and she was far too innocent. He would not have them ogling her.

"Whitby, Bridport." Jack gave a bow, keeping his voice even, hoping his greeting would indicate that he was not in a fighting spirit that evening. All he wanted was to take Louisa back to the ballroom. He took one step forward, keeping his hold on Louisa's arm.

Whitby stepped forward, a sneer on his chapped lips. Jack couldn't quite understand why someone with two missing teeth would choose to bare them so readily. "Where are you going? You have neglected to introduce us to your wife."

Jack stopped, keeping his expression stoic. He glanced

at Bridport. What did he make of Whitby's constant harassment? How could he tolerate being near the man so often? It had only been a few seconds and Jack was already prepared to bury him in the back of one of the hedges.

Bridport was the host of this ball—he wouldn't forcibly stop Jack from crossing the path. He would wish to keep a pristine reputation at his own event. If Whitby tried, Jack would simply throw another facer at him. It wasn't good form to ignore a request from Bridport, but it was Whitby who had asked for an introduction, and Jack had no qualms about ignoring *him*.

"Come, Louisa," Jack said in a quiet voice. He took a confident stride forward, keeping her close.

"Look at the way she obeys him," Whitby said, nudging Bridport's arm. "It is no wonder she is so submissive. She fears that he'll kill her if she doesn't listen."

Jack's stomach lurched, and he gritted his teeth.

"I feel a sense of obligation," Whitby said, stepping in front of Jack, "to tell your wife exactly who she is married to." With Louisa on one arm, it was difficult for Jack to push past Whitby without risking injury to her.

Louisa remained silent, holding tightly to Jack's elbow. Her eyes were wide, flickering between Whitby and the earl.

It wasn't until Bridport laughed that Jack lost his sense of composure. He turned on the man who he had once called his friend. "I wondered why you invited me here tonight. I should have known your intentions were not apologetic."

Whitby's laugh was just as vexing as everything else about him. "He invited you here at my request. He has proposed to my sister, and it was the only favor I asked of him in exchange for her hand."

Bridport looked down, rubbing his nose nonchalantly. He must have felt some measure of guilt for luring Jack there. But why the devil had Whitby wanted him to attend?

"I didn't know you enjoyed my company so dearly," Jack said, turning back to Whitby. "I'm glad you could find me while the night is still young."

Whitby laughed in his throat. "Do you see what you did to me?" He gestured at his missing teeth. "Teeth don't heal like a broken nose."

Jack groaned. He would have checked to ensure Louisa was all right, but he didn't dare take his eyes off Whitby as he drew another step closer. If this man was about to challenge him, he needed to ensure Louisa was somewhere safe. Her hands were wrapped tightly around his arm, fingers squeezing tighter with each step Whitby took. "I'm not looking for a fight tonight, Whitby." Jack leveled him with a cutting glare. "Leave us."

When Whitby came close enough to see Louisa more clearly, he tipped his head to one side, craning his neck to examine her from over Jack's shoulder. He seemed surprised to find her clinging to Jack's arm. "Have you not heard what your husband did?" Whitby asked.

Louisa's quiet voice floated up to Jack's ear. "He knocked your teeth out."

Whitby laughed, glancing back at Bridport. He had obviously been drinking, evidenced by the crookedness of his gait. "That is not even the start of it. Five years ago, he killed a man—his own uncle and his father's elder brother—in order to secure the inheritance of Haslington in his own father's line. He framed it as a hunting accident." Whitby grinned as he watched Louisa's reaction. Jack was too afraid to look at her. Did she believe him? His heart pounded as Whitby opened his mouth to speak again, still directing his words at Louisa. "I suppose once he tires of you, he'll simply take you horseback riding or something of the sort and stage another *accident*."

Jack's fists clenched. "I would never tire of her, and I would *never* hurt her." He pulled his arm away from Louisa. Whitby seemed to have been anticipating Jack's outburst, because before Jack could reach him, he lunged forward, thrusting his fist against Jack's mouth. He fell back, already tasting blood.

Louisa screamed.

Jack charged forward, shoving Whitby away with both hands. "Stop!" He didn't want Louisa to be afraid. Her scream still rang in his ears. He glanced back to ensure she was all right. It was his second mistake. Whitby's fist collided with his jaw. His head spun as he fell to the ground, cursing under his breath. There was no one else in this part of the gardens, but someone must have heard Louisa's scream.

Jack heard Whitby's voice as his vision cleared. "Hold him down."

Bridport glanced at Jack, then at Whitby. He didn't move.

"Hold him down!"

Jack rolled to his hands and knees, spitting the blood that had gathered in his mouth. His teeth all seemed to still be present, so that was a relief. Jack met Bridport's gaze as Whitby kicked him in the side. Jack groaned, rolling over. Why was he so off his guard?

"No." Though he had hesitated for several seconds, Bridport's voice was sharp. "This is enough. Enough!" He pushed Whitby hard enough to send him flailing to the ground.

Jack managed to find his feet, blinking away the stars in his vision. He immediately found Louisa, her hands pressed to her heart as she watched him. He breathed a sigh of relief to see that she wasn't harmed. Returning his attention to Bridport, Jack watched as the earl pulled Whitby back to his feet by the front of his jacket. "I'm finished with you. Away with you. Now."

Whitby wiped the dirt from his cheek, throwing one more glare at Jack before turning toward Bridport with the same expression. "You'll never marry my sister."

"I'll find a way without witnessing another moment of this."

Whitby laughed, as if amused by the entire event. Jack's face throbbed with pain, and so did his ribs where Whitby had kicked him. Guilt spread in his stomach. Louisa's perfect evening had been ruined.

"Jack." Her small voice was filled with concern. When

he looked down at her eyes, they were wide as usual, but he couldn't tell if her terror was directed at him or at the events that had just occurred. If she believed Whitby's story about him, then she had every reason to be afraid. He took her hand, leading her past Bridport and Whitby. His breathing calmed once they were away from the two men, but only a little.

"I'm sorry," Jack said, his voice breaking. "I didn't know they would follow us to the gardens. I'm so sorry to have ruined the ball for you." He cringed at the stinging on his lip. He could still taste blood. His heart beat frantically, and he released her hand. She likely didn't want to be near him after what Whitby had just told her. He needed to explain, but there were too many people watching them as they walked out to the drive. Their carriage was stopped there. The coachman jumped to attention when Jack and Louisa approached, climbing back to the coachbox.

"I think it is best that we leave now," Jack said, wiping at his chin.

Louisa touched his arm. "Jack, please look at me."

He turned back, his throat tightening.

A tear glistened on her cheek as she stared up at him. She drew a shaking breath. "I know it isn't true. I know it." Determination burned in her eyes, but there was also a hint of fear.

He extended his hand to her, helping her into the carriage. The moment he was inside and the door was closed, he put his face in his hands. "I wanted to be the one to explain everything to you." He shook his head, raising his gaze to hers. "What you heard from Whitby were the rumors—the version of the story that has been twisted by society whispers and gossip papers." He paused, wincing as the carriage began moving, the motion jostling his sore ribs. "But the story isn't entirely false."

Louisa looked so small in the corner of the carriage, round eyes fixed on him. Jack's heart ached at the hint of fear that still lingered in her features. His throat tightened as he looked out the window. "My uncle did die at my hands. Five years ago, he came on a hunt with my father and me. I was not well-practiced with my gun, and I was careless in the way I held it." The memory blinded him, and a tear fell down his cheek. "It fired, and I still do not know how, but I was the one who held it when it did. My uncle was in its path, and he never recovered from his wound." Jack took a deep breath, shaking his head. "My uncle lost his life because of me. It is the reason my family's reputation has suffered. It is the reason Cassandra has not married. The effects have reached all of them, and especially my father, who is believed to have conspired this murder with me in order to inherit his elder brother's estate." Jack turned his face away from the window, looking down at his lap. "Thankfully my uncle didn't have a wife or children to leave behind, but that doesn't make it better. It only adds to the suspicion that has been placed upon my father and me." He swallowed hard. "I have prayed every day that the events could be undone, but I know they cannot."

He waited in silence until Louisa finally spoke. Her hand touched his knee as she leaned forward in the carriage. "You must feel so horrible." Another tear fell from her cheek, soaking into the knee of his trousers. She sniffed, the moonlight reflecting off the moisture in her eyes. "Oh, Jack." Her voice was a broken whisper.

"The amount of guilt I have felt...I wouldn't wish it on anyone. Guilt doesn't simply leave or fade over time. It grows stronger. I'll feel it forever. It isn't my father's forgiveness that I require, it is my uncle's." His voice cracked. "But he isn't here to give it, and perhaps that is why my father is so reluctant to give his."

"But you do not have to contend with it alone," Louisa said in a persuasive voice. "You should have told me sooner." Tears continued to streak down her face. "You cannot carry such a burden all by yourself."

Jack could hardly believe how understanding she was, how kind and compassionate. What had he done to deserve Louisa? Absolutely nothing. She was a gift. He certainly hadn't earned her through any virtues of his own.

"Does your father know it was an accident?" she asked.

Jack nodded. "He knows."

Her eyes fluttered to the window as the carriage moved up the drive of Benham Abbey. They were home. "I still think you should try to speak with him," Louisa pleaded.

Fear jolted up Jack's spine, and he started shaking his head.

"I'll go with you." Louisa's gentle voice touched his heart, providing him with a strange sense of calm.

He gave a slow nod, wincing again as the carriage came to a

halt. Being thrown out of his childhood home would be much harder than being thrown out of a gambling party or ball. That was why he had been too afraid to go back. But Louisa's courage had tethered itself to him, and it refused to let go.

He stepped down from the carriage, turning to help Louisa down the step. His head ached, still spinning from Whitby's strike to his jaw.

"Are you all right?" Louisa held onto one of his arms, guiding him inside the house.

He would have immediately nodded, but he quite liked the way Louisa was trying to steady him. Even with his bruised face and cut lip, he couldn't stop himself from smiling down at her. "I am fine."

She shook her head hard. "No, you are not. There is blood all over your face." She let out a distressed sigh, guiding him toward the staircase. Her eyebrow arched as she glanced up at him. "Again."

He chuckled, but the movement hurt his side.

"That is a disagreeable habit to have, you know," she said, her face still devoid of a smile. The tears that had streaked down her face were still drying. With both hands wrapped around his left arm, she walked up the staircase with him. Her grip was more of an interference than a help, but Jack allowed her to think she was assisting him. It was far too adorable.

When they made it to his room, she instructed him to lay down on his bed. He obeyed, and she reached over him to grab two pillows, tucking each behind his head. A crease marked her forehead as she worked, and Jack could have been entertained all day watching her movements.

She fetched a maid who came with a bowl of water and a rag. Louisa instructed her to leave it by the bedside. This was a side of her he hadn't seen, but he found it highly amusing. When the maid left the room, Louisa removed her gloves and dipped the rag in the warm water, wringing out the excess.

She sat down beside him on the bed, pressing the corner of the rag to his chin. He watched the intense focus on her features. Her brows scrunched and her lips pressed together, causing a dimple to form in her cheek. Each movement was slow as she cleaned the blood from his face.

"The last time I did this, you were fainted on the floor." She shook her head as a laugh escaped her. "I didn't imagine I would *ever* be doing this again."

Jack grinned, disrupting her work with the movement of his mouth. "You must be grateful. I am well aware that you enjoyed every second of it."

Her hand shook as she laughed, cleaning the blood around his mouth. "I most certainly did not."

"Tell me…now that you have another experience to compare it to…how much of your enjoyment of the task is influenced by whether or not I am fully clothed?"

Her laughter echoed and her cheeks turned a lovely shade of crimson. "I was terrified of you."

Jack met her gaze. "Are you still?"

She turned to dip the rag in the water. When she faced

him again, she shook her head, delicately wiping away the blood around the cut on his lip. "Of course not."

Emotion clawed at his throat, relief flooding through every inch of his body. Her gaze lingered on his face as she set the rag back on the table beside his bed. "There." Her hand settled on his chest as she leaned closer to his face to examine her work. "Now you ought to sleep." Her fingers brushed the hair away from his forehead, and for a moment, he forgot how badly his head hurt.

"I'm not tired," he said in a defensive voice. He wanted her to stay beside him, even if his vision was a bit blurry. He tried to smile, but it stung the cut on his lip.

"Go to sleep," she said with exasperation, leaning even closer to his face. Before she could sit up again, he wrapped his arms around her. She tucked her head against his chest, and he rested his chin on her hair.

Her body trembled slightly in his arms, and he heard her sniffle. "I thought that man was going to kill you."

Jack closed his eyes. He hadn't realized she had been just as afraid of losing him as he was of losing her. The realization brought him a new sense of strength. He ran his fingers through the loose strands of her hair. "He never would have succeeded. I am much stronger than him."

"He did manage to break your nose."

"It takes much more force to dislodge teeth."

Her body shook again, but this time it was from laughter. Jack chuckled too, ignoring the pain in his side. He lost track of the minutes that Louisa lay there on his chest. She stopped demanding that he go to sleep. They talked and laughed instead, until both their voices were slurred and tired. When the candle on his bedside table was burned to the base, Louisa sat up halfway, her eyes drooping. "Shall we go see your family tomorrow?"

Jack swallowed hard. No matter the outcome of the visit, he had Louisa. He hadn't lost her as he had feared. Everything he could ever need was there in front of him. "Yes."

A faint smile crossed her lips as she slid off the bed. She still wore her ballgown, the sleeves crumpled from laying against him. Before she left, she turned back toward him. She hesitated for a moment before pressing a soft kiss to his forehead, then the bridge of his nose. She pulled back an inch, color creeping over her cheeks. "Goodnight."

Jack grinned as he watched her hurry toward the door. "Goodnight, Louisa." He waited until she looked at him again, one final glance as she exited the room. "Thank you," he added. There was far more that he wanted to express than could be contained in those two words, but he couldn't speak adequately while he was so tired.

She gave one of her shy smiles, slipping into the hallway.

CHAPTER 25

Louisa held Jack's hand as they walked through the gates of Haslington. She studied the signs of nervousness in his posture and expression. She gave his hand a reassuring squeeze.

They hadn't left an official calling card with the Warwicks. It shouldn't have been necessary considering that they were all family. The walkway to the front doors was made golden by the afternoon sunlight. It filled Louisa's chest with hope.

The butler let them in through the front doors. Making their way to the drawing room, Louisa sat beside Jack on the settee. After several minutes, Cassandra finally came into the room, followed by her mother.

"Jack." Mrs. Warwick's eyes rounded. Her lower lip quivered and she pressed a hand to her chest. Cassandra steadied her arm, casting her brother a look of concern. "Jack—your father…"

"I know he doesn't wish to see me." Jack stood, crossing the room to his mother. "But I wish to change that." He took her other arm, guiding her to the sofa with Cassandra's help. Mrs. Warwick seemed near to fainting at the sight of her son in the house.

"Where is he?" Louisa asked. "Where is your husband?"

"In the study." Mrs. Warwick swallowed. "I do not wish to hear the two of you argue again." A new flash of distress crossed her features. "And what happened to your face?"

Jack shook his head. "It does not matter." He sat down beside his mother, exchanging a glance with Louisa from across the room. "I didn't come to argue with Father." He looked down at the floor. "I came to ask for his forgiveness. Louisa brought it to my attention that I have never asked him." He paused. "I have never asked you either."

Mrs. Warwick's eyes flooded with tears. "I have nothing to forgive you for."

"Because of my mistake, the family has suffered much. I'm sorry. Please forgive me."

"There is a difference between accidents and mistakes." Mrs. Warwick shook a finger at him. "I have told you this before. Mistakes are often deliberate in the moment, but regretted later. What happened the day of the hunt was an accident." Mrs. Warwick clutched Jack's arm, emphasizing her words. "An *accident*."

Louisa watched the exchange, holding her breath.

"If it were up to me, you and your dear Louisa could come here every day." Mrs. Warwick wiped a tear from her cheek. "You must forgive me for not arguing more with your father on the matter. I wish you had never let Benham Abbey and moved away from us."

Jack shook his head. "I'm still glad I did. If I hadn't become a tenant of that house then I never would have married Louisa." His gaze traveled to her, a soft smile on his lips. Louisa's heart skipped, and she was distracted enough to fail to notice the drawing room door as it opened again.

She had only seen him once, but she recalled his intimidating stature. Mr. Warwick, his greying hair slicked flat against his head, walked into the room. The aging hadn't yet reached his eyebrows, leaving them dark and full like Jack's. He froze near the settee, his eyes taking in the room and settling on his son.

Cassandra moved from her place by her mother, crossing the room to Louisa. She whispered as she passed, gesturing at the door. "We should leave them."

Louisa nodded, casting one more concerned glance at Jack as they walked out the door. Louisa followed Cassandra through the hallway and all the way to the back door of the house. She seemed intent to escape the walls of the estate, her strides quick and determined as they stepped out onto the grass. Cassandra took a deep breath, turning to Louisa with alarm. "How did you manage to do it? How did you convince Jack to come here?"

"It was with great difficulty, I assure you." Louisa clasped her hands together, squinting up at the many windows of the estate. She could hardly believe she would be mistress of such a house one day. Her thoughts and worries still lingered in the drawing room with Jack. "Do you think your father will forgive him? At least enough to welcome him back here more often?"

Cassandra hesitated, her pale brows drawing together above her thoughtful brown eyes. "I'm not certain. There are times I do wonder if my father regrets his harshness toward Jack. And there are times I think he does miss him. But they are both so stubborn."

"Perhaps all it will take is Jack's actions today. Asking for your father's forgiveness is not a stubborn thing to do."

"You're right." Cassandra exhaled, long and slow. Emotion flashed across her features. "It is my only hope that our family can be whole again. I don't care what society thinks of us. I only care what we think of one another."

Louisa let Cassandra's words sink into her skin. That *was* all that mattered, wasn't it? There was nothing that could not be endured, no outside forces that could break apart anything if it was bound from deep inside.

When Louisa looked up, she caught Cassandra watching her curiously. "Jack must truly love you."

Louisa felt her face grow warm as doubt crept over her skin. She wanted to smile, to agree with Cassandra's observation, but her tongue was tied. How could she know for certain that he did? Love was a mysterious thing, working in different ways with different hearts. Simply because Louisa loved Jack did not mean *he* loved *her*. Neither of them had ever spoken their feelings aloud, at least not in such plain terms. It was fine if Jack did not love her now, in that very moment. He could spend the years to come falling in love with her if that was what it took.

Though she hoped he loved her already.

When he had held her in his arms the night before, she had never felt more safe or comfortable. Jack made her feel like precious gold, meant to be cherished and collected, not a stone to be tossed from one place to another. He was so aware of his faults, yet so unaware of his strengths. He was surprisingly humble, kind, generous, and he made her laugh more heartily than anyone could. Unexpected tears sprung to her eyes, but she blinked them away.

Oh, how she hoped he loved her already. Because she had never loved anyone so much.

The summer breeze tossed her hair, and she crossed her arms over her chest. "I do know he loves your family, though he doesn't know how to show it."

Cassandra laughed. "That has always been Jack's way. He struggles to bare his emotions, but I suspect he has a very soft heart."

"He does." Louisa's own heart ached with longing. They had only been minutes apart, yet she was eager to see him again and discover if he had succeeded or not. She turned back toward the house, sending a prayer to the heavens.

∽

"I'm asking you to forgive me." Jack leaned his elbows on his knees as he held his father's gaze. He hadn't always found him intimidating—only for the past five years. His father had grown hard and cold, but with each passing moment, Jack saw hints that he was beginning to thaw. Jack had expressed his remorse many times before, but never with as much sincerity and emotion as he had just now. His father had never seen Jack cry, not even the day his uncle died. Jack had always kept himself composed in his father's presence, but Louisa had taught him to be vulnerable.

He cleared his throat, wiping at the tear that hovered on the edge of his eyelid. "Please, Father. I know the burdens I have caused you cannot compare to what I have felt, but I ask that you give me the opportunity to move forward with you and with our family." He paused, shaking his head. "My wife is the reason I'm here today. She helped me see that I needed to communicate with you, to tell you how very sorry I am and to ask for your forgiveness. She wishes to know you and to be free to visit this house. We both do." Jack knew his relationship with his father wouldn't be mended in an instant, but the fact that he was sitting with him on the sofa, Jack's mother between them, gave him hope. He hadn't yet demanded that Jack leave the premises.

His father rubbed at one side of his face, letting out a slow breath. He blinked as he looked down at his lap. The room fell silent, and Jack's mother held a hand against her heart. When his father finally looked up again, his face was stoic. Jack had rarely seen any emotion besides anger from his father, but there might have been just a hint of something more spilling through the cracks of his facade. His father's brow twinged as he blinked again. He nodded. "Very well. You may come here if you wish." He turned away, fixing his gaze on the floor. He had always been a man of few words, but these were the first that had given Jack any measure of hope.

"Thank you, Father." Jack smiled, the split in his lip stinging all over again.

His father glanced back as he stood. "I will not ask what happened to your face." The exasperation in his father's voice would have usually vexed him, but instead Jack laughed.

"I would not tell you even if you asked."

One of his father's eyebrows lifted, but he said nothing. "Where did Cassandra take that wife of yours?"

"I'm not certain." Jack could hardly wait to tell Louisa of his success, no matter how small it was.

His mother sat forward, raising her eyebrows. "I wondered the same thing. She does seem to be a remarkable woman." Her eyes welled with tears again. "I haven't seen you so happy in a very long time."

Jack hadn't *felt* so happy in his entire life. He no longer had to be afraid that she would resent him, or hide from him, or refuse to be near him. His heart was hers, every last piece, whether she wanted it or not.

"Is dear Louisa just as happy as you are?" His mother asked.

Jack let out a sigh, rubbing his hands over his knees. He didn't particularly enjoy speaking to his mother about matters such as this, but it was better than Cassandra, with all her wiggling eyebrows and speculation. "I—I'm not certain. I hope she is."

His mother touched his hand, calling his gaze back to hers. "Does she know how much you love her?"

Jack hesitated, recalling the night he had first kissed her at the pianoforte. She had expressed her doubts to him then, and he had thought her mad for doubting his affection. "She should know. Surely she does."

"Well, have you told her?" The gruff question came from his father, who still stood nearby, listening to the conversation.

Jack crossed his arms as the realization crashed over him. "No. I haven't."

"How can you expect her to know if you haven't told her?" His mother shook her finger at him again. "You tell her this instant, or I will."

He laughed, his stomach tugging with sudden nerves. He reminded himself that it didn't matter if she loved him yet or not. If he loved her, which he did—far more than he could ever explain—she needed to know, without a single doubt.

He bid both his parents farewell, eager to find Louisa. Urgency flooded his limbs as he strode out the door to find his wife.

CHAPTER 26

Sitting down on the ground, Louisa tucked her ankles beneath her, twisting a blade of grass anxiously between her fingers. Cassandra sat nearby under the same tree, her bare feet extended out in front of her. She hummed an unfamiliar tune, weaving several blades of grass together on her lap.

Jack had been inside a long time. Louisa didn't know whether that was good news or bad news. Her heart gave a sudden leap when she caught a glimpse of his brown jacket from across the lawn. She nudged Cassandra, pointing at Jack as he walked in a circle, seemingly searching the grounds for them.

"He's still alive," Cassandra said. "That is very good news."

Louisa laughed.

"Jack!" Cassandra shouted, waving both her hands in the air.

He turned, finally seeming to catch sight of them. His sister stood, brushing the grass from her skirts as she approached him. "Did Papa send you out here or did you come of your own accord?" she asked.

Relief flooded through Louisa as she noticed his smile. She remained where she sat beneath the tree, listening as he relayed the details briefly to his sister. "And he didn't object when I said Louisa and I would like to visit more often." His eyes slipped past his sister for what must have been the tenth time, settling on Louisa with a weight that kept her planted on the ground like the tree beside her.

Cassandra glanced over her shoulder at Louisa, a knowing smile twisting her lips. When she faced Jack again, he had already taken one step around her, headed in Louisa's direction. "I'll leave you two alone," Cassandra said, her grin persisting as she meandered back toward the house.

Louisa interlocked her fingers in her lap, looking up at him expectantly. His determined strides set her heart pounding. The same determination flashed in his eyes as he sat down beside her on the grass, rotating until he faced her fully. In the shade, his hair appeared even darker, the freckles on his cheekbones more prominent with the contrasting shadows.

"I'm proud of you," she said in a quiet voice. "It could not have been easy to tell your father how you felt."

Jack gave a subtle shake of his head. He stole her hand from her lap and wrapped it up in his. "It wasn't easy. I've been wasting the years wishing he understood what I was feeling rather than explaining it in words." His eyes wandered over every feature of her face. "It was a mistake I have no intention of ever repeating. I don't want the same fate to occur between you and me, so I will no longer keep my feelings from you. Not in word, nor in action."

He drew a deep breath, a half-smile pulling on his lips as he traced a circle over the back of her hand. "You've signed your name on my heart, Louisa. I didn't plan to marry you, and I certainly didn't plan to fall in love, but that is what has happened. You give me a reason to arise each day, and you give me something to aspire to. I will spend all of my days striving to be worthy to call myself your husband." He touched the side of her face, cradling her cheek as she leaned against his hand.

She watched the emotion playing across his face, completely entrapped by the sweetness of his words. Her heart raced.

"I make another revision to my proposal," he said. "I propose a life together that is what you have always dreamed of. I am far from perfect, as you well know, but I promise to try. I want to share every moment and hardship with you. I want our house to be filled with laughter and children and fond memories that they can tell the people they love one day." His voice cracked. "I want you. I choose you."

Louisa's throat constricted with emotion, a broad smile on her lips. Her heart soared. He lowered her hand to the grass, leaning toward her until his forehead touched hers. His arm curved around her waist, warm and safe and strong. "I love you, Louisa. Quite madly, in fact." The raw sincerity of his words caused tears to sting the back of her eyes. Louisa had always thought that one day a man would fall in love with her and then marry her. She had never expected that he would marry her first and then love her.

She drew a quaking breath, unsure whether to laugh or sob or kiss him. "I wish you could see how wonderful you are," she said in an accusatory voice. "There is nothing more you need to do to obtain my good opinion or forgiveness."

"I thought your forgiveness could not be won until I procured you a pineapple? I have been working with my man of business in having one imported, you know."

She covered her mouth. "You cannot be serious."

"I am."

She practically snorted as a laugh burst from her mouth. "I love you." The confession flooded her with strength, and she leaned toward him with a smile. "Just as madly," she added with another laugh.

He touched her face, his fingers grazing her cheek as a grin curled his lips. "Are you certain my snoring won't be enough to change your mind?"

She took his face between her hands. "I'll learn to tolerate it." The poor man could hardly smile with the cut on his lip. She wanted to kiss the pain away, but she feared kissing him would only make it worse. He seemed to have forgotten his injury, brushing his lips across hers. He winced, and she carefully drew her thumb across his mouth, stopping him from making a second attempt. Her heart skittered wildly as he groaned with frustration.

"Blasted Whitby," he muttered.

She giggled, wrapping her arms around his neck as his arms encircled her waist. He tipped backward on the grass, pulling her down with him. She could feel his heartbeat against her own chest as she left a trail of kisses over his bruised jaw, caressing his face as she pressed her lips slowly to each injury. There were so many after all.

"Will you allow me to drive the curricle over the bridge today?" Louisa asked, propping herself up on his chest. They had missed her lesson the day before, and he had promised that he would finally allow her to take the reins on the bridge that spanned the river.

Jack smiled, tucking one hand behind where his head rested on the grass. "I confess, I would rather stay right here all day."

Her face warmed, and she wondered if she would ever become accustomed to his flirting. Still, she couldn't stop her smile. "Jack, please?"

He gazed up at her with a mischievous grin. "Very well, but I have three stipulations."

A laugh bubbled out of her chest, and his own laughter rumbled against her. He beckoned her closer, whispering his stipulations in her ear.

They were far too flirtatious to repeat.

NEXT IN THE LARKHALL
LETTERS SERIES

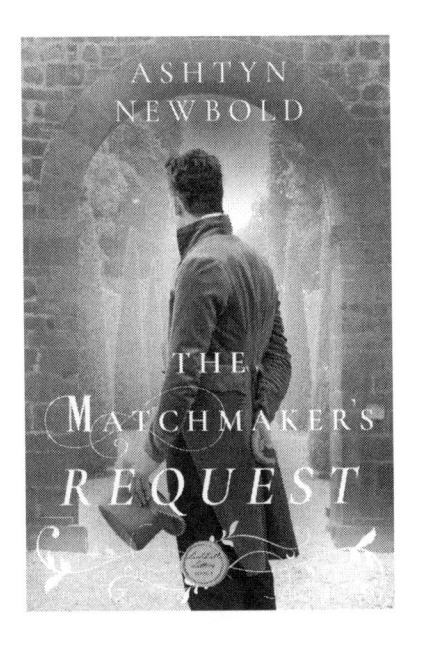

Matthew's new challenge: Keep himself from falling in love again at all costs.

OTHER BOOKS BY ASHTYN NEWBOLD

Larkhall Letters Series
The Ace of Hearts
The Captain's Confidant
With Love, Louisa
Brides of Brighton Series
A Convenient Engagement
Marrying Miss Milton
Romancing Lord Ramsbury
Miss Weston's Wager
An Unexpected Bride
Standalone novels
In Pursuit of the Painter
The Last Eligible Bachelor
An Unwelcome Suitor
Her Silent Knight
Mischief and Manors
Lies and Letters
Road to Rosewood
Novellas & Anthologies
The Earl's Mistletoe Match
The Midnight Heiress
Unexpected Love

ABOUT THE AUTHOR

Ashtyn Newbold grew up with a love of stories. When she discovered chick flicks and Jane Austen books in high school, she learned she was a sucker for romantic ones. When not indulging in sweet romantic comedies and regency period novels (and cookies), she writes romantic stories of her own. Ashtyn also enjoys baking, singing, sewing, and anything that involves creativity and imagination.

Connect with Ashtyn Newbold on these platforms!
  INSTAGRAM: ashtyn_newbold_author
  FACEBOOK: Author Ashtyn Newbold
  ashtynnewbold.com

Made in the USA
Columbia, SC
17 December 2023